REVIEWS OF
BY L M S

Mel Harris trilogy: *Utmost Good Faith*, 1988 (republished as *Lodestar*, 2012), *The Gentlemen's Mafia* (1989), *The Messenger* (2012)

"A dizzy-makingly clever scam in which an over-tired and emotional underwriter is taken to cleaners by some powerful shipping magnates." *The Spectator*

"*Utmost Good Faith* has done for Lloyd's what Dick Francis has done for the turf." *Mail on Sunday*

"A thriller that ignites from page one... Compelling." *Publisher's Weekly*

"L M Shakespeare ... is a smooth and even elegant stylist." *Lloyd's List*

"A remarkable achievement." *New York Times*

"Shakespeare deftly weaves arcane insurance lore with psychological insights... a top-notch mystery thriller." *The Times* (on *The Gentlemen's Mafia*)

"A thriller that goes on moving briskly and compellingly, like a rocket, against the background of the Lloyd's insurance market." *Publisher's Weekly*

"A well written exciting thriller from an author who not only writes well but knows his subject inside out.. One of the best financial thrillers I have read this year. An absolutely first-class book." UK Amazon review

Malice, 2006

"A witty, finely researched feat of the imagination. Compulsive reading, enchanting and original." Colin Thubron

"Malice is not so much an historical novel as a novelised history. The fictional parts bind together a fascinating and detailed account of life in the court of the Sun King.

Laclos himself could not have invented such seething intrigue and wicked plotting." Kate Saunders, *The Times*

"this story... with its vivid characters and authentic detail, had me racing through the pages... Intense and compelling." 'Book Club Book of the Month', *Woman's Own*

"Ms Shakespeare has previously been noted for financial thrillers. This historic pageant is a departure – and a brilliant one. My book of the year so far." 'JB', *Nottingham Evening Post*

"... feel the very nap and texture of 17th century France under your hand." Jonathan Keates, 'Best Books of the Year', *Sunday Telegraph*

"*Malice*, a stylish and highly readable novel. Part...love story...told with wit and boldness." Isabel Quigley, *The Oldie*

"This is THE BEST historical fiction novel I've ever read about Louis XIV's court! I could hardly put it down. The characters are so real and you feel like you're there. This book is a keeper; I can't wait to read it again..." US Amazon review

"In this beautifully detailed novel you are transported directly to the court of Louis XIV where intrigue and deception are around every corner and evil ambition meets loyalty and the best of the human spirit head on. Monsieur De Brisse is our unlikely champion in a world of unreality and ambition. Follow him in the shadows, passages and nooks of Versailles and cloak yourself in the drama of this age. A magnificent read. Researched deeply and wonderfully readable. Historical novels don't come much better." UK Amazon review

L M SHAKESPEARE

Monsieur Law

AUSTIN MACAULEY PUBLISHERS™
LONDON • CAMBRIDGE • NEW YORK • SHARJAH

Copyright © L M Shakespeare 2023

The right of L M Shakespeare to be identified as author of this work has been asserted in accordance with sections 77 and 78 of the Copyright, Designs and Patents Act 1988.

All rights reserved. No part of this publication may be reproduced, stored in a retrieval system, or transmitted in any form or by any means, electronic, mechanical, photocopying, recording, or otherwise, without the prior permission of the publishers.

Any person who commits any unauthorised act in relation to this publication may be liable to criminal prosecution and civil claims for damages.

This is a work of fiction. Names, characters, businesses, places, events, locales, and incidents are either the products of the author's imagination or used in a fictitious manner. Any resemblance to actual persons, living or dead, or actual events is purely coincidental.

Cover illustration: 'The Rue Quinquempoix, 1720', by Antoine Humblot. This engraving, held by the Rijksmuseum, Amsterdam, is in the public domain.

A CIP catalogue record for this title is available from the British Library.

ISBN 9781528917339 (Paperback)
ISBN 9781528925785 (ePub e-book)

www.austinmacauley.com

First Published 2023
Austin Macauley Publishers Ltd
1 Canada Square
Canary Wharf
London
E14 5AA

DEDICATION

For my late husband, David Harvey-Evers

HISTORICAL NOTE

Monsieur Law (John Law) is the hero, or antihero, of the history of the Mississippi bubble. His birth was registered in Scotland on 21st April 1671. As a young man he went to London and there fought a duel in which he killed his opponent. Because of some circumstances of the duel he was accused of murder and sentenced to death, but escaped from prison and fled to the continent. He worked at first for the Wittlesbank in Amsterdam, where paper money was already being used. From his experience there, and using money, which he had won at the gambling tables – there was never any question of his honesty, but he had a phenomenal memory for figures – he worked on a system which eventually he had the opportunity to test in France in the years following the death of Louis XIV. His financial experiment was recorded in detail by some of the most famous diarists in French history.

The Mississippi Company was created as part of John Law's scheme for the revival of the French economy, and for a while it was brilliantly successful, with John Law himself becoming the richest man on record, at the time, in Europe. With many similarities to the South Sea Company, which almost certainly influenced John Law in the formation of the Mississippi Company, its failure was scarcely less dramatic than the revolution at the end of that century, in which the Royal family were executed.

Our history, *Monsieur Law*, begins in France, after the death of Louis XIV in 1715. The king was succeeded by his five-year-old great-grandson, with his uncle Philippe, the Duke of Orléans, appointed Regent during his minority. France is bankrupt when John Law arrives in Paris with this plan to revive the economy, and succeeds in securing the backing of the Regent for his scheme.

Monsieur Law is a sequel to the historical novel *Malice* in that the narrative is again recounted by Berthon, the idiosyncratic hero of *Malice*. Unlike the Regent and his opponents and friends, Berthon is a fictional character: a nobleman whose physical debility is typical of the period of 17th and 18th century France, but whose natural intelligence and character makes him very attractive.

There is no shortage of contemporary records which have been researched to produce this scholastically accurate account of one of the most dramatic periods of French history: the time of the Regency, and of the Mississippi bubble, from 1715 to 1720.

"... that stupendous game of Chance, played by an unknown man, and a foreigner at that, against a whole nation."
Voltaire, referring to John Law

"The fatal charm of England."
The Duke of Saint-Simon

CHAPTER ONE
December 1722

I AM alone, sitting in my carriage at midnight on the outskirts of Paris. This small clutch of trees and scrub are now reduced to restless skeletons, and the air itself has the texture of water just before it turns to ice. I am neither a thief nor a beggar. I am a witness. A rise in the ground here – not too steep for the horses – seemed to be familiar to my coachman; and there are remnants of what may once have been a paved way, which was enough for the carriage wheels. They dug in to hard core. They crushed the earth, spat out small stones, lurched over boulders. There may once have been a house here, but it is a forgotten place now.

From this deserted vantage point, I can see across part of the city of Paris to the Pont Neuf, which is the object of my vigil. I am here to witness a funeral cortege which will cross that bridge on its way to the royal mausoleum of Saint-Denis on the other side of the river Seine. It will be lit with flares when it arrives, but very little ceremony and only the attendance of servants. If there is any truth at all in the legends of the immortality of the human soul, the spirit of the former Duchess of Orléans will know that I, the most devoted of her court, am here to watch over her last journey.

I have kept one torch alight; enough to write by, although hardly enough to see the paper or the marks I make on it. The night is thin and bitter. Now that the horses have been taken out of the traces and the carriage is still, it seems exceptionally quiet as well as cold. A moment ago I stopped moving, and with my hand arrested, suspended every sign of my own presence, even my breath. I listened for the counterpoint of nature, briefly smothered by the disturbance of my arrival, to reassert itself, like an invisible body stealthily settling. I heard the tap of a dried leaf still hanging to a tree; a silence, a hesitation, but then a muffled creak of wood from a branch strained against the wind.

I have a long time to wait, and I decided to pass the time and distract my mind from the infernal cold of Winter by inscribing an account of the dangerous last years in France. These scraps of paper may outlive Madame's ample form, her kind and greedy heart, and the indomitable progress of her great life in a foreign court, but will not be enough to contain more than a fragment to remember her by.

Madame, as she was called at Court, was the second wife of the brother of Louis XIV, the Duke of Orléans, and mother of the present Duke of Orléans, now Regent. Her life, despite the efforts of her enemies, was not cut short. She has outlived the Chevalier de Lorraine, who would have poisoned her if he could. He was very handsome once. There was a harshness to his features which made the occasional softness of his glance peculiarly telling, and a manner as witty and cutting as his tongue. Most men envied him, but I did not. I knew that one day the poison in his soul would leech into his body and become visible. So it did. He was not beautiful any more after he had suffered twice from the French disease, as Madame called it. His love of depravity was still not assuaged, but in the end the exchange between the poison of his spirit and that of his body became evident because when he was old and sick enough, he became a better man, but an ugly one. And Madame, in spite of his evil past, was reconciled to him.

She also outlived Lorraine's friend, d'Effiat, who was

responsible for murdering her youngest baby son in his cradle; but she never knew about it. No one knew but myself and the enemies who had killed him. Had she known about it – had I not hidden it from her – she would have died of grief or rage long ago. If I must, I will relate that story again, but I have already given it, and the memory disturbs me too much.

There, in the distance, I can make out some flares already lit on the bridge. My own solitude throws into relief the extraordinary loneliness of the city at night. The buildings seem to hold their breath as do cows that stand stock still in freezing weather, in order not to disturb the warm air rising from their own bodies. At some point during the hours of darkness the light of more distant torches from far away below the south bank, like sparks blown from a fire, will be the first sign of the approach of the funeral cortege.

I have lived long enough myself, if Madame, with all her life's vigour and strong heart, has left this world behind. Of all the people I have met in my lifetime, she has been the most precious to me. Despite her age, and the occasional remark to the contrary, she had not finished with living. She recently devoted more time to her religious duties and said that she looked forward to the call of almighty God putting aside the complications and vanities of court life, but I did not believe her. In the next breath, she would ask one of her ladies to repeat every detail of one of the scandalous evening entertainments given by her son, now the Prince Regent, and an entire account of the food and wines served, with close attention to the ladies and especially his wife, her daughter-in-law, the present Duchess of Orléans, and what was said, and done. She simply did not have the mentality of a lady who was tired of life.

When Madame herself was young, and first arrived at court from her native Palatine, I was still a child. Even before she showed me such extraordinary kindness I thought her pretty. Monsieur, the Duke of Orléans, who was the brother of the King, did not think his wife attractive because she was plump and would not paint her face. But to me, even before the event which precipitated such a change in my whole life, she appeared, in her manner and her movements, extremely pretty. And despite the elaborations of court dress and the jealous snares of strangers, she radiated an appetite for enjoyment and happiness. It showed in the brightness of her eyes, but was sometimes held in check by her dignity and her awareness of the necessary formality of the role she now occupied as the sister-in-law of the King of France and first lady in the land after the Queen.

At the age of nineteen, I remember she had a clear complexion, naturally very red lips, and was tall. De Largillieres did not do justice to Madame when he painted her, and certainly not Rigaud. Both depicted a silk ribbon or the intricate beauty of lace to perfection, but to treat the face – the eyes, the mouth of a living soul – to the same scrupulously tactile observation is, in my opinion, barren, and in the case of a person like Madame, whose presence was so much more the matter of her spirit – her character, the rolling tides of her robust humour and intimidating dignity, her simplicity and innocence, her appetite for life and rich food, which made her company so animated – was a travesty.

I possess one portrait of her which is the work of one of her ladies at court and is a far more true representation. Madame gave it to me years ago when I returned from Italy, having found proof of the Chevalier de Lorraine's guilt in the matter of the murder of Monsieur's first wife, and I treasure it more than anything else I have. She made me promise never to show it to anyone else, and to fix her intention and make sure I kept my word she looked away from me as she put it in my hand and then turned her head back and frowned at me.

I had it set in gold. On Madame's birthday, I wore it hung on a chain inside my coat, and I am wearing it now. I see her in my mind's eye at this moment, as she was in those early days, her great skirts of silk weighed down at the hem with the sleeping body of Charmille or another of her pet dogs. How she would settle herself with a shuffle of cushions and animals and papers when she was pleased with something she had written in the letters which, often for as long as five hours a day, she would write to her extended family in all the courts of Europe. She would even occasionally read something out to me, and I will never forget her laughter and the accent of her voice, which retained its distinctive but small inflexions of German.

A moment ago I thought that someone here approached my carriage window; maybe a beggar unable to sleep because of the cold, or one of those women who wander through the country. If so, they withdrew quickly enough to merge with the scrub. There is nothing out there now but the familiar elements of cold wind, fitful moonlight, and shadows which shift with surreptitious zeal between the bushes and the rocks. But what if such a wanderer had indeed been there and actually tapped on my window, and I had opened it to allow them to speak to me? They might have taken me for something like themselves, being here at the dead of night. I am not an impressive figure of a man. I am unusual. My name is Berthon Collet de la Tour de Brisse, and I was brought up in Court, where my father was a courtier among many hundreds of others; but I was exceptionally ugly from birth, and I am still.

I am small. But I must make it clear – I am not a dwarf. Those dwarfs who were always at our court when the Queen was alive – the dwarfs she brought with her from Spain – they were of a particular make, and I do not share it. Madame herself called me her goblin, and that was a different matter. When I was old enough to be a man and took advantage of the court tailors who knew so well how to disguise the physical defects of those of us who were born crooked or made crooked by various plagues (and there were many at Court), Madame abandoned this pet name for me, but I still treasure the memory of it.

I put these thoughts aside a moment ago, lowered my carriage window, and let in the night air and as clear a view as I could get of the scene below. The breeze on this small rise is restless as well as very cold, and it immediately replaced the thin draughts which squeeze through cracks in the glass and wood of a carriage, with an annihilating chill. I made out no movement on the distant bridge. Nothing yet stirs. Between those banks it could be the river Styx that flows, so neatly does the Seine at this point separate life from death. On the south bank vitality and light are epitomized by Madame's palace at St. Cloud, where she loved to be happy whenever she could, surrounded by her ladies and with good food and wine and gossip. On the opposite side of the river is the territory of death: the regal mausoleum of St. Denis, with its hidden population of the dead royal families of France. It has been waiting for Madame in silence all these years.

CHAPTER TWO

I ALSO wait in my way. This night that encircles me is more like a presence than an element; neither body nor spirit but in a sense watchful, subject to the surreptitious shifts and whispers of an undecided predator on guard. From time to time the wind blows some bare twigs so that they catch on the carriage window like claws; followed by a sudden silence.

The horses, tethered nearby, make their presence felt by the occasional clatter of a hoof against a stone, or the sound of them blowing through their noses as they do. As for this icy wind, I am resigned to it. Most members of the royal family who have died in my lifetime have been interred in cold weather, but for Madame particularly it is appropriate. She was always robust. Like her brother-in-law, the King, she loved fresh air; so for her the moon shines tonight as if it has been freshly polished by each cloud that briefly covers it, and the air is as sharp as the newly ground blade of a knife. I am made of warmer stuff. But until I have witnessed the last journey of Madame, whom I loved and whose friendship was the greatest blessing of my life, I refuse to stir from this place.

If Bonhomme, my servant, was still with me, he would have found a fur or another rug to cover me with, but he is gone too. I can't even muster the will to summon the two ordinary servants I brought with me. They are probably asleep or drinking in the bushes. I neither know nor care. But I do miss my old servant and friend, Bonhomme.

It is on his account that I keep this carriage as I do. I have kept the inside covered with the same cloth and colour as it had when we travelled together to Italy and he was murdered by agents of the Chevalier de Lorraine on the way back. So it is not very splendid-looking, it has got rather worn; but it suits me, and reminds me of a time which must be rare in anyone's life. Even tonight, just the sight of the interior – the familiar small woven flowers, like stars, on a background of indigo, or the way the seat is braided – has the power to snatch me back in time. I hear again the sound of Bonhomme whistling as he prepares food for us in some lonely valley where no inn offered shelter, or when he drove the carriage or attended to the horses. The way his real self emerged, like a fine jewel once casually dropped into the mud of human suffering and then reappearing, is something I learned by. I never forget him. I first saw him – in the sense that you see a man with more than just the skin of your eye – when I realised he had betrayed me. It was in my apartment in Versailles. At that moment his entire frame, his thin trunk and oblique look, his lips like desiccated rind and his wandering uneasy sullen gaze, suddenly claimed my attention as if he had only just been born. I knew in that instant what he had done. There flashed in on my mind a remembered fragment of a casual observation, when he was bent over a coat of mine and rubbing something into it. I had thought he was cleaning it. But he started on seeing me pass by, and for that reason alone the image of his occupation hooked itself in my memory like a small thorn. And then, some months later, I realized that he had not been cleaning it at all, but rubbing something into it, to deliberately madden the huge wolfhound of the King, which would be returning from the hunt at the same time as I crossed the inner court. As planned by the Chevalier de Lorraine, it leapt furiously on me, attracted and made savage by the powdered *Dra-*

cunculus vulgaris that had been rubbed into my jerkin. I remember the smell of my own blood on his breath and how nearly those jaws, dripping with the slime of rage, had killed me.

Bonhomme had been paid to do it by Lorraine. Bonhomme was my servant at the time only because no other courtier wanted him, and I was in no position to choose. It was hardly surprising that one of my enemies had found it easy to corrupt him, and although it had nearly cost me my life, I did not dismiss him. I could not afford to. Instead, I agreed to take him with me when I travelled down to Italy in the service of Madame, and somehow, in that time, he changed. He became the man he always should have been. He worked at his redemption, and by the time that he was killed I had learned to value and even love him as much as any man, including those in my own station in life. How I wish he was still with me. He would have found a way to frustrate the night wind now prising open the cracks in my carriage doors with icy fingers in search of an inch of warm flesh to feed on.

Madame, on the other hand, although I mourn her and am in this place because I want her spirit to have the company of mine on her final journey, had – in spite of what I felt a moment ago – reached the natural limit of her days. She, who had been only plump, had become stout. Of the great circle of those she loved, many had died already, although she still wrote letters almost every day to those who remained. She no longer needed to complain of censorship of her letters now that her own son was the Regent, but like a warrior whose adversaries have perished, she had begun to turn her back on the field of battle.

She left instructions regarding her funeral rites, that once the mass and other stately ceremonies had been observed in the cathedral in Paris in keeping with the dignity due to her rank, the carriage which carried her body on its last journey to St. Denis should not be attended by the court, or even draped But at least the carriage will be lit, and the servants who walk beside it will have flares, although it was her wish for her body to be carried without even that ceremony, in proof of her abandonment of all worldly things. This order was so unlike her it made me smile when first I heard of it. And yet, considering the dangers we were – and are – all in, her spirit may have failed her. She may indeed have felt comforted, rather than threatened, by the thought of silence and an end of so many years of the daily drama of court life.

It is almost as silent, on this abandoned small lookout over the city, as the grave where her body will be left. I wonder if, once a body is entombed, there is some part of that person which lingers long enough to be aware of it. And how does the silence of the grave compare with this, which I thought so significant a moment ago? Here there is the rattle of dried twigs and grasses every time a mouse or a bird stirs, or a finger of wind lifts the corner of my paper as if to read it. And the horses fidget more than I thought. They shift, and I can hear the grinding of their teeth as they chew the grass and the occasional chink of the metal on their tethers. The silence of the tomb must be one to which this cannot be compared.

CHAPTER THREE

AND so who am I? I must give some description in case these words are read one day by a stranger. I was born an outcast. My mother died giving birth to me, and my father, when he saw what sort of a malformed child he had been given in exchange for his wife, rejected the bargain. He continued, after I was no longer an infant, to pay a pittance to the peasant woman who had been hired as a wet nurse when my mother died, in order not to be associated with me. He gave her instructions to keep me in the country, well away from Paris and the Court.

From then onwards I slept with the pigs and was afraid of the night. When I grew a little older my foster mother amused herself by terrifying me with inventions of monsters waiting in the dark, and as for work, I was used like a slave. When I was three or four years old, she would order me out at night, and I would have to obey. I was sometimes so terrified I forgot my direction, and I remember standing in the bitter cold, my wet rags flicking against my shins, and holding my breath to listen for the snorting of the animals to guide me. The smell of mud and pigs still sometimes haunts me in my sleep, although it is now more than thirty years ago.

I was still only five years old when a discarded mistress of my father found out about my existence and conceived a spiteful plot to shame and embarrass my father by bringing me to Paris. Some strangers came to the hovel in the country where we lived and took me from my foster mother and her dreadful husband. They took me just as I was, full of lice and dirt and still bleeding from a graze where one of the pigs had crushed me against the wall of the sty. At the end of a long journey, when it was dark, I was dragged up some stairs and then roughly thrown on the polished floor of the great gallery in the palace of St. Germain. A wall of silk skirts and jewelled shoes surrounded me. But only briefly, because after a few moments my tormenters drew back at the approach of the King.

I made an attempt at standing, whether to defend myself or to try to escape, but my uneven legs never did allow me to stand easily once I had fallen. Also, my body had wet that polished wooden floor, and I slipped on it. I looked fearfully up at this tremendous stranger – and remember even now how his expression, as he looked down, taught me, once and for all, the majesty of not being afraid. His regard seemed to control my terrified breath instantly. There was no spite or malice in it, but an air of calm observation. He seemed not to despise me, like other men did, for my appearance. He made no gesture either with his eyes or in any other way, to express the usual reaction of disgust that I expected. He spoke and was answered by others who could understand him.

What he heard was that scandalous story concerning my father, who was one of his own courtiers, and lived at Court. At the time I could not understand what was being said. They towered over me and spoke a language that only from time to time dropped a native word that I could recognize. I can still hear it, if I pause as I do now, and listen; so raw was my attention at the time that all the years since have not served to erase the echo of it.

One of the ladies laughed, a brief high trill that was quickly stifled. Another lady spoke in a mocking tone, interrupted occasionally by another more tense and insistent. Whenever the King spoke, his voice was calm and immediately silenced all others. I can piece together, now, fragments of words which I did not understand then. And besides, the whole story is no longer a mystery to me.

Once the King understood the circumstances, he ordered that I should be restored as well as possible to the position that my birth should have given me. I was to be cleaned and to live at Court as any other son of a nobleman should live. He provided me with the appropriate pension. And so I did live at Court after that, and at least I was clean and fed.

For me the memory of that time, when I had clearly possessed absolutely nothing and His Majesty had nevertheless given his attention, unimpaired with haste or smallness of mind, to rescuing me, it was not surprising if the admiration and gratitude which the King then inspired in me has lasted the rest of my life. But when His Majesty was on his deathbed, I saw that the same was not true of others. I observed the indifference of some courtiers, on whose live affections the cold draught of death seemed to cause instant atrophy. Until His Majesty had expressed his wishes, completed the codicil to his will, said his farewells to his family, his servants and all those in attendance, they kept the busy whispers of ambition, the rustle of elbows jostling for future positions, at a discreet distance. But with what seemed to me then like indecent haste, the moment the King was dead – even before – the entire temper of the court swung around to the new sovereign and the question of the Regency. Five minutes after His Majesty Louis XIV had breathed his last breath, if an order had been given to take a cup of chocolate or a biscuit to the King no one would have been the least startled or confused, so instantaneous and absolute was the transfer of all attention to the five-year-old child who was now Louis the Fifteenth.

Following my ignominious introduction to the court, my new life gradually evolved. When not eavesdropping on gossip or the conversation of clever people, I was able to read in the King's library. I missed nothing of my former life, except, occasionally, that version of solitude which you can have in the country, where the sound of the grasses rustling in a breeze, the clumsy affection of pigs, the prodigal displays of glory in the skies liberated one with their indifference. Here at court, my father was far too ashamed to acknowledge me or give me any attention. It was several years before his own reputation recovered from the catastrophe of his angry mistress having found out about me and exposed his shame, because it was considered shameful that he would have left me all my life to look after pigs and starve if it had been up to him. But I understood him better than many of his former friends at court. I pitied him for my marred face and crooked back and smallness. For myself, like an animal that escapes from a burning building which destroys all the men and women and children in it, I cherished my new life.

But until Madame found me I was as lonely as I had been in my foster-mother's hovel before. As I already wrote, my own father never came near me. Until I had lived at court for three or four years I still didn't know which man he was. I believe I even missed my pigs.

Only animals seem indifferent to a human being's physical disfigurement, and they used to treat me like one of themselves, leaning their warm bodies against me during the night, snorting and rubbing their heads against my legs with pleasure when I scratched them with twigs.

As I write this, my mind conjures a scene which I can see as clearly as a painting. I see my own hand. My hands were always well formed. My hands are the one part of me that will bear normal scrutiny. I have good hands. The moon is up now, and full, and if I rest my palm on the corner of this sheet of paper they can be seen to be perfect. Since my father died I wear his rings. It is the closest we ever came to any sort of a reconciliation. Sometimes, by accident, he would notice me, but then he would move away. I bore no resentment towards him. He could not be expected to want my friendship. I wonder if now, wherever the dead dwell, he may occasionally think of me.

The paper on which I am writing is the same colour as the hide of the white pig in daylight, and likely to become as patched and smudged in this writing venture of mine. I picture it now in my mind with my hand small again, and filthy, gripping a twig of hawthorn to gently scratch the middle of the pig's back. Even the wet mud of Spring is there in my memory and a scattering of peel half-buried in it, the sow grunting with pleasure and two of her piglets pushing at her to turn over and feed them.

If Madame could see me now, she would not recognize me. She would say that if a gentleman is to be up at this time of the night, he is to be in company, not sitting all alone bent over some notebooks in the dark. But I have never spoken to a living soul about these things of my childhood, and if I write them here it can do no harm. My father would never have enquired about them, and if he had I would not have dared to tell him. And yet I feel glad to know that those words are now written. I can see well enough to write, but scarcely to read again, and yet I was just tipping the page this way and that to catch enough light to look over them. It is almost as if an undetected obstruction in my spirit has escaped; words imprisoned in the dungeon of my heart for too long.

I would always have been an outcast at Court if Madame, when she arrived at the age of nineteen to marry the King's brother, had not taken pity on me. I have said before how she came upon me in an unused room of the palace when she had lost her way, and how my bitter tears moved her. She did not recoil on seeing me, as I expected. The moment was terrifying. I remember my despair. The screen behind which I had hidden almost fell over. A great sob blocked my throat; was washed out with a flood of tears. I expected to hear her run away; the slamming of the door. I heard nothing. Panic-stricken, I froze. She looked steadily at me for a moment; and then she bent down holding out her arms that were white and slightly plump and smelled sweet. My heart jumped out of my body and I felt her take hold of me. She embraced me. I swear it. She was the first person I had ever known, in all my life, to do so. She took me in her arms and comforted me. It is as if that embrace has held me captive ever since. And she spoke those words which I have never forgotten: "Don't cry, little goblin. What's the matter?" Is it any wonder that I loved her with all my heart?

It is for her that I am waiting on this cold dark night. Hers is the corpse which I am waiting to see drawn across the bridge, to be interred in the royal mausoleum of St. Denis. I am old now, but my feelings of devotion to Madame are, as they have always been, unchanged. I would have let my heart be carved from my living body rather than see her harmed. It may seem unlikely that I was ever in the position to do her any useful service, and when I grew older I was not any the less ugly and insignificant. But as a result of those very characteristics, as I became familiar at Court I was also not often noticed. It was as if I was invisible when I wanted to be. I often overheard or saw, or guessed, when Madame's enemies plotted in secret to harm her. I became useful to her as time passed. She would not have lived so long if I had not guarded her.

As it was, she outlived her husband the Duke of Orléans, and his brother, the King. I am glad that she lived long enough to witness the triumph of her son, Philippe, becoming Regent on the death of Louis XIV despite the desperate plotting of M du Maine and the bastards. Madame loved her son deeply. I have studied her expression when he entered her drawing room, which he continued to do on most days even after becoming Regent. A faint blush of satisfaction, almost a gathering of repose would minutely change the contours of her face. For example, she had a way of sometimes tucking in her chin while looking out of the corner of her eye at his approach. She was occasionally severe, at which others would step back in order to be, in theory at least, out of hearing, but such encounters did not last and at the sound of her laughter at some witticism of his or, better still, a joke of her own, the whole court would visibly relax and step closer to her again.

She loved her son's nature, his talent for all the arts, his intellectual curiosity, and marvelled at his industry in serving the country. He works with his ministers and advisers from early in the morning until six in the evening. But once that hour has struck he retires into his own house accompanied by the most dissolute group of familiar friends, and particularly his eldest daughter, Mme de Berry, among them. It is said that he was too fond of his eldest daughter. No strangers were allowed to interrupt him there or to intrude uninvited. The Marquis de Saint-Simon tried for an entrée once and was refused, but swore ever after that it had never been his intention to participate in such wild and immoral behaviour. And I believe him; but the fact is that he tried once.

Things have not changed in that direction even now. Madame spoke to me about it recently. When she was in residence at St. Cloud I attended her court as often as I could. On the occasion when the Regent, in response to Madame's request, appointed my own son to that latest position at court where he soon won friendship and approval, I remember I attended at St. Cloud in order to express my thanks to her. She happened to be looking in the direction of the door when I approached, but not in expectation of myself or anyone else, I believe. She was deep in thought on some other matter. But having made my bow, when I looked up again I saw that her eye had cleared, and she was giving me a very searching look.

The very temperature of my skin and all my awareness was attuned to that scrutiny. My comfort depended on it.

"Well, Berthon," she said, "and are you content with what we have done?"

She was referring, of course, to my son's placement attendant on her son, the Regent. I knew her views of the Regent's lax moral standards in his private household. Madame herself let her ladies flirt and indulged their love affairs, but the repugnance she felt towards depravity was an entirely different thing. That very day the behaviour of Mme de Berry at the Regent's private parties was the occasion of numerous scandals and was being celebrated by the common songwriters of the city, just as they had circulated scandalous ditties about Athenais de Montespan before her disgrace. Madame held a sheet in her left hand which proved her point and she gave the piece of paper an indignant flick before screwing it up. I wished she hadn't done that. I would have liked to see what was written and now I would have to send Fanette's manservant to get another copy.

As for being content with what was done, as I said, she was referring to my son's acceptance at court by His Highness, the Regent. But what else can you do, when your son becomes a man, other than wish to see him given an entrée among the greatest in the land? The Regent's dissolute tastes were at least confined to his domestic life. His attention to the affairs of state belonged to a different part of his life altogether and usually the two were kept apart. Except in the case of a chosen few, and unfortunately my son was soon among them.

My son's name is Armand. How many men born as ugly as I, and in such circumstances as to have to stumble along a path in life so precariously laid with traps, have yet found love with a beautiful woman and had an unmarked child by her? Very few, I imagine. And in such circumstances, you hardly know when to relax your guard. Before his birth, I feared so grossly, so painfully, for the fate of any child of mine; whether he would inherit my physical defects. I doubted that cruel Nature would allow him to avoid them. I found it difficult to keep still during the day, and I could not sleep at night. No sooner had I recovered my wits when finding that Fanette was bearing my child, than this terror gripped me. My entrails turned to water when I contemplated the possibility of a version of myself emerging from the body of my beautiful young mistress; a child malformed like me. I felt how trivial and unimportant were my recent adventures in Italy compared with this. What does it matter if one's throat is cut with a dirty knife wielded by a scoundrel? In comparison, I had been at peace when I expected to be killed within seconds, whereas this other matter gave me no rest at all.

When Fanette was in labour, I heard only muffled cries from the room where I crouched waiting for the infant to be born. I was a coward beyond the very concept of cowardice. My sister Climene, who was with me, could hardly make herself heard for once. "Look at me!" she commanded repeatedly. "Look at me? Berthon, you fool. Am I ugly? Am I malformed? We have the same father, and your mother was faultless." I tried to look at her. She stood on the tip of one toe and spun round. The confection of her embroidered bodice, her silk skirts, her ribbons, threatened to catch on the furniture; and her radiant face above lit with the flash of her green eyes, from which I hid my own. And when Isabel, Fanette's maid, was at the door, with something in her arms, I fainted. At last, I squinted through the narrow gap that opened into consciousness, and they were showing me a child unwrapped, unhidden; a naked baby with a perfect body.

"Are you satisfied now?" exclaimed Climene. "Oh Berthon, this baby is extremely nice. I like it. Look at his hands and little feet. Mine was not anything like so pleasant. Don't contradict me."

Neither did the child die in infancy, as they so often do. He flourished. I was able to love him without restraint, because to him all things in this world were strange, myself no more so than a cup or a mouse, or another man. He was never afraid of me. He laughed when I came near him because of the sweets I carried, the stories I told him and the toys I made. He would run to meet me, take my hand, walk with me.

But when he was eight years old he was as tall as myself. Then I dreaded the moment when he would outpace me, when he would become a grown man and I would still be the way I am, and how he would first question, and then withdraw, and then, perhaps, hate me.

I hid my dread of the future. I told myself that soon he would begin to withdraw his affection and confidence from me, and I must simply bear it. He would be ashamed. I must be prepared for him to turn away from me. And there was a short time when I glimpsed the beginning of a strangeness. There was just intermittently an air of assessment in his look. I gave no hint of noticing, and I braced myself. I remember having a confused image in my mind; a pattern like an abstraction from a reality that either I did not fully know or did not dare to look at. I can describe it now; a diagonal, coloured as if it were dim glass with a third of it obscured with a jagged slice of a sharp sea-green. A combination of shape and colour without apparent connection to any representation of my son or me, and yet that abstract form summed up, in unfamiliar language, the disaster which threatened me. If an artist should do something so inappropriate to his craft as to paint that pattern, the rest of the Court would laugh at him, but I would not.

And then my son came back to me. I can't explain it. I have never known why. I suspect Fanette will have arranged it. He simply cleaved to his friendship with me in a way which was both new and familiar, and which never afterwards altered.

He is now a full-grown man and not at all like me. His limbs are straight. He is long. He has broad shoulders and an unmarred face. In fact, he so completely escaped the inheritance of my body that his mother's honour would not have been safe at Court. I must assume that he had some suffering on my account. He fought a duel in secret, when still very young, and he could have been dismissed for it. I was not allowed to know the quarrel that caused it, but I think it was almost certainly in revenge for some remark about myself. That is most likely. It would surprise me very much if other young men of his age had not, at some time or other, spoken disrespectfully about me.

CHAPTER FOUR

SINCE I must entertain myself with my own thoughts while I wait here, I will take leave to please myself with a study of Armand. He has light brown hair, thick eyebrows, blue eyes, and a graceful tall frame. He is almost as tall as the man who has come some time ago to court, called John Law, and about whose restructuring of the finances of France there has been such a tumult. I mention him because on his account – I mean Monsieur Law's – my son's aptitude for the affairs of State and finance have been most particularly trained, and it has been in Monsieur Law's great venture that he became employed when the Regent was pleased to notice him.

There is no doubt that when two dangers threaten us, it is often the least hazardous which monopolises our attention. Between the arrival of John Law at Court and the depravity of the Regent's community of friends where my son was housed, I was almost as fallible as every other fool at Court. It did not at first occur to me that Monsieur Law might be a more dangerous threat to life than drunken lascivious company. Nor did it occur to me that both would possess a third of my heart; the remaining third belonging to Fanette.

The first time I saw Monsieur Law was a chance meeting in the King's library at Versailles. I never entered among those walls of books without the sensation of wonder that settled on me in my childhood. The library at St. Germain – the old palace which pre-dated the Court's move to Versailles – was the first place that I ever felt was mine. Like a field mouse trespassing in the King's kitchen with a banquet all spread out, I crept on that first occasion through the massive doors opening from the South gallery when no one else was about, and stood in silent astonishment. The air smelled of paper and leather with none of the sharp tang of human occupation – of garlic, piss and other smells familiar at Court. This scented hush was not disturbed by me when I stealthily advanced into it. For that first year and a half, I read without ever being discovered. When eventually I was found out and taken to be punished, I was questioned by the old father of the Marquis de Villeroy (that tells you what a long time ago it was) and being himself a scholar and a kind man, he told my governor that I was to be allowed, with his Majesty's permission, to frequent his store of books. I owe my education mainly to that decision.

When the construction of Versailles was complete and the King and the whole Court moved there, the new library was furnished from the old and I frequented it as often, although I always hid myself a little. I was very rarely seen. And then one day in the year 1716 when I, now a father myself, and of an age when most of my contemporaries were either involved with the army or affairs of state, was absorbed in a study of Pythagoras, I suddenly became aware that a tall man with a brown wig had crept up on me.

Being so much older by then, I no longer felt the fearful caution of an intruder. Even so, his appearance gave me a shock. I saw that he was a handsome man. I have since learned that Scotland, which is the country he came from, breeds men like him who are tall and rugged, with great bones. At the same time he had a refined manner and spoke French reasonably well, and above all appeared not alarmed or offended by myself. In fact, there was a glint of humour in his eye which made me afraid, for an instant, that he might try to pick me up. But the next moment he said, with great courtesy, "Sir, I am an elephant admiring a diamond. Forgive me for disturbing you."

There was such charm in what he said that I did not remember in time how much worse I look when I smile. But still undisturbed, he said he had been hunting for a certain study of Pythagoras. This astonished me, as all coincidences invariably do astonish, and I pointed at the volume I held and asked him if it was the one he had been seeking. He looked very surprised, and explained that the study of mathematics was his present preoccupation, whereupon we became mutually absorbed in the subject, and had a lengthy discussion, and our friendship began.

This man – this great tall traveller from across the sea – had no support but his own wits to get by with. And yet here he was, in the King's library; not an intruder, nor yet a courtier, but an individual with such a sharp and intricate mind as I had never yet found in anyone at Court. Even his Highness the Regent, when he was still only the Duke de Chartres and would converse with me often, having known me since his childhood, never entered into any study with such consistency as to acquire the depth of knowledge which ultimately sharpens the mind of the man who discovers it. This man had.

To talk with him was to enter a space in one's own mind which was sparklingly lit. He was fortunate – or perhaps just very well practised, and of necessity – in having a very pleasant manner. But such a refinement, for real value's sake, needs to be linked to a firmness of character, and that this extraordinary man also had.

I soon found out more about him. He made his own money by gambling. He did not cheat, and yet he amassed very great sums, and was usually rich. The explanation was that he had an extraordinary memory. Madame de Clérembault, who had reappeared at Court after the death of Monsieur to resume her devoted friendship with Madame, was to be seen again still wearing the black velvet face mask which she thought essential for the preservation of her skin, and still as keen on cards and gambling as she ever was. And she was soon in awe of this new gentleman on account of his skill at the gambling tables, and his interest in money.

The explanation for Monsieur Law's appearance at the French Court lay in the coincidence of his needing employment, and of France needing a solution to the bankrupt condition of the State after the death of the old King, Louis XIV. Monsieur Law had such a solution in mind. I was soon fully acquainted with his financial plans and his ingenious system well in advance of most others at Court. I discussed it with Armand, my son. And His Royal Highness, the Regent, who was alight with enthusiasm for Law's scheme and who had from the beginning been attentive to the theories expounded by him, was favourably impressed to find among the newest members of his household a young man like Armand able to understand and support these ideas. In fact, it was probably a significant reason why my son became such an intimate of his Royal Highness the Regent.

This was not the first time John Law had travelled to Paris, but I did not meet or hear of him on the previous occasions, and neither did he succeed in interesting King Louis XIV, who was still alive then, in his proffered solution for the financial difficulties of the State.

That such difficulties existed was no secret. His Majesty was a very great man, with a magnificent and generous heart. But his understanding of finance was another matter. With wars, and with extravagant expenditure at home, he had spent all the gold and silver generated by the industry of his subjects and he was at a loss to know how more was to be come by. The solid silver benches which at first graced the gallery of mirrors in Versailles were melted down for coin. Imagine. Those great solid benches, which glittered with all their multiple reflections in candle or sunlight, reflected from, and in, great panels of glass, were carried by footmen in full court dress and loaded on carts by which they were delivered to the mint, where they were melted down into coin. Many silver candelabra and chairs from Versailles shared the same fate. To these sacrifices the King expected his subjects to add from their own stores, and they did, with plate mainly, although a large amount was hidden. I saw, with my own eyes, the secret cupboard of the Duke de Saint-Simon. But a sovereign country can't be financed on such terms anyway, however heroic in scale.

By his revocation of the Edict of Nantes, the King had already lost yet another great source of income since the experienced Protestant artisans, the Huguenots, deprived of the protection of the treaty, deserted France. I know about this particularly because my English friend, Francis, married to my half-sister Climene, says that nearly 400,000 Huguenots have arrived in Britain, and I heard similar figures referring to Savoy. Since the wars that Louis had waged throughout his reign in pursuit of the greater glory of France and the expansion of his own sovereignty in the Lowlands, and in the Palatinate and elsewhere, had been the chief drain on his purse, that source of wealth was entirely dissipated. He could not reconvert it. The taxes he levied did not repair the ravages of war made to gain them. And yet, at the same time, the expenses of his magnificent Court never flagged.

After the death of Louis XIV, John Law had returned again and approached the Regent, and it was during this visit that I met him in the library. The imminent bankruptcy of France had reached the point of being almost unavoidable, and it was in these circumstances that Law was granted a hearing and eventually succeeded in gaining a foothold at court both for himself and his financial scheme. He approached the problem of the bankruptcy of France from an entirely different point of view than that held by others. I think that from the beginning he was influenced not only by his own earlier apprenticeship in the Wittlesbank of Amsterdam, where paper money had already been introduced, but also by the recent formation of the Bank of England in 1694.

To those who had never imagined the possibility, he set himself to present the idea of a State becoming independent of the supply of precious metal for coinage by replacing gold and silver with paper. It was a subtle idea, and not inviting to a man or woman familiar with the age-old satisfaction of gold and silver coins, their weight, the sound they make, and the security, built up over so many centuries, that gold like the sun, and silver like the moon, actually represented the value of man's labour rather than being a figment of our imagination. But John Law was able to be very persuasive. His intellect and his imagination worked together with astounding range and precision. I was fortunate in happening to meet him and in being considered useful by him, as one to whom he could describe his ideas and thereby refine and improve the method of description, with some hope of being both tolerated and understood.

CHAPTER FIVE

HAVING spent a great deal of time in the King's library since a very early age, a number of subjects of study have attracted me, but none so fixed my attention as this scheme that John Law described. He had an attractive and very clear use of our language when he gave all his attention to the persuasion of an audience and spoke with an intriguing mixture of cool intelligence and vivid passion. I made a particular note of it. Later on, he honed his wits, as he put it, in his discussions with me, having all the time the object in mind of winning the debate he knew he must have with the Regent's advisors and other courtiers. The Regent himself he had already captured, but the Prince's temperament was mercurial. Despite the precision of his own remarkable intellect, he could vacillate exhaustingly according to the persuasions of others.

Monsieur Law's 'system' for exchanging the coinage for printed paper bills of exchange involved intricate peripheral planning dovetailed into the matrix of the new scheme. The bills of exchange, for example, would be printed with a specific value in silver at the time of issue and guaranteed by a national bank to hold that value. I could clearly imagine how convenient this could be. Coinage is expensive to mint and heavy to carry, especially when large sums have to be transported in the course of business. Covered carts have to be used to carry it from one part of the city to another when merchants are to be paid in gold and silver for the cargo unloaded from the holds of ships. The noise of these huge carts, usually at night, and of the armed guards who had to accompany them was familiar to those who did not live at Court. And all coins are prone to suffer the despoiling of their original weight by shavings-off or the addition of alloy metals, so that any piece could not be sure of representing the value engraved on it. In contrast, a paper bill of exchange, if regulated in the way Monsieur Law described, and printed with the weight in silver which it represented, could be exchanged at any time for that exact value, provided that the value is underwritten by a Bank. He argued that for the sake of commercial convenience bills of exchange (or banknotes as they were soon called) would rapidly replace the common circulation of specie, and the great convenience of this method of exchange would cause an expansion of commerce which would, in turn, replenish the State's stores of actual gold and silver held in an as-yet non-existent National Bank, to underwrite the commerce in paper.

I could see that my new friend would have a problem persuading the Regent's Council of Finance of this idea. My own problem here and now is not dissimilar, but I am weaving my explanation with so much care purely to satisfy myself, and not a rapacious audience of courtiers competing for power. The most immediate problem for Law was the recent failure, or depreciation, of bonds (the *billets d'état*) issued by King Louis before he died, and which would strike most people as not dissimilar from the paper money which Law now proposed. The great difference, however, lay in the fact that *billets d'état* were merely records of a permanent loan made to the Crown, on which a yearly payment was promised, whereas Law's paper would be printed with the value it represented in silver and could be exchanged at any time in a National Bank for that sum stated on it, in specie. And about that national bank, which featured large in the early discussions

I had with Law, France did not have one. Our 'national bank' was the King.

John Law seemed to think that there would be little or no problem establishing a national bank over which the King would have no control and would need no control. I thought it very doubtful, here in France, but refrained from annoying him with my speculations. This bank would be funded to maintain payment at the figure printed on the paper; certainly a very necessary expedient. If the Regent still had the power to alter figures, he would certainly do so; already he had reduced the dividend on *billets d'état* from 12% to 7% since the death of the old King.

I took only a mathematical interest in these arguments at first. Subsequently, when I was at court, and more especially when paying court to Madame, I soon noticed that M. Law began to be often spoken of by everyone. The existing *billets d'état*, now on the brink of being declared valueless, were still at that point yielding seven per cent *rentes* (as dividend was called), and despite the general anxiety about cash, Law was most often spoken of in terms of his personal manners and style of dress, which were exemplary.

In this very crux of the problems of State, that right of the King to alter, and devalue, the *billets d'état* if necessary, was the very 'solution' put forward by Chancellor Desmarets, the successor of Chamillard, when he became Director of Finance shortly after Monsieur Law appeared at court. He proposed the arbitrary reduction of the bond-holder's dividend from the prevailing 7 per cent, to 4 per cent, and a state lottery to raise the means of paying even the 4 per cent. This scheme was adopted with all the disastrous results predicted by John Law. He said that such a programme would destroy public confidence in the state bonds, which would lose their value as a means of exchange in the money market, and that was precisely what happened. Only days after the scheme was initiated, the value of *billets d'états* dropped by 80 per cent in the Paris money market. I went to the Rue Quinquampoix to see for myself. There was an atmosphere of febrile fatalism in the way they were trading, like condemned prisoners tying the knots in their own ropes.

Later that day I met John Law as usual in the library. I already had a very different attitude to the coming storm and I was eager to hear what Law would say about the day's events. Yet again, the quality of his strong character impressed me. He strode in looking for me, his great long legs and huge feet making very little noise despite the fact that he did not walk in the court manner. The events of the day must have impacted greatly on his plans, and I supposed that he had already discussed them with the Regent; but his manner was discreet, although clearly buoyant. At this distance in time I have forgotten the detail of our conversation, but what I remember – apart from the fact that the Regent had called a meeting of the Finance Council for the following day – was that extraordinary physical impression of equanimity and buoyant strength which was so much a part of Law's attraction. He spoke about the coming trial like a man relishing the prospect of a fight which he would enjoy and had reason to hope of winning. I know it crossed my mind to warn him of the depth of ambitious men's abhorrence of new solutions which are not their own, but fate had clearly struck the first blow in his favour, in the collapse, which he had predicted, of the market in bonds.

I can recall the apartment prepared for the Council the next day. I failed to slip in when the Council assembled. The room was too bare. There were no women, whose skirts normally create a malleable crowding in an assembly where I wish to make my way unobserved, and in addition, the members of the Council made a distinct and formal group. Not being myself a member, I had to wait outside and listened to a certain amount of mindless gossip. One man described Law as very handsome – which he was – and "a gambler, adulterer, convicted murderer and coward with beautiful manners." All that was true, except that he was no coward.

After the meeting, the members of the Finance Council came out of the chamber and stood about, still discussing the measures Monsieur Law had proposed and which – apparently very much to their satisfaction – they had yet again rejected. The State was bankrupt and they knew it. You would have thought that in these circumstances the Council would not have rejected Law's system again. But they did.

I heard one gentleman say that what was needed was the philosopher's stone to turn paper into gold. Despite the keen interest with which many of us viewed alchemy and especially at Court where the transformation of base metals into gold always fascinated certain gentlemen with a scientific turn of mind, he meant it only as a witticism. He stood there smiling in the brief burst of laughter which followed, but behind him Law himself had arrived in time to hear what he said.

"I know how to do that," said Monsieur Law. "I know how to turn paper into gold."

As his expression was not humorous but almost severe, his audience did not know quite how to take this. One of them said,

"Are you going to tell us, Monsieur?" This was the Duke of Noailles. He was always against Law and the rise of the man's fame. He knew too well that men of moderate intelligence like his own needed to keep a constant eye open to suppress those who might rise above them.

Monsieur Law, with no change of expression except for

a slight glint of merriment, replied, "I will explain it the next time we meet."

It certainly was a most extraordinary statement. Did he want to be believed? Or was it a poetic expression? Those standing around him at the time demonstrated the sort of variation in their faces that you might see in men who, half way across a fragile bridge, hear a loud crack. Shock; annoyance; indecision. The Duke of Noailles laughed very unpleasantly. I always understood why the Duke of Saint-Simon so deeply disliked that man. Ambition that makes a man frigid, as it did him, also made him very thin. That is no crime, but in his case his mouth, under the influence of not infrequent mean thoughts, could look as if it had been eaten by a worm. Clearly, he considered that M. Law had made a fool of himself now, and his tone was insulting when he said, "How do you expect to do that?"

Monsieur D'Agessau and the young son of de la Rochefoucault were just turning away with the air of abandoning a discussion that would no longer bear the weight of their intelligence, but they paused to hear what came next. I noticed that Samuel Bernard, who was present to advise the Council, and in all probability to lend the Regent yet more money in addition to the six million livres he had already given to the late King, showed instead a demeanour of benevolent interest towards Law. Bernard was watching him intently, but with a cautious smile and a look of acute interest. Law himself, being such a great tall man and being wanted for murder in his own country, as I well knew, neither stiffened nor heated up at Noaille's manner. Indeed, he seemed quite unprovoked, and I challenge any man who would fail to recognise the courage of a gentleman capable of standing up with unaffected dignity and even humour to the bullying scorn of his peers. It is true that, later on, when it came to having his throat slit, he had a different attitude. But for this kind of danger, he knew exactly how to resist. He stood there, his expression being candid, his eyelids being slightly lowered on a gleam of amusement, and gave them that reply: "Gentlemen, I promise to explain it to you, but not yet." And then he bowed and got away with the apparently satisfied calm of a man who knew precisely how to do what he said.

Considering that his system, as he called it, for the reform of the economy of France had just been refused by the Council for the fourth time, and that he had worked on it so diligently and for so long, it was a miracle of endurance, self-discipline, and diplomacy on his part.

I believe that after that meeting he retired to his own house, while those who had rejected his advice set about implementing the ruinous alternative favoured just that one last time by the Regent. I, who had such good reason to appreciate courage and an indomitable spirit when I saw it, marvelled at him.

I discussed this later with Armand. I visited my son's mother in the evening and found him there.

CHAPTER SIX

ARMAND'S mother still lives in the same house in the village of Versailles with her maid Isabel and the blackamoor servant, as she did when I first knew her. I have my apartment in the palace, as always, but Fanette very rarely comes to Court, whereas I am forever in her house and most happy there.

I saw her first on the stage in Paris where she played the part of Aricie in a performance of *Phèdre.* When she appeared, for myself it was as if a sudden silence swallowed all evidence of normal life in that space except for her, and I had an undiluted experience not only of her, the beauty of her face and figure, but the essence of her gentle and strong nature, her grateful mind, her steadfastness, even more. I am not sure that I didn't in that moment become aware of the colour of the tapestry on the chairs in her house, and the presence of the black servant who cooked for her, but of course, that must have been an illusion. But it was not an illusion when my life's happiness slipped so unexpectedly into view.

I made Fanette my wife. This miraculous state of affairs need not trouble my friends too much. What many others are used to I must not try to astonish them with. Unlike the expectations of other men, I had never imagined that the love of a beautiful woman was for me.

I kept my apartment in the palace of Versailles but I rarely pass a night in it now. I was still devoted to Madame while she lived, and still attended her court and watched over her with undiminished determination to frustrate the threats of her enemies. But I lived with Fanette in our house in the village of Versailles and it was there our son was born. The moment when I first really looked at him is imprinted on the inside of my very eyelids, as if by some supernatural process, for me to verify whenever I close my eyes. No doubt I am repeating myself but I saw the little body lying very still, breathing and perfect; not marked with any gashes of careless nature, nor splits or unevenness. The limbs lay like those of the baby Christ painted by Raphael. The skin was smooth. I reached out and took one of the hands. It was perfect. I counted the fingers. He woke and opened eyes that were set within little lids and orbs as symmetrical and pure as any I had ever seen, and the mouth, when he opened it, was pink and sweet. When fed, he sucked with clean lips like the mouths of the goldfish in the fountain basins of Versailles sucking the surface of the water.

Now that Armand is a grown man, on the subject of Monsieur Law he has been eloquent. He admired him not quite inordinately, but enough. For example, when I gave him an account of my impressions of that Council meeting, he clearly already knew the state of play and judged it to be inconclusive. In fact, now that I consider it, he no doubt already knew how his Highness the Regent was on the brink of rejecting the advice of the Council of Finance.

Perhaps Monsieur Law also knew it, and that accounts for his *sangfroid* when he made that remark about turning paper into gold and parried so excellently the scornful riposte of de Noailles.

All this revolved in my mind as I spoke to Armand that very evening. I was to be at Court in waiting on Madame at St. Cloud the next day. I no longer rose quite so easily at five in the morning in order to be in attendance at eight. On those occasions I needed to sleep in my apartment in the palace, and not rest here with Fanette, and I must have Gaudet with me, to dress. I felt unusually tired that evening. There are times when my body is very restless, and I have no means of knowing whether this is something that others suffer or whether it is unique to me, as are so many of my features. I remember glimpsing Armand as he exchanged a glance with Fanette as if they had some subject under discussion that I did not know about. I sensed, rather than knew at that very moment, that the dangerous environment in which he shared the Regent's pleasures had reached some threatening point.

The shadows of evening were now lengthening. Armand must be expected elsewhere. His Highness the Regent returned at six for his hours of gaming, eating and other pleasures and if my son had the honour of being expected, he must go. I found him bowing to me before I had even reached this point in my reflections, and with no time to guard my expression I must have looked agitated because he took my hand, but still left.

"My dear," Fanette said, "will you not sit with me a moment? I know you must go soon but surely you can dine with me, and here is the glass of wine that Isabel has already brought for you."

Fanette was wearing blue silk; not the powder blue that Madame wore all those years ago when she first arrived for her marriage celebrations at the old palace of St. Germain but a brighter and darker shade. The colour of bluebells. The sight of her calmed my heart and I sat down and waited. Whatever accident or treachery or misjudgement threatened our son, she would know it and would tell me if I waited. I hoped that it would be a small thing. But how could anyone scape injury if they play constantly in a house that is on fire? That was how I viewed the Regent's household at the time.

"He is in love," Fanette said. Was this all?

"Do you mean with the Princess? Armand has been devoted to Louise Adélaïde for a long time," I replied. "Surely he won't break his heart over her now?"

"It is not her," she said. I waited again.

"He is in love with Louise Adelaide's sister, the Duchess de Berry."

I almost laughed. The Duchess de Berry, although beautiful, is very sick, and also considerably older than Armand. Her spirit is in a constant state of laughing despair, and she is always drunk. Her father, the Regent himself, dotes on her, and she returns his passion to a degree which has aroused scandalous speculations at court. I must admit that. She is married to the Duke of Berry, grandson of Louis XIV. She would be Queen if de Berry's older brother had not given birth to our present young king before both he and his wife died of smallpox.

I say I almost laughed, but of course, the romantic fantasies of the very young are a serious matter, and Fanette herself looked troubled. She said,

"Monsieur, he is too much in love."

"The young often are," I said, remembering Ernst and La Belle Adaire.

"But she is a dangerous woman. What if he persists?"

"Surely he won't. She may play with him an hour or two, like a cat with a mouse..."

"Cats kill mice," said Fanette.

I went in my carriage back to the palace that evening. It was Autumn, but there was a full moon, and the landscape displayed, as an etching does compared to colour, the noble harmony of the mind of Le Notre when he designed the whole. The old King had loved it. No shortage of gold and silver had cramped him then, when the visions of his own imagination and those of Le Notre had called for millions of expenditure to create the gardens, the fountains, the lakes, the terraces, the great paved way: the palace of

Versailles itself. And once made, they could not be turned back into mere coin.

However, if Monsieur Law thought paper could be turned into gold, and he was as clever a man as I thought him, who could tell what feats of alchemy he might strive to perform? At that moment – although I ignored it at the time – I remember a sensation as if I was looking through a corrupted glass at the scene I went through. Philosophers tell us that we presume too much on our limited perception of nature as solid and truly existing; those great trees, the avenue, the water laid like cut glass reflecting the night sky. But for once I saw them all as shadows. One day they would not be there.

CHAPTER SEVEN

AFTER the death of her husband, Madame's household at St. Cloud was exactly as she liked it. She always had preferred the palace at St. Cloud to being in Paris, and now she visited her son in the Palais-Royal in Winter when she moved there herself, whereas, years ago she had been obliged to go whenever Monsieur, her husband, chose. Besides, she complained very much that her son's wife was too lazy to keep a proper Court there. That her daughter-in-law certainly was. And Madame's granddaughter Madame de Berry never left her bed in the mornings, and although she was beautiful she often looked slovenly, even when wearing cloth of gold and fine jewels. It was something about her, and what was more it attracted certain men very much, not forgetting her own father who she indulged by kissing him and sitting in his arms. Even more.

At the Regent's private suppers, the ladies and even the gentlemen dressed however they liked, and none of the graceful formalities Madame approved of were observed with any rigour. At St. Cloud, Madame held her own Court, and all who attended on her there knew what was expected of them. His Highness the Regent, when he visited his mother as he often did, found himself in the familiar environment of his youth and, when there, never offended her by transgressing any of the practices which she considered essentially civilised. And yet there was an atmosphere at St. Cloud of lightness and freedom, entirely in keeping with that other side of the character of Madame who, at the same time as insisting with quelling dignity on the correct observances of precedence and other matters belonging to her royal position, loved gossip, allowed her ladies to flirt and play, and delighted in good food.

As soon as she decently could after the death of Monsieur, who had banned Clérembault from appearing at Court, Madame recalled her dear friend from exile, and the two of them and the lady Theoban were as good friends as they had been when I was very young. In those days of my youth, I would often be inconspicuously sitting on a cushion on the floor, as near her as Madame allowed me to be. Now, when Clérembault had returned to court, she always had a sour smile for me. She remembered lending me the money needed to travel into Italy for evidence of the past crimes of the Chevalier de Lorraine at the time when he contemplated poisoning Madame. I think she had a certain affection for me as probably the only person to whom she, rich and miserly as she was, had ever lent money. Of course, I was only the means to an end, that end being the protection of Madame from the most dangerous of her enemies at Court.

Although I never referred to it, my memory preserved, almost verbatim, her words of passionate love when describing to me the moment when she first met Madame. I never heard, or read, a more moving account of complete adoration from any man for his mistress than that I heard from Mme de Clérembault for Madame. I'm sure she had momentarily forgotten my presence when she spoke those words aloud. I'm sure she assumed I had forgotten them now.

I watched her sometimes after she returned to Court after the death of Monsieur. Although many years older, she retained that unlined and radiant complexion which she was sure she owed to almost always wearing a velvet mask over her skin. She also retained her love of gambling. I think she was of the party when Monsieur Law first met His Highness the Regent playing lasquenet. Age made absolutely no difference to her stamina. Four in the morning still meant nothing to her, if she retained good cards; or bad ones. She made so much money, no doubt she possessed the powers of divination that she claimed were hers. Her latest dictum was that Madame, who had begun to suffer with her health, would not die until shortly after she herself, the Marquise de Clérembault, had expired. No doubt this was meant to reassure Madame, who suffered several difficult illnesses. But when Clérembault died just recently in November, a sense of inevitability must have weighed on Madame. I saw it in her eyes; in the solemnity of her step when she attended Mass. I regretted it.

Surely the change in the body's humours, when resignation slows down the pulse and thickens the blood, leads to ill-health. Clérembault's powers of prediction were certainly upheld, but her dear friend might not have wanted to follow as close on her heels as she had foretold.

On the day after the session of the Finance Council which I began to describe before other thoughts distracted me, I was in attendance on Madame. John Law was also present at St. Cloud. After her morning devotions, which were much more drawn out than in the past, Madame ate well and then walked in the gardens until dinner. For a good deal of the time, she walked with Monsieur Law. She did not call me to her side, but as usual I lingered near and heard much. She enquired about the meeting of the Council of Finance the day before, and he replied. He gave her a very accurate account of it. He did not dwell on the enmity of de Noailles that day or the vacillation of d'Aguesseau's loyalty, but if she was expecting something of the sort he made it possible for her to infer it, and I well imagine how she must have rolled her eyes, as she would do when listening to such tales. Afterwards, she told Clérembault that she thought Law a handsome fellow, and remarked that he spoke French better than other Englishmen.

When Madame dismissed him, Monsieur Law noticed myself and drew me aside. By this time Madame had retired to write her letters.

"Tell me, Berthon," he said, "what impression had you yesterday?"

"I was not able to be present at the Council," I said.

"You missed an interesting scene, but you were in the adjoining room afterwards and must have heard the discussion that took place there, I fancy."

He stopped and snapped off the head of a perfect small rose, removed his pocket book, and laid the petals carefully in the page before shutting it tight. There was a pause. The sky was utterly blue. It was hard to remember that in June, a year ago, hail the size of pigeon's eggs had fallen so thick on the fields of Bordeaux and the region of Toulouse that all the harvests were ruined.

"Before he retired," Law continued, "I attempted to remind His Highness of the difference in the income the French throne can expect resulting from the disappearance of factories and artisans of the weaving trade since the Edict of Nantes was revoked. It has taken some years for those branches of former commerce to become completely bare, but..."

I could hardly believe what I heard.

"Tell me," I begged him, "please, that you said no such thing."

"Isn't it true?"

"What of that? Many truths are better not spoken of."

"Well, there I'm afraid, I do not entirely agree with you..." He paused. He was so tall that it was inconvenient for me to raise my eyes to his face. If I saw a bench nearby

I could persuade him to sit on it. But he breathed deeply, as if he was pleased, and looked over my head, repeating, "There, I am afraid, I must *dis*agree with you, my friend. Those of us in search of a clear view of reality cannot afford such a trick. But timing is everything, and I do accede to your prejudice enough to admit that I reminded his Highness of that at the wrong moment."

I was sure of it.

When the Regent was a child – known then as the Duke of Chartres until his father, the Duke of Orléans, died – he had a compliant and easy nature. But I, who knew him so well in those days and used to tell him stories and sometimes made him toys, knew better, now that he ruled the country, than to correct him or try to tell him of things he would not want to hear.

"Is that so?" Law replied casually. "However, here I am. I have not been sent to the Bastille. I believe you may be right to the extent that a better time and place would have been when others were not present. I'm afraid several of them leapt on what I said and twisted it, and His Highness always listens to everyone. That's convenient when it includes oneself, but it makes him, with the broad range of sympathy and understanding which he possesses, difficult to convince when he listens to everyone else as well."

I could not resist laughing at the way he put it. His description was so accurate and targeted so exactly the problem which Madame herself complained of: and the Duke of Saint-Simon and many others.

"His Highness will sometimes weary of argument, and he vacillates, but he is very intelligent," I said.

"Precisely. So he understood perfectly well that losing so many factories and artisans in the weaving and cloth trade when thousands of Protestants fled France was not a good thing. It damaged the means of repairing the finances with that amount of profitable commerce. And that is only one example. Healthy trade and commerce are absolutely necessary, but so is a monetary system, which helps that commerce. Both are essential. My scheme will replace an outdated monetary system with one which frees the trader from the encumbrance of coinage and liberates France from the threat of bankruptcy."

These were the words of a man who had spent the last eighteen years refining and tirelessly offering this scheme to the rulers of France, Italy, England and Savoy and had been every time rejected. I thought that perhaps his reluctance to sit on the bench which was now in front of him might be a reflection of his determination not to submit to any move even remotely connected to the deportment of a man defeated. Then he seemed suddenly to remember my dilemma, and sat down.

"Berthon," he said, "you are very courteous to listen to me."

"On the contrary," I replied with complete sincerity, "I am interested in the science of alchemy as well as mathematics." I had had to crane my neck to say it, and then it was that he suddenly stepped forward and sat down on the bench. "And you have such skill with figures," I added, "that you even surpass, by the use of memory alone, a clairvoyant gambler like the Marquise de Clérembault. You have beaten her at cards, Monsieur. She will never let you out of her sight until she has her money back."

He laughed. Who ever heard a man, who had completely failed for eighteen years at the same endeavour, laugh like that? The sun shone on his face as he threw it back and I got a glimpse of white teeth, which is more than you could say for many of us at Court.

Even so, it did seem to me at that moment that a man who had made such a groove for himself might be stuck in it.

"She will have her money back," he said. "If I can persuade His Highness to adopt my system, all France will get her money back." And seeing that I showed no inclination to end our discussion, he righted himself on his hard seat which brought him level with myself as I stood before him, and leaning forward said, "Members of the Council of Finance wanted to reduce the income paid on existing government bonds or *billets d'état* from seven to four per cent. At the same time, his Highness knew he needed to issue even more bonds because, without them, he cannot even finance the payment of the reduced interest on those that already exist. So when the new bonds are issued, who did they think would buy them? Those whose *billets d'état* were nearly halved in value last week? Not likely. In fact, my estimate was that the value of the newly issued billets would drop in value by fifty per cent in the space of one day and that is exactly what happened."

If I recall correctly now – and this is years later, remember; I am no longer talking in the Autumn sunshine to the man who became my friend Law, but sitting here in my freezing carriage at night and keeping myself from starving of cold by writing this. And of course, the banknotes which were issued had done as he predicted. In fact, they had fallen not by fifty, but by eighty per cent, in the space of twenty-four hours.

I heard that Noailles went in person to the Rue Quinquampaux to remonstrate with those who he thought had control of the money market, but needless to say, he fed the bitterness of his own spirit without succeeding in forcing his point of view down the throats of the tradesmen and bankers he found there. The demand for gold and silver rather than *billets d'état* of any sort was instantly twice as determined as before, and the Regent had to explain that the Crown simply had no more specie to give. What choice was left to him? It was either bankruptcy or Law's system.

But I must not lose sight of the man himself – Law as he

sat in the garden that day – or of the prospect of success which radiated from his entire bearing, in complete contrast to his predicament. Perhaps his remarkable mental quickness at calculations exceeded the range of mere numbers but extended to the faint hints of the weather in other men's minds so as to be able to add up the value of a sigh of impatience last week, a suppressed smile observed today, an adviser who stumbled over his conclusion and failed to quite convince, a blink of an eye, a trace of interest in a quickened glance. He behaved so much as if he knew, not guessed, his eventual power to persuade.

"But if the Council and Parliament have their way now," I said then, "despite the result having been as you foretold, surely it will be too late for you to persuade the market to use paper of another sort. Presumably, no one would trust it. Will you leave France in that case?"

"Oh no," he said. I kept silence. "I have my methods. And I have my secrets." He stood up. "Believe me, Berthon," he said. "I am confident that I shall have the pleasure of your conversation here in France for many years to come."

I hoped that what he said was true, because I greatly enjoyed his friendship.

Before I left St. Cloud, the Maréchale de Clérembault took me aside and said, "I should like to know, Berthon, what Monsieur Law confided to you in the garden here. And in case you wonder at my curiosity, let me tell you that I do not trust that man."

"Trust him with what, Mme de Clérembault?" I said.

"Ideas, of course. He has dangerous ideas."

Theobon was just out of hearing, but she came nearer to listen. I noticed such a sideways peep from her eye that I had a most uncomfortable feeling of being once more a small boy tolerated only by the kindness of Madame, and not that of anyone else. Madame was absent, writing her letters, and the other ladies had retired. I realised that I had no chance of getting away without an explanation, and I gave the Maréchale the most lucid account that I could, at that point, of Law's reactions.

She would have no detail excluded. Madame herself would not, at the time, tolerate discussion on the subject with her ladies, because it bored her, and consequently the Maréchale was afraid of being behind in the world over a means of enrichment; or the reverse. Fondness for money seems to be an appetite which grows with what it feeds on. There was no doubt that with her surpassing intelligence she might have insight into the likely result of this system, and eventually I asked her if that was the case.

She did not grudge me this small return for my lengthy explanation. She thought severely for a moment, and then said, "It will not work." She paused. "All that you told me is very interesting. I would say he is a most clever man. But that idea of his for a National Bank, or *Banque Privée*, is not feasible for us in France. In England, they have a different institution of monarchy. Their parliament, not their king, has the control of the country's exchequer. Here, our king rules the finances of the country, and I am telling you now, Berthon – and as you know I love his Majesty as much as any subject, and His Highness the Regent perhaps even more so – that very difference would be ruinous to the plans you have described. What they can do in England, we in France cannot. In every other way, it is a good scheme. But this flaw would be fatal." She remained silent for a moment in a pose which made it clear that it was not yet time for anyone else to speak. "I must conclude that Monsieur Law is a very pleasant man, since Madame already says so, and the Duchess de Maine permitted him to kiss her hand last week. But charm can be fatal."

I think she must have mentioned this idea, of the constitutional difference between the two monarchies being a bar against the project in France, to the Duke of Saint-Simon, because later I heard him proclaim it as his own opinion.

CHAPTER EIGHT

MY English friend, Francis, Lord Claydon, who many years ago married my sister Climene, returns often to Paris. I still have the saddle that he made for me, which enabled me to ride on horseback when otherwise my deformity would not have allowed it. Francis has changed in appearance a good deal since his father died and he came into the title and the estate. Either the climate in England is as dreadful as Climene insists on telling me, or simply being married to my sister is the cause.

I can best describe Climene as a loving shrew, whose beauty and innocence, combined with a warped sense of humour and fearlessness, have held Francis in thrall since he first met her.

When he was younger, he was handsome, and he still is, but those cold winters and too much fresh air and open bedroom windows (I quote Climene) have toughened the skin on his face, and he has the aquiline look now of a man always scanning the horizon. But when he brings his eye to bear on a near object, like oneself for example, it is surprising to encounter more amusement than anything else, as if he was permanently occupied with some private joke of a kindly nature.

I found him and Climene in Paris on my return from St. Cloud. I felt that I had had enough conversation of late on the subject of finance, even for me. In general, there was too much emphasis on fantasies of the imagination that all extremes of wealth or poverty seem to let fly, whereas it is the mathematics which hold my interest for longer without my becoming weary. In the case of Francis and Climene I could have it both ways, but have it I must.

It was the South Sea Company which Francis had dealings with in London. Since I had to, I listened to Climene first, on the subject of the exotic spices and jewels which the trade with such a fecund area of the world would undoubtedly make available to all who were lucky enough to live in England, and how much she looked forward to being especially rich. Whereas Francis was hungry for reciprocal information about Law and eager to explain the details of the new British Bank in exchange for what I could tell him of Law's future ideas for a Private National Bank in France.

"Francis has invested in it," Climene announced triumphantly, referring to the South Sea Company. "There are five of them."

Francis darted a look at her which, as always, held a glint of humour in it; but his lip also narrowed. He had probably not intended to mention it. I remember suppressing a smile myself. I could not help loving Climene, and not least for her wayward wit. She will, with delicious and frivolous titbits, tempt the unwary whose tender parts are then brutally pinched by a sudden release of logical insight.

To relieve Francis, I appeared to pay no attention to Climene's information about his involvement and mentioned instead the English bank and, incidentally, the Clérembault's comment on that matter. He looked relieved, and nodded. As far as he was concerned, of course, he was encouraged by the judgement in favour of a bank under English jurisdiction. If I ever wished to converse on any other topic with him – for example, that excellent English gentleman, Matthew Prior, who had been acquainted with Law in Holland, and as a diplomat here in France, had recently published some more poems – I had to promise him an evening with Law and Armand first. I took some time explaining the various connections which made that possible, at which point Climene, of course, expressed an ardent interest in being invited to one of the Regent's *soirées*. Not quite for the first time, I spotted the dark stain of a storm cloud in Francis's eye and realised my mistake, not only for his sake but my own. What if Climene witnessed some evidence of my son's infatuation with the Duchess de Berry? Her observation could be much sharper than her discretion.

"Don't look like that, Berthon," she already said. "Since when did you expect me to be a hermit?"

I would have preferred not to smile, but I couldn't help it. In that instant, with a flash of penetration, I perceived how like the Clérembault was my half-sister: a sharpness of spirit born of an unusual intelligence, but in her case trapped like a butterfly behind glass, emotionally denied the outlet of scholarship which the Clérembault enjoyed, but defiantly flinging her brightly coloured mind in all directions. Francis held his lips between his teeth in a characteristic gesture, but the corners of his mouth escaped upwards.

"His Highness the Regent only invites his especial circle: his own household," I said.

"But I'm sure he sometimes includes you, Berthon," countered Climene immediately. "Think of all those toys you made him when he was a child and how he loved to play with you. He is not changed. I don't believe it."

"Yet he has never invited me to his evenings," I pointed out. "And so I am in no position to promote you, Climene."

"Then I shall ask Louis Armand."

I was afraid she would say that. At which point Armand came into the drawing room accompanied by the Princess Louise Adélaïde and Madame's godson Ernst. The Princess hardly allowed Climene to rise from her curtsy before seizing her and kissing her absolutely on the face, while laughing like a boy. She was dressed as usual in the plainest clothes allowed even at the Regent's court. I caught a glimpse of her shoe at one moment and it must have been designed for a young man to wear when out walking. And yet her unpainted face had great charm, and so far the constant exposure to sun, wind and rain from hunting and walking had not affected her complexion. I had once suggested to Armand that he should perhaps desist, now that the Princess had reached marriageable age, from taking her with him when he went hunting on foot with his dogs, but neither her father the Regent nor her mother the Duchess of Orléans seemed the least concerned, and so nothing changed.

Francis, being free to talk with Armand after the general courtesies of meeting, broached the subject of Monsieur Law and his 'system'. His interest was very keen. There was a penetration in his manner which, while familiar, was so sharpened that I wondered again if he was uneasy about his own situation in England. In the month or so since I had last seen him in France, he had aged disproportionately. It crossed my mind that he might be ill.

My son, in response to pressing questions from Francis, discoursed on the relative merits of Law's project of the Banque Générale (it had a slightly different name, it seemed to me, each time it was mentioned) compared with the Bank of England, and Francis listened with a sharpness and attention which made me proud of Armand. No doubt his main teacher in all this was John Law, but that was entirely satisfactory to Francis, who, as I began to suspect, had made this particular visit to us with the express objective of meeting the financier.

Monsieur Law could not go to England himself without risking imprisonment and worse, because of the judgement still outstanding against him for murder. And so Francis had come here. Realising the urgency implied in his coming at this time, my curiosity for news of the progress of the South Sea Company which the English Bank was supporting, quickened a great deal.

The English were well ahead of us at that stage. The South Sea Company had been established already for about four years in London. That John Law contemplated something similar for us in France in terms of colonial expansion was news which Francis received with enthusiasm, but Law had only referred to it once, and then as a principle alone when illustrating his suspicion that land would ultimately prove more reliable than specie as a means of generating security for his system. But I digress. I myself am too good an example of the allure of mathematical speculation, even now. It still has the power to warm my blood, even on this night of freezing vigil. Back then, I was piqued with curiosity for why Francis should be concealing such an edge. If I did not know him so well, I would almost have thought he was afraid of something. Since I knew him to be indifferent to any physical threat, I wondered if he was in danger of losing his money.

At that moment Climene put her hand on his arm to regain his attention. I remember it well. The emerald on her third finger was the very same as that worn by the late Queen of France when I was at court as a boy. Louis XIV had needed, in the year before his death when he found himself nearly bankrupt, to sell jewels, as well as melting the silver benches in the galerie des Glaces for coinage, and accepting a gift of six million livres Tournois from Samuel Bernard.

And Francis?

Given the ring Climene was wearing, I had not realised that he was such a rich man.

The next time I attended on Madame she had moved from Versailles to Paris, the weather having become cold and the trees losing their leaves. The apartments in the Palais-Royal have smaller rooms, and reminded me of the old palace, and the time spent there. I shouldn't dwell now, when the night is so dark and cold and prone to grief, on how cruelly those four favourites of her husband hounded Madame. They hated her not for anything she had ever done or said, but because her very existence threatened their privileged status as the favourites of Monsieur, her husband. I have seen Lorraine follow Philippe with his eye when Monsieur approached his wife in her drawing room. It was the same sort of look that a wolf might give, on observing a stray lamb. After a brief interval, during which he appeared to be listening to some gossip, as before, we all heard the duke of Orléans laugh heartily at something Madame had told him, and their mutual enjoyment was more than Lorraine could bear. From my usual point of view, I could see the point of Mme de Grancy's shoe peep out from under her skirt and nudge Lorraine's foot. Lorraine did not turn his head, but he seemed to flex the muscles in the back of his neck, and then bent gracefully forward for the lady to whisper in his ear, after which they both laughed as if they were flutes playing a coda to the conversation of Monsieur and Madame. He won. Orléans heard him and abandoned his *tête-à-tête* with his wife. Whether or not Monsieur had continued to prefer the Chevalier de Lorraine to Madame, he clearly would play his flatterer's game in preference to that of the declared friend and defender of his wife. Lorraine would have poisoned Madame if he could, as he had poisoned Monsieur's first wife. Until her death, Madame would on occasion mention these events of the past in talking to me, and she did so quite recently. She even referred to the Chevalier with reference to her reconciliation with him a mere month ago, before her final illness settled on her; to the fact that he was so altered since he had endured the French disease twice, in spite of which he still died in the midst of his usual excesses.

Although the Duke de Chartres has long inherited his father's title of Orléans and is now a grown man and has become the Regent of France during the minority of our new King, the bond which formed between myself and him when we were both children is not broken. It is set aside because he is become so great and I am still so small, but it is there.

Madame's husband was also handsome, but her son has inherited none of the thoughtless cruelty of his father. For example, the Regent's first action, in the week following the death of his uncle, Louis XIV, was to demand to see all the *lettres de cachet* from the offices of the various secretaries of State. He then freed more than a hundred wretched prisoners from the Bastille, and the condition of some of them was so pitiable that when they appeared the population of Paris was outraged; but I had the impression that unjust imprisonment was so linked to the monarchy in the minds of the people that they scarcely noticed whose hand it was that set the prisoners free.

Whenever the Regent is unjustly criticised – which is often – I feel for him almost as much as Madame, his mother. She used to know this. She was of the sort who truly loves her children. She used to tell me that this was because she came from Germany; but I love my own son just as much and I am from France. If Armand now got into difficulties because of his close association with the Regent's debaucheries when his day's work was done, it would grieve me very much. Madame might have deplored her son's private life in this context, but naturally she did not consider Armand as in need of protection from being involved in it. I did. Armand was still so young, and at the very age when a boy is not quite yet a man, but very attracted to manly virtues; and vices. Sometimes he reminded me of a cat picking its way along a narrow shelf the further surface of which has lost its support. I spent many wakeful hours pondering the enigma of how to keep him safe.

So I had no difficulty understanding the feelings of Madame when she was mortified by the ingratitude, criticism or scorn of the Regent's enemies. It was infinitely painful for her to know that he deserved so much more praise for his good nature and his talent for the arts and sciences and also his devotion to his duties regarding the State, than he received from others. She would complain often and bitterly at how he abused his body with excessive food and wine, but far more dangerous, in my opinion, are the other substances he indulged and still indulges in, and the unbridled sexual profligacy of his entire circle of friends, not to mention his own daughter. It was this excessive affection– or, so they said, adoration – of his eldest daughter, Mme de Berry, and his behaviour with her, which attracted the poet's comment. That is why M. Arouet, or Voltaire as he calls himself, has been exiled to Tours.

Mme de Clérembault was enraged because of it. She said Arouet was a great poet and should be forgiven if some of his verse was scurrilous, and when Madame disagreed with her she changed tack and said that Voltaire (she used that name) did not, himself, write the worst of them, but his imitators wrote them, and passed them off as his.

On the afternoon which I began to describe, I was already uneasy on my son's behalf. How could he, being so young, resist the temptation to imitate his betters when they became habitually very drunk so that they did not know what they were doing? And how would such a young man's sense of honour and beauty survive when he saw those around him, in that condition, take off all their clothes as they were said to do in licentious entertainment of each other and without retiring to a private space? A young person can be ruined in that way. I have seen it. Madame's young protégé, Ernst, nearly died of it.

I remained in attendance at the Palace on this occasion while Madame dined, but she did not address me. She had recently received fresh supplies of some of her favourite butter from Germany, and also sausages. Madame eats neatly. She enjoys her food, but her hands are always delicate. Among those, besides myself, who were standing in attendance was Theobon. With the passage of time, her tongue is no longer as sharp as it was. She came over to me and whispered that Madame wished to speak to me after her meal, and also to add – whether on her own account or that of Her Highness – that I was looking too morose, and would cause Madame to have indigestion simply by looking at me. As usual, she expressed herself with sharpness, and it made me smile, whereupon she put her hand on my shoulder and congratulated me dryly. But there was kindness in her manner. She has known me since I was seven, and like many of us at court, each year that passes adds some tiny bloom – or abrasion – to the sum total of familiarity. Between Theobon, the Maréchale de Clérembault and myself there had developed a bond of association because we had been for a long time united in defending Madame from her enemies. When I returned from Italy with such proof that the Chevalier de Lorraine had poisoned the first Duchess of Orléans, that he was disarmed from further attacks on Madame for fear of being exposed, these two ladies had both been overjoyed. They hardly ceased congratulating themselves and especially me for weeks, and each had given me small and exquisite portraits of themselves, both framed with gold. The Maréchale must have parted with a whole day's winning at the gambling tables to pay for hers, which was not her custom.

I digress; but why not? I have many hours here to wait and my heart will be too sore unless I think of the past.

To return to the evening of the visit I began to describe, after she had left her table Madame took me aside and spoke to me at length about John Law. She had now met him several times. With her usual frankness, she noticed his attractive manners and said that he was very desirable to the ladies. That was true. But that Madame herself should be so taken with him I had not expected. For one moment I even wondered; but indeed I was completely mistaken because her concern was Law's growing influence over the Regent.

"I hear that my son has invited him to his evenings," she said. "So what do you think of that, Berthon? Do you think he will lead him down the wrong path and ruin him, as Clérembault fears?"

I was so utterly distracted by my own concerns for Armand on the same account that for a moment I thought it quite extraordinary that Madame herself should have reached a point of such disapproval of the Regent's dissolute habits as to worry about the wellbeing of Law under his influence. But fortunately, I gathered my wits before I opened my mouth, and realised that she meant it the other way around; that Law's ideas might lead the Regent financially astray. Even so, she scolded me.

"You are not paying attention, Berthon. Why, oh why, has the Good Lord seen fit to place me where I can't look after my own children! This Law may be a clever man, and they do say that he is, but I do not understand money matters, and Clérembault says that if his Highness gives him a free hand he could ruin the whole country. I am speaking to you because you understand mathematics. You have spoken to Law. Armand is actively involved as his secretary. My son is talented and clever, but too amiable. He is easily led, and he finds the country in such debt that combined with all the tangled affairs of state he will make himself ill. And now he has this new 'system' as Law calls it. You know the Council are all against it?"

"I think Monsieur Daguesseau is in favour of it," I said. And then unfortunately I added, "and the Abbé Dubois."

"If you think, M de Brisse, that I should be comforted by the opinion of the Abbé Dubois you must be about to forget your own name."

It was true. I had momentarily forgotten the trouble he had caused between Madame and her husband years ago, and how she had opposed his appointment as tutor to her son. Nevertheless, his influence with the Duke had increased as a result of his role as tutor, and he had not lost it since his pupil had become Regent of France. I knew that he was trying to help Law sway the mind of the Regent because Law had said so. However, at that point I did not know that Dubois was being bribed, and by John Law. Law paid the Abbé 30,000 livres for his help in persuading the Regent to favour the financial scheme. It makes me very thoughtful now, in retrospect. Just as that bramble can scratch at my carriage window and plant a jagged sound like a thorn in my mind to distract me tonight, so the concatenation of events never ceases to generate random conclusions which may disturb the settled reflections of the past.

His Highness the Regent also wanted to reward Dubois in other ways, but Madame would not let him make her old enemy a Cardinal.

I hastened to respond more effectively to Madame's questions at the time. I pointed out the ingenuity of the decision to induce the merchants to trade with paper instead of gold and silver. Individual banknotes issued by the King, with a value in silver printed on them, would be infinitely preferable commercially. If the issue of paper could be carefully regulated in relation to coin kept in the vaults and trade prospered because of the ease introduced in this way into the system so that the money supply recovered, all might do very well.

"I can't argue with you, Berthon," Madame said, as if I had attempted any such thing. "You know the Duke de Saint-Simon is against it?"

"I don't think he is completely opposed, Madame."

"If not now, that is because my son has asked the Duke to see Monsieur Law once a week, to discuss the state of affairs with him. And the Duke de Saint-Simon had to agree, and of course it provides Law with the very opportunity he needed to influence Saint-Simon, not the other way round."

"His Highness, the Regent, is far more astute than is always obvious to careless observers, Madame."

"Yes, indeed. The Duke de Saint-Simon always insists that he knows nothing about money. But when my son required him, nevertheless, to give an opinion, you know what he said. He thinks that the charm of the English, by which he refers to Law, who has that dangerous talent as I think we both know, will persuade His Highness to agree to a scheme which may work in England, but not in France." And at that point, the Maréchale de Clérembault came and pleaded with Madame to take her place at one of the gaming tables, and so Madame left me.

CHAPTER NINE

I RETURNED to my own house late that night. Fanette had already gone to bed. I let myself be helped out of my carriage because the first cold draughts of the turning year had already affected my legs, and my court dress and particularly my shoes hampered me. A man is glad of the darkness if his wig catches on the carriage window as he climbs down, and the heel of a shoe – and mine are steep of course – lands on uneven ground. Gaudet was waiting for me. I stood for a moment when I had landed safely, and the dark air shifted down through the remaining leaves of the ash which stands there, filtering the cool memories which rapidly gather around any man who is alone at night. I would have gone to my own bed but I saw from a light burning that Fanette was waiting for me. The house smelt very sweetly of lavender, which my wife burns when the bushes are cut before the Winter months. She was upstairs but waiting for me sitting in her bed, reading by candlelight.

Fortunately, when this night's bitter vigil is over, I will be able to see her again in much the same fashion. It is not as if the finding of her at home waiting for me is over, as it is over for me to wait upon Madame and cherish in my mind, at any time, the thought of speaking to her.

Fanette does not seem to get old. Neither, in a curious way, do I. I am so ugly to begin with that time and Nature pass over me with indifference. There is not really space available to be marred further. My hair is still black, my skin no less smooth than it ever was. Madame once said pityingly of Athenais de Montespan, the King's former mistress, who was withering in her abandoned old age and lamenting the lines and folds which smothered her once beautiful face, that the change from beauty into ugliness is a tragedy which plain people are lucky that they can avoid. Madame congratulated herself on not having had to lose beauty which she had never possessed. Apparently, according to Madame, the Montespan's skin in old age resembled that of pieces of paper which children in play had been folding and refolding.

Of herself, Madame was not entirely accurate. Rigaud showed, in his portrait of her when she was young, that Madame had her share of prettiness. But just as she undervalued this advantage, she also escaped the mortification she might have felt when later portraits showed how altered she became. It was her own complete lack of vanity which saved her any regret.

On that evening I knew, as soon as the quiet of the room had closed around us, that Fanette had been sad while I was absent. She smiled now, but I put my gloves down carefully near the fire, and turned to her and said, "Madame asked me to greet you, and to thank you for the recipe which you sent her cook."

Fanette smiled in acknowledgement and looked round the curtains at the side of her bed to call her maid. There was a rustle through the dark door in the corner, and Isabel appeared. She came in her very quiet way, much the same as she first was when she brought a message to me in the palace from her mistress – the message which so very much delighted me.

She curtsied to me, kissed Fanette's hand, and left the room. So we were alone then.

In the silence that followed I think I said something like, "What's the matter?"

Fanette looked at the door as it closed behind Isabel, and sighed very deeply. "Oh, Berthon!" she said.

My heart stopped. What news? I stayed standing where I was, but I was no longer conscious of the comfort of the fire behind me, or the remembered conversation at court which I had planned to recount to Fanette, but only of that gap in time, in life itself, before she spoke again. It may seem that I, who, after all, had lived through perilous times and always kept my head, must have changed a great deal if my own wife could give me such a shock with one word. But I knew instinctively that this was something to do with Armand. I knew it.

"Louis Armand came to see me, my darling. He is not at all well."

"In what way? Has he got a fever? Don't say ..."

"No, no. He is not sick in that way. It is to do with the Duchesse de Berry."

"But surely..."

"I know," she said. "But he is not normal, Berthon. Your son is beside himself. She has taken a new lover."

"What!" I said, in an attempt to deflect the gravity of her tone, "Another one? Surely Armand knows better than to imagine that Mme de Berry will ever change her appetites."

"Of course he does. But there is something wrong here."

I think I actually laughed. As if there could ever be anything right where Mme de Berry was concerned. But Fanette started to cry. I couldn't bear it.

"Fanette," I protested, "Surely the romantic torments of young people are nothing new."

I was no longer so anxious myself, now that I thought I saw which way the wind was blowing. But she could not be so easily consoled. Apparently, Louis Armand was either drunk or affected by something else when he had called on his mother expecting to find myself, otherwise

Fanette thought he would not have presented himself in such a state. His clothes were dirty and disordered. He had not dressed properly from the previous night. His face was cut, and shortly after he arrived he was violently sick. Fanette could not make out the details of his story, but evidently the Princess had become unusually infatuated with that boy the Countess de Mouchy has brought to court. I have seen him myself. He is slovenly, short, and only someone as depraved and odd as the beautiful Mme de Berry could possibly notice him, leave alone fall in love. Apparently, Armand, driven mad by this new situation, had opposed Rions (the wretched fellow is called Rions) publicly, and Mme de Berry has forbidden Armand to come to her ever again. And he fought Rions, but not as he should have done. It seemed to have been an affair with dogs and knives and goodness knows what else. If it came to the ears of the Regent, Armand could lose his place. "And besides," said Fanette, now weeping bitterly, "it is making him very ill, Berthon."

But my own extreme anxiety was partly assuaged. I thought I could see him the next day, and persuade him not to take romantic quarrels home to his mother. I somehow forgot my own foreboding, seeing this as not part and parcel of the conditions of the Regent's intimate circle, but more a touching example of the fiery passions of youth.

I was wrong, of course.

Having roused the ghost of Rions with this recollection, I can't so easily get rid of him.

He was – probably still is – the most unpleasantly ugly young man. But once he was perceived at court to have attracted the Duchess, others paid him more attention, and then he was able to display a remarkable underlying ability to please. The Duchess soon insisted on having him with her at all times, and since he treated everyone except the Duchess herself with unfailing politeness, he began to be well-liked. But it was quite extraordinary how he behaved to the infatuated princess.

He was rude to her. He treated her like a servant and controlled everything she did from a contrary and spiteful point of view. For example, on that occasion when Armand had been so infuriated I learned afterwards that the Duchess had already been dressed for the opera when Rions appeared. He demanded that she should go at once and change into different apparel because he did not like her gown for that evening. The one matter beyond contradiction was the Duchess's own amazing beauty. She was taller than the squat little Rions, and that evening she had a collar of blue diamonds, and matching ribbons in her hair. Others who were present, including Armand, scarcely knew where to look, as her eyes filled with tears and she begged Rions to tell her what he would prefer. He had a habit of getting his chin up in a certain way when baiting this lady who loved him with such an inexplicably servile adoration, and Armand imitated it to me as he recounted the story. Apparently, Rions on that occasion snapped his fingers in her face, at which Armand could control himself no longer. He stepped forward and shouted a challenge at Rions, when immediately the Duchess herself, with a strangely sudden rebound of her normal temper, drew herself up and cursed Armand, and sent him away. Rions laughed. Armand said he laughed. That was why he waylaid Rions later on that night and did his best to kill him.

I could see how very distressed Armand still was the next day. Although he was well enough dressed now, and certainly not drunk anymore, he was very pale. But what gave me the false confidence which I then had was the conviction that his mind was firm and that he knew what he was doing. He told me then that he saw that he must wait until Madame de Berry had worn out this infatuation, and that he was resigned to it no matter what the despicable Rions would do. I left him, turning over another matter in my mind, namely the affair of Rions' great uncle Lauzan, who had had just such another relationship when he had wanted to marry La Grande Mademoiselle, but the King would not allow it. It was she who died of a broken heart as a result, although Lauzan was rude and unkind to her in exactly the manner apparently inherited by his nephew. It is not just history that repeats itself; it is we who do the same. We are dealt to each other generation after generation, like a worn pack of cards.

About a week after Louis Armand's quarrel with Rions, the Duchess de Berry herself, who is Madame's own granddaughter, visited Madame when I was in attendance at the Palais-Royal and I had an opportunity to see her again myself. It is hard to describe her in such a way as to reproduce her extraordinary charm. To begin with, she has a most commanding and beautiful body despite the fact that she is painfully thin. She walks, of course, in the court manner seeming to float over the ground, and as she approached her grandmother her expression was quite strange. She seems to be elsewhere in spirit; a devastating trick, because the beauty of her face, her pale skin lit with a rosy light of fever, her dark blue eyes, the tendrils of her hair, cause all who see her, to want to be acknowledged as occupants of the same world. When she curtsied low to Madame and came forward to kiss her, she seemed to stumble and even to be in danger of fainting. But one of her ladies caught her and she gave a little laugh as she embraced Madame.

Not so Madame. Her mouth remained turned down at the corners, and as much as she could she withheld the ample folds of her own body from the emaciated touch of the Princess. It was quite evident. Eventually, they were seated together quite close and others were expected to keep their distance.

Theoban came behind me and pinched the cloth of my collar to get my attention. We spoke together, but I was reluctant to be distracted from observing the princess who had so captivated my son. Despite her exquisite beauty, there was something about her which repelled me. I could not work out if it was a new sensation caused by recent scandals and the predicament of my son, or one that I had always had on the comparatively rare occasions when I had encountered her. She looked sick, with a feverish glow to her skin and a tension in her carriage, even sitting, as if the effort of remaining upright devoured all her energy. And yet she looked inordinately proud; as if she needed to call upon the forces of contempt for her attendants and anger for her life itself in order to remain upright. While, at the very same time as this burning quality, she could also look as soft as a flower just dampened with rain, and even as I watched her she gave a smile like a quiet suppressed laugh at something Madame said, and with one exquisitely ringed finger actually caught back a tendril of Madame's hair and kissed her, and without being reproved.

I had encouraged myself to think that provided he kept himself in his own control, and provided that no malign chance should cause Mme de Berry to return his love, Armand need come to no real harm. But this one encounter disabused me.

That very week, Climene succeeded in persuading the Regent to invite her to one of his private suppers. She demanded that I should attend her toilette because she was determined to look her best, and she says that I am unusually good at advising others who wish to be beautiful. She wore emerald earrings and green ribbons to bring out the colour of her eyes, and a gown of red and green shot damask. Her shoes were crimson.

I heard all about the evening's entertainment afterwards, but from Francis, as Climene herself was indisposed for five days. Francis himself did not look very well, but he said that he had not experimented with certain potions which everyone else was taking. He contented himself with just getting drunk. He told me that unless he had done at least that, he thought the Regent might have had him thrown into the Bastille. His description of the room after a few hours was incredible. There was a lady dancing naked on the table, the Regent had his daughter on his lap and she was very drunk and so was he. Francis blushed and clearly suppressed something in the narrative relating to what they were doing. The hem of the Duchess's gown had been torn in a game where the men had pretended to be wolves with the ladies as deer – an entertainment which they all had enjoyed immensely, including Francis and Climene, as he admitted to me. Several of the hunters and their prey vomited because of the exertion. Some of the servants were also drunk and they did not clear the mess at all well, but no one seemed to mind very much. When Rions arrived, his Highness was discourteous to him, so his daughter was extremely angry, jumped away from her father and turned her back to fling her arms around her lover. Climene then seemed to be not herself. Her eyes were wild and she started to undress, laughing the while at Francis until he took hold of her. There were musicians, and conjurers and finally desserts so elaborate, I had a vision of crème Chantilly and sugar spilt all over the floor. Francis was remarkably philosophical about it, even when Climene allowed a fellow guest to kiss her. He said that he was too drunk really to care very much, but that he was taking Climene back to England as soon as she was recovered. I think that sometimes my fellow countrymen misunderstand the demeanour of the English. They mistake a manner of stoicism and dry humour for lack of passion, as if the best way to prove the heat of a flame were to set fire to one's own clothes.

Climene and Francis had not planned to leave Paris until after the inauguration of the Banque Générale the following month, but a day or two after the Regent's entertainment they disappeared. The next time I paid court to Madame at the Palais-Royal where she lived when the weather became cold again, the Countess Theoban said that the Maréchale de Clérembault had been asking for them, with a particular wish to question Francis about the South Seas Company. Apparently, the English ambassador had been boasting about Mr Hoare's bank, and the minute she saw me the Maréchale broke off a conversation she was having with Monsieur de la Rochefoucault at the far end of the drawing room. I had time only to make my bow to Madame before she caught up with me. I still had the letter that Francis had left for me in my pocket and at one point I almost thought I would have to show it to her, to prove that my sister and Lord Claydon had left France. I explained that Climene had been unwell after the Regent's last supper the week before, at which point Clérembault said peevishly that my sister could have recovered her health perfectly well in Paris. She demanded to know if I was sure that news of the Duchess du Maine's support of the Spanish ambition to claim the French Regency had not affected the London money market.

I did not know, at that point, of the Duchess du Maine's most dangerous plot. If the Maréchale de Clérembault had heard rumours over the card tables at four o'clock in the morning, I hoped she would continue to confide them to me. But she lost patience with me when I clearly did not know exactly when Francis might return. Neither was she willing to give credence to the supposition that Francis, despite his interest in long conversations with John Law, had only the influence of a private investor in the new London bank.

CHAPTER TEN

THE ceaseless battle waged between the Regent and Parliament over Law's licence to create a French bank on a similar national level as England had been turning every day into a wild clatter of argument from the kitchens to the ballrooms of every house in Paris. I truly wondered whether Francis would be able to tear himself away for long. It was from John Law himself that I heard, second-hand, the advice of Saint-Simon, with whom he had weekly interviews every Tuesday morning at the Duke's house, entering privately by a side door.

Law recounted a good deal of these conversations to me, or I should probably not even have known of their existence.

The Duke would not have spoken to me himself, naturally, being of a rank so much above my own. His Highness the Regent had, and still has, a great opinion of the Duke de Saint-Simon and treasures his friendship. He constantly asked his advice on financial matters even though Saint-Simon had resolutely refused to involve himself in any of the financial decisions of the state. He claimed that of all subjects finance was the one on which he was most ignorant. It puzzled me why, in that case, he had agreed to give an hour of his time once a week to a private interview with M. Law. The Regent must have made a very particular request for some other reason.

His Highness the Regent, for all his interest in the sciences, had always that taint of the dilettante which deters certain brilliant minds from the hard core of achievement. Madame constantly complained of this fact, holding as she did such a high opinion of her son's many talents, and she was not mistaken. Whether it was music or literature or any other of the arts; whether it was the science of alchemy, in which he took a great interest for a time, or the study of plants, or astronomy he had a mind capable of devouring knowledge; but when he came to the heart of the matter he would become rapidly sated. Having known him since he was a child and not so much younger than myself, I admire and love him almost as much as I did his mother. He has sharp intelligence and sometimes wisdom which his air of insouciance, his malleable smile and polite attention to the words of others, mask from general appreciation, and all combined with creative talents in painting and writing. He even composed an opera, but I didn't hear it. In this very matter of his insisting on John Law developing a constant dialogue with the Duke de Saint-Simon, I had always thought that he showed just such a wise grasp of the essentials of any issue, and in this case the actual character of Law was bound to be vital. I had always thought that the Regent instigated these meetings to have the benefit of Saint-Simon's famously penetrating observation of Law's qualities as a man. However, a significant advantage of being alone here myself, independent, a man whom no one else is concerned with and around whom the quiet dark air of night holds no fear of intrusion, is that on this page I can open my mind as to no other recipient. For example, all my life I have seen the Duke de Saint-Simon come and go at court, and I have often listened to him speak when he was not aware that I was within hearing, or if he was aware he assumed that it could not matter to him. And he is right. I am his inferior and I am undisturbed by any feeling of discontent that it should be acknowledged. Besides, he is a great man in terms of the importance that the Regent particularly, but also many others, ascribe to his opinions. I myself can vouch for his strong feelings of friendship and obligation; he is a very feeling man, when his pride and attention to precedence are assuaged by the correct manners from his peers. Saint-Simon has, as well as a remarkable talent for judgement (for example, England's system of monarchy as opposed to ours, and Stair their ambassador, although he was wrong about Spain) a consummate ability to remember every single detail of history, scandal, rumour, to do with every notable individual at court, their families, antecedents and, indeed, many of those in Parliament. His wit and attention to detail; his amazing vigour in the pursuit – if necessary over a period of years – of one man's lack of integrity or another's virtue, have always amazed me. I believe he is capable of remembering whether one dignitary was said to have signed a paper when he must actually have been unavailable because he was in bed with his mistress at the time, and Saint-Simon might know that. He knows every member of every important family for three generations, their income, their establishments, and if he chooses to do so he may punish with an almost vulgar relish. He showed this side of his nature when he drew the Regent's attention to the need to dismiss the Duke de Noailles, from his seat at the Council Chamber before continuing with the business in hand in 1715. He gets great enjoyment from a triumph of that sort. When I use the word vulgar I am conscious of being very accurate, despite the scandalous contradiction I seem to make to the Duke's idea of himself as a noble gentleman; after all, I saw the way he looked covertly at the Duke de Toulouse to make him laugh as Noailles slunk from the room. That sort of triumph against an enemy, even if he deserves it (and I am not sure that Noailles did deserve it), is what I myself call unworthy of the behaviour of a gentleman. At the same time, I would not underestimate his good qualities. Among them, a very sharp eye is included, and on those occasions when I am present but unobserved I am particularly careful that he should not see me. I escape because I am beneath his notice, but should he once be disabused he would make it impossible for me to find my secret ways anymore.

But to return to the subject of those weekly *tête-à-têtes* between Law and Saint-Simon, I now wonder who was the hunter and who the prey. I have no doubt that the Regent thought that the Duke would serve to advise and moderate the financier. But here I pause, and a new idea presents itself. We are lucky to be able to cast our minds like baited lines, into the pool of past memories. The same fish does not always get caught, and I have an example of that before me now. I see, in my imagination, the Regent as he was talking to Law, the one so tall and strong, His Highness of only medium height with such a gentle look. The Regent has taken off his wig, and the financier is sitting, and the subject under discussion is the projected programme of private interviews for Law with Saint-Simon. It is not His Highness who has had this idea at all. It is Law himself. But Monsieur Law so expresses himself that the Regent is given the impression that he is the one who requests this arrangement. Saint-Simon, whose opinion His Highness values so highly, began with opposition to Law's scheme. After all these private conversations, John Law has almost entirely reversed the opinion of Saint-Simon who would have been a formidable opponent. It now seems to me that John Law may have wished to protect himself against the Duke's influence with the Regent, and what better device could he use, but to see the Duke regularly himself and depend on his own potent powers of persuasion? He cannot, however, engineer this for himself. But if the Regent requested the Duke de Saint-Simon, as a favour, to agree to a weekly interview, that would be a different matter. And so it turned out.

Such a thought is disagreeable to me now. This is a prize I would willingly throw back into the pool of my memory. For all that happened, I have always resisted the tide of opinion which sought to drown my friend Law's reputation for fundamental probity in the poison of personal ambition and even lying. But here I am, and here is the sharp clear air of solitude and the night, and a truth has emerged. The Duke de Saint-Simon did not exert himself to deter the Regent from Law's scheme in the end, and now I think I may have stumbled on the reason why. If I have I would be sorry.

Any man likes to be able to look back on his life with a reasonable conscience, and some pride. This was a turbulent and passionate period in the history of France. At court, the real prospect of actual bankruptcy was emasculated by the unbroken luxurious habits of the Regent, and also by the fact that if, on these gentlemen's country estates, the peasants had to be squeezed to keep up their payments to the bailiffs, the courtier who received a smaller dividend from his estate could always turn to the Regent's kitchen for his dinner table. I think my father was as short of money as anyone, and I never noticed him wear an old pair of shoes, or unfashionable gloves.

Ever since the old King had the idea of keeping the nobility at Court where he could keep an eye on them, rather than on their country estates conspiring a repeat of the Fronde, which was the rebellion nightmare of his youth, we courtiers had had very little contact with the provinces. Even I, who had travelled to Italy and seen many sights of famine and degradation which frightened me, might have forgotten them when I returned to Paris and Versailles. On my journey into Italy with Bonhomme, I had seen for myself some of the devastated landscapes where Nature, unaided by man, had stripped the harvests from the fields and fruit from the trees in June, with unseasonal frosts and hail. By the onset of Winter, the poor had eaten all that they had stored, and had nothing left. I saw with my own eyes icicles in a ditch near Toulouse in May. But even if I had the memory of my own childhood blotted from my mind, which it never could be, I would have learned then about the famine that resulted from ruined harvests, and the effect that extreme poverty has on the peasantry if the national economy does nothing to help them.

Ruined harvests won the peasants no pity from the tax collectors and the bailiffs. They were still held to account for every sou they should have made if the weather had not turned against them. The nobility, of course, pay no taxes, as their sole duty is to defend France from her enemies. I doubt if that will ever change. But there was a time I read of in the King's library when the nobility lost a battle in Crecy against the English when the peasantry thought they should have won, because they so greatly outnumbered their English foes. The poor rose up, led by a man called Jacque Goodman, and slaughtered their masters. It could happen again.

I also dredged up from my reflections the memory of one man fallen on the ground at that time of my travels. He lay almost at his length half under and half across the roots of a hedge. I called out to Bonhomme to stop the carriage so that we could attend to that man, and got down onto the track. When I got near him, I could hardly believe he was still alive. The few rags he had lay across naked bone, over which skin of a strange colour and texture was rather loosely collapsed. His head was caught in the thorns, so that his face was exposed. The Winter weather was closing in on the land, and the wind was cold; and yet his eyes in that face burned deep like live coals. He looked as if he was in hell. I told Bonhomme to fetch some food from our saddlebags for him, and some water; Bonhomme was about to turn back for it when something caught his attention. He stood suddenly aghast, and following the line of his eye for a moment at first I noticed only the thin line of blood around the man's mouth, which I had seen already. Sometimes this is caused by starvation. My own mouth bled when I was a child twice for that reason. But Bonhomme grasped my arm and said, "Come away, Monsieur. Come away." I'm not sure what I saw in spite of him. I could not bring myself to name it. My heart hit my ribs for a long time after, while Bonhomme, having once more taken up the reins, urged the horse forward almost too fast for the rough ground, and my mount, Maud, on his lead rein, broke into a canter.

I did not forget. This awareness was with me when I took so much interest in John Law's scheme to avoid the bankruptcy which threatened ourselves, and even more the defenceless poor in France. The fact that in him I found such a friend, and through that friendship was included closely in the unfolding of events, gave to my life at that time a great vitality. At the dawn of each day, I awoke to the awareness of a distinguished group of friends such as Madame, Clérembault, Theobon, The Regent, Francis, Armand, John Law himself –whose frame of mind I could engage with as soon as Gaudet had shaved and dressed me.

I assumed that Armand's priorities were the same as my own, but they were not. His nascent maturity had encountered nightmares I did not dream of. Fascinated as I was at the time by the political and financial forces at war with each other, I was blind to the sufferings of my own son.

Then, like someone waking from a nightmare, I became conscious of Armand waiting for me to speak. "I was remembering something," I said. The expression on his face was anxious, as if he expected me to say something amiss. "It's nothing," I said. "I was just remembering something which I saw once – a starving man who had eaten in his desperation..."

Armand still waited. I realised my thoughts were too confused to be useful. After all, the famine that year had been caused by nature, not by man. No miscalculation on the part of any master had snatched the harvest away from the peasantry. When I explained it to my son, he actually laughed and said, "Shall I tell Monsieur Law that you had a vision of his scheme blighting the harvests and drying up the vineyards of the whole land?"

"No. Certainly not."

But he wouldn't stop. "And the populace turning to cannibalism, while the nobility eat their own servants!"

I thought I had better smile.

"If Law's system fails it will be the nobility who will have to bear the brunt of it," Armand said, and then he set about explaining to me why, if the discipline of the system was compromised for any reason, it could be the rich who would lose everything they once had overnight. But on that occasion, he said it with such verve, and in such a tone, that I did not think for a moment that he meant it.

No one disputed the fact that the State was devoid of the means to pay its debts. Bankruptcy is one answer in such circumstances. But for France to declare bankruptcy and by that means to draw a line under the hopes of all her creditors was a disgrace that the Regent's advisers wanted to avoid on behalf of the honour of our country. Monsieur Law's scheme offered one alternative, but at the cost of a fundamental revolution of the established financial culture. Whereas the Duke de Noailles, in his new role as Director of Finance, came down on the side of a 'partial' bankruptcy, balanced by fixing the rate of exchange permanently at the current value – a trick, in my opinion, and Law agreed with me. It could only be suggested by someone either naïve or completely disingenuous.

Noailles was specific in his plan. He proposed to fix the rates of exchange between banknotes and remaining specie in gold and silver at 14 livres the gold Louis and 3 livres 10 sols the ecu. To this, de Noailles claimed, a collection of individual devaluations of debt or basic economies of the State could be added, and legitimised if necessary by a new Chamber of Justice. Armand had not heard this full story until then. He could hardly contain his indignation as he waited for me to pause. He actually shifted from foot to foot – I remember – and in the end, brought his hand down so carelessly on the small table near where he was standing that he scattered some papers that I had been working on.

As he bent to pick them up I noticed a mark on his neck which looked like a deep wound half-healed. But before I could say anything he was so taken up and voluble on the subject of de Noailles' shortcomings that I could almost have mistaken his attitude for that of the Duke de Saint-Simon himself, who so unaccountably loathed that gentleman. I then mentioned that Rouille du Coudray had pointed out that cash deposited in a bank can also be removed, and that this was a sore point with Law and His Highness. They maintained that despite the authority that the King (and therefore the Regent) undoubtedly possessed, and despite the possible pleadings of temporary necessities, specie deposited as the balance of printed paper notes would be sacrosanct. It would be an act of theft to remove it, and His Highness had no intention of doing so. This he said, most sincerely, at the time. I had my doubts. But to express them would tend to impugn the honesty of Law and the Regent and even, by association, Armand. Then I thought of an apt illustration; or what seemed so to me.

"Let me give you an example," I exclaimed. "I hear that the Duchess de Berry has boarded up all the entrances to the Luxembourg gardens except the one which leads out of her own house."

My son froze. Looking back, I can hardly imagine how I can have been so obsessed with what I myself wanted to say in illustration of my argument that I failed to be aware of the effect my words were having. A dark flush gathered on his face, but I ignored it.

"The Luxembourg gardens," I probably said, "are a precious resource of the people of Paris, who frequent them at all times. They are sacrosanct. They belong to them, and not her. And yet Madame de Berry has had all the gates locked except the one which leads from her own house. Because Mme de Berry is a member of the royal family, she can remove that benefit from the public just as, in the future when M. Law's system is in full operation, her father could remove coin from the bank – if he so chose."

I fell silent, to see the effect of my argument, and then I did notice the condition of Armand. There was a colour in his cheek that was almost black. He held a handkerchief to his lip as if to gag himself. Eventually, he said something like, "Forgive me, Sir. I cannot see any parallel between the actions of Mme de Berry and the possible bad faith of a member of the Council of Finance."

Plunged into the utmost distress though I was, I could not apologise. If I did, he might assume that it had been my intention to insult the Princess.

But he saved me from embarrassment by taking a chair and sitting as if he would talk with me. Unluckily at that moment, Isabel appeared with a message, and he was obliged to leave.

CHAPTER ELEVEN

I WOULD like to say that I was more cautious after this, but I was not. My emotions were so involved with the extreme danger that France was facing, and the character of John Law, whose strength and intelligence were so vitally and heroically engaged to defend her, that I was almost blind to other problems. I was pleased and relieved when Armand himself sent me a message the next day inviting me to dine with him, mentioning that we could discuss the new developments which ensued from the Duke de Noailles' meeting with the representatives of the businessmen of Nantes. As I was very interested to hear more of that meeting, I somehow allowed myself to completely forget that I had offended my son at our last encounter. I will curse this strange night if, stumbling about in the uneven ground of memories from which Time has removed the blessed light of any remedial action, I fatally injure my own peace of mind. Because I know now that I ignored a vital moment when my son needed my help. A hot flush of shame sweeps through my blood, instantly setting fire to my skin. How trivial the bankruptcy of a country seems compared to the loss of a child; because that was very nearly the bargain I struck that evening. Other fathers who love their sons have probably made the same mistake, but what is that to me now?

It was not exactly that I was completely unaware of the turmoil of preoccupation in Armand, but it suited my mood of the moment to believe that he wished me to forget his passionate reaction to our earlier discussion. I thought no more about it, and we talked only of the absorbing alternatives of finance until he had to retire to prepare to join the rest of the Regent's roués for the evening entertainment.

The Regent himself, by the way, called and still calls his debauched companions his roués. But although I was so interested and engaged in this financial debate, which incidentally was the prevailing topic of conversation wherever you went at that time, there lurked in the background of my mind a nostalgia for the past, and the authority of the old King. Louis XIV had a firmness in his character which was different from the volatile good nature and cultured intelligence of his nephew the Regent. When the old King was on his death bed, his body poisoned and his limbs black with gangrene, he confronted his own death as if it were his servant, and not his master. He must have been in great pain, but he withheld any sign of it. From my hiding place, I watched to see his face, and when those around him shifted their positions, I glimpsed his head and saw not a man who was sick with a mortal illness, but one whose majesty could not be dimmed even by the moment when, for the first time in his life, he stood on the brink of that version of poverty when a man owns nothing; when the poorest live person in the whole kingdom possesses more than does a dying king. Louis XIV, who bankrupted his country, had, at least, an invincible courage when he confronted his own annihilation.

And yet, in spite of my knowing that he was such a great man, like everyone else of my own persuasion, I was not influenced by the fact that Louis XIV had refused to consider Monsieur Law's advice. The King had clothed his decision in that remark expressing contempt for the notion of allowing a Protestant to advise him. But what if a man knows what is right by instinct and yet needs to excuse his opinion? He may use just that sort of facetious device.

The fact that the King had preferred to send the solid silver benches from the galerie des Glaces in Versailles to be minted into coin rather than listen to the inventions of a Protestant and a foreigner simply made an excuse for his own wisdom. Or so I now speculate. Perhaps he just instinctively knew that the course Law was advising would eventually lead to disaster, but did not know how. Desmaretz, who was the Minister of Finance at the time, said so. Decisions made on such grounds would not command respect from an ordinary person, but a king can say what he pleases. And perhaps a king should be believed even if he cannot express appropriately the thoughts which, by the mysterious process of Divine Right, he may have. Consider. Here I am now, alone this night, and there is the landmass of France asleep under the stars; and invisible in the darkness, a whole army of peasantry and nobles alike lie stripped of their wealth in cold beds – if they still have them at all and are not reduced to sleeping in the ditches.

Sometimes those who are touched with a particular kind of divine wisdom, as was the old King, do not know how or why they arrive at their conclusions, and then the rest of us can laugh at or dismiss their reasoning and brush their opinion aside. Unless, of course, some priest has put his seal on those opinions to turn them into beliefs. It seems to me, who long ago slipped the leash of clerical authority, that there is no point in attempting to follow any God so obsessed with obscuring His own footprints that even a man with the Divine Right to rule, and who may occasionally be wise, can be mistaken for a fool for following God's track in the wrong direction.

And in this frame of simple bad temper, or as such I remember it, I believe I returned to Fanette. She never allowed me to be unhappy for long.

My half-sister, Climene, was always very dear to me. When I was a boy I was not allowed to speak to her at court unless she gave me a sign. I thought that entirely reasonable. She was not only older than myself but also beautiful, and she wanted to be seen with other beautiful and distinguished companions. I was nothing if not aware of how far short of such flattering associations her relationship with myself must fall.

When she was eighteen and I twelve she was not only beautiful but very spirited and amusing. She was briefly in love with the Chevalier de Lorraine at the time, as was just about every other pretty woman at court. I did not let her know, until many years later, the fearful enmity I felt for that gentleman on account of his dangerous and vindictive treatment of Madame. By the time I achieved my revenge on him for the misery he caused Her Highness, Climene had fallen in love with Francis, my English friend, to whom she was now married. I was fortunate in that, despite being so ugly, I had always been allowed to love Climene, whereas now that we were both older she seemed almost as fond of me as I of her.

Now, whenever she was in France she spent a great deal of time with me. She would come to see Fanette; she would take lessons in cooking from Fanette's Namibian servant, and she would be forever consulting me about the colour of her ribbons, or some rearrangement of her hair, by which I need scarcely to point out that she was not so changed as to have lost her taste for all the frivolities of life. For example, after that first occasion she and Francis were always welcome at the Regent's suppers, and she seemed to enjoy them very much. Predictably, she caught the attention of de Noce, who pursued her with such ardour that Francis would have called him out. But de Noce could never be persuaded to be serious about anything, and he would certainly not have survived so long if he had not been born with the necessary charm to make an angry husband feel it would be ridiculous to attack him. After a brief but brilliant courtship of Climene full of wit and song, and that measure of romance combined with indifference for which he was famous, his attention drifted elsewhere. The Regent, when he was the Duke de Chartres, always visited de Noce whenever he was in Paris. De Noce rarely appeared at Court in Versailles. He said it was too serious for him.

After a long absence, I saw him only the other day walking on his way to the palace of the Luxembourg. He is still very tall and still upright and walks well. He was looking about him as he went along with a slight smile of mockery on his face as if he had just seen or overheard something ridiculous. Knowing the sort of person most likely to be the butt of his wit (having occupied that place myself a few times) I looked for his likely target but made none out.

The fact is that if de Noce had met God Himself in the garden of Eden he would have thought of some quip to make the Deity laugh at one of his own creations. I never found it surprising that the Regent had been so fond of his company, and for so many years.

But I digress. I was remembering a late morning in Fanette's drawing room with Climene when the three of us were drinking chocolate. Then Fanette was called away by Isabel, and Climene, giving me a sideways look as she put down her cup, said "Berthon. I want to talk to you."

This surprised me, as you can imagine, not least because she was talking to me already. But then, as she had waited for Fanette to go out of the room, I thought it must be to do with her private affairs; some problem with Francis, or with money.

She waited rather a long time with her head tilted to one side and her eyes flexed as if to sharpen their ability to penetrate beneath the surface of things. I found afterwards that I remembered this image of her very well, and I still do. She had her hair tied à la Fontanges again – a style no longer in fashion, but it always suited her particularly.

"I was at the Palais-Royal last evening – or nearly all night," she said. "Do I look tired? No. Don't answer me. I'm perfectly well aware that I have a line under my right eye, but that was not what I wanted to say. It is that Armand is not well."

"Not well?"

"No. He isn't. Naturally, everyone gets drunk at the suppers. I'm not bothered about that. Or by his vomiting – excuse me for mentioning it."

After a pause, I said, "I know that he is very much in love with the Duchess de Berry, but is that so unusual?"

"You mean everyone's in love with her?" A certain sharpness of tone. "Or just that Armand is always in love somewhere?"

"Both," I said, still floundering.

"You are making it sound stupid," she said. "I wouldn't mention it to you unless there was good reason, Berthon. Have you ever known me to concern myself with other people's behaviour?" I thought of her first husband, who so conveniently drowned in the Rhone, but said nothing. She had been eloquent on the subject of his manners. "Well then, I just thought you should know that Armand is more roué than the roués. He will make himself ill."

Looking back on that conversation, I am surprised that it was the absurdity of Climene in the role of governess which preoccupied me. So much so that I was diverted into teasing her, and by the time Fanette came back into the room Climene was sitting on a cushion on the floor pulling faces at me, and we were both laughing.

Fate has a knack for waylaying fools, as I was soon to discover. Not so long after this encounter with Climene, I was returning one night from St. Cloud in my carriage when, on the outskirts of Paris, one of the horses swerved, the coachman tangled the reins and we came to a stop. The road was very dark, but I could just make out some poor fellow stumbling as if he had been hit by the side of the carriage. I thought he was just one of the homeless wretches who, securing a few sous to spend, had got himself drunk as well as filthy. It had rained, but it had not rained mud, and therefore he must have fallen as well. He was holding onto the guard of one of the front wheels and my coachman was roughly telling him to let go, when the moon came out from behind the clouds and I saw his face.

It was Armand, my own son.

I almost leapt from the carriage and without falling myself despite my uneven legs, I called to the coachman to help me and together we managed to get Armand inside. He had no idea who we were.

I had – I still have – a horror of the decay which a crumb of corruption, warmed by a passionate disposition, can cause in any man. Or woman. And here was my son showing every sign of being mortally infected by it. He was not only drunk; he seemed to be trailing something that was rotting behind him, and in his own shoes. When he was seated I sat beside him to hold him in place on the carriage seat as best I could. He had no control of his body. He smelt vile. When I called his name, it meant nothing to him, and the repetition of it made him laugh in an ugly gurgling way which turned my guts to water.

Fortunately, I had Gaudet, my man, waiting for me at the house, and between him and Fanette's massive strong black servant, and my coachman, we got Armand indoors. But the whole house was disturbed. I could not keep it from Fanette. Once he was at least partly washed and wrapped in a clean sheet on his bed, I sat beside him. He didn't fall asleep. His eyes were open, restlessly moving about the room, and his voice in a mumbled mess of words and sometimes that laugh, sickly and repellently disconnected. I myself felt what my mind forced me to confront, so that although I had no physical pain I could feel my body disintegrating at its very core. This was not because he was drunk, but more because some drug or poison had him in thrall, and I could not imagine him recovering.

Neither could I cure my inner eye of what it had seen. Long after Armand was sleeping I sat awake, accompanied by this insidious, this wavering and unwholesome caricature of a splendid youth. It stalked my consciousness. If I turned in my bed stealthily not to wake Fanette, this dreadful incubus followed me and was waiting on my other side. If I was on the brink of sleep, it would wake me, scratching on the closing door of my mind. I think until then I never knew what fear was. I associated fear with physical danger and also with the reflex of excitement and an intensified awareness of living. But I was mistaken all along. It is dread. Real fear is dread. And grief.

Before dawn, I spoke to Fanette. She lay with her head on my arm, and with my other hand I stroked the silk of her hair and lied about the inevitable recklessness of young men, and how they dived as boys into what seemed disaster, and emerged as men. Strangely enough, my own words, although I thought I knew them to be false, displaced the dreadful haunting of the night. A trickle of courage slowly drained from my own mind into my body, and I felt able to face the day.

We found Armand already improved. He would not physically die of whatever it was, then, I thought, as I looked at him sleeping. Fanette busied herself with his comfort, and mine. We ate. I went back to my dressing room, and let Gaudet shave and dress me. But this time I was not in danger of forgetting the harm that had entered Armand's life.

Following my own words, Fanette seemed to be reassured that almost all young men get drunk and that Armand was no different. I can say that I, too, seemed to accommodate myself to this new situation, but this time it was only a pretence on my part. From then onwards, whenever I saw Armand I would look for any small hidden signs of his continued depravity, and if I thought I saw something, it made my heart drag in my ribs with a sickly reflex and fear which caused my pulse to race like a galloping horse. It was as if the normal landscape of my life was fatally undermined. That sensation of secure well-being which happy men experience had simply gone from me.

If Armand crossed a room or opened a door, I would watch for a different walk and a different opening. I watched, with dread, how my son moved today; whether his bearing bore the traces of someone who could not trust his own body; who displayed a confidence about to be unmasked as a sham, despite valiant efforts to avoid miscalculating a step or knocking over a glass. Like a threatened traveller in dangerous territory, I often sensed a residue, a trace in a tone of Armand's voice, or a gesture, or a slight miscalculation of balance which immediately triggered a sudden and devastating fear; it was like an incipient refrain; like a sound one dreads but dare not fail to hear. In fact, I suspect I must have behaved towards him rather as I feared he would behave toward me when, after the innocence of childhood, he first realized that I was different from other men.

He must have spoken to Climene because she took me aside one evening and, in a manner most unusual with her, teased a confession out of me. Looking back on it now, I do wonder how she, the most frivolous of women, learned such a lesson about a man's natural instinct to shrink from other men's pain, and in that way desert the friends who need them.

Whatever the explanation, I forced myself to recover my confidence in Armand, or at least to behave as if I had and

I found myself free to resume my interests in other things rather than being continually harassed by my fear for him.

I followed the political manoeuvres of John Law, the Regent and the Council of Finance with apparently renewed interest, to the extent that Law said to me one day, when we were drinking chocolate together in his house, that he was glad that whatever had troubled me was now mended. I hadn't talked to him of Armand, for fear of harming my son's character, knowing how strongly he was indebted to Law for his position at court. But that morning I had the distinct impression that my friend already understood the dilemma of a father with a wild son.

Francis, who was constantly going backwards and forwards to England at that time, had financial preoccupations with the South Sea Company in London as we in France had with our debt and Law's scheme for solving it. He brought news of the progress of their bank in London, and the development of trade with the South Sea Company, which seemed to me to be stillborn. John Law would listen to him intently on those occasions. He would come to the house which Francis and Climene owned near the Luxembourg, arriving often in the morning. In my memory now, I see him standing in the embrasure of the window where the drawing room overlooked a rather bare section of the garden, and where he could give all his attention to the discussion at hand. He used to stand elegantly and despite his physical height and burning ambition for his own view of finance, managed to convey an attitude of pliancy. This was not entirely assumed either. I believe he had such a voracious appetite for all forms of gambling, including this erudite and intellectually most exacting version where he pitted his own system against the national debt, that every nuance and variation – even those which threatened to unpick his own arguments – fascinated him. There were elements of the French political system about which he was secretive. To one like myself, for whom a crumb that falls from the overloaded surface of the mind of another is always worth scrutinizing, a more detailed picture did emerge. For instance, I suspected that in the wake of a successful introduction the National Bank shares sold in the South Sea Company would have to begin to prove their worth. And with the English/Spanish level of existing enmity on account of the Catholic cause, Spain would be reluctant to promote trade between her colonies in South America and Britain. That morning Law was listening intently to Francis who, although tall himself, had his face lifted to speak to Law. Not being within hearing, I was particularly attentive to their expressions. Time, as I said, had hardened Francis superficially. When young and exiled from England by the danger which threatened him from his father's murderous insanity, he nevertheless retained an air of careless wellbeing, whereas now, as I looked at him, I thought that quality quite gone. It was the first time that I was really aware of it, and it disturbed me a great deal. It had seemed likely to me that being married to Climene had made Francis less reckless, as he might have argued that one of them needed to be moderate and that was clearly not going to be his wife. But this more profound change very much upset my temper once I had noticed it. It could not have been caused by living with Climene. I was, I still am, in the habit of amusing myself and occasionally others by exaggerating her wilful character because such behaviour in such a pretty woman is something men enjoy; but at heart, she is too good to cause pain deliberately. Neither, or so I imagined for some reason, could it be any financial worry. In England, Francis had his estates and considerable wealth, as witness that ring which Climene wore. In addition, what had he to concern him? His land was in the North, but not so far north that he needed to be anxious about the machinations of the Pretender. I knew that Francis did not now support the Scottish rebellion. I myself had dined with Francis and the English ambassador, Lord Stair, at the Residence in Paris and in fact the whole miserable saga, seen from their point of view – and indeed my own, in so far as I cared about it – was that France and England were the more suitable allies than England and Spain. Stair was at pains to imply that any attempt to promote the fortunes of the Pretender to the throne of England, in order to unite England with Catholic Spain and improve the chances of trade with Spanish colonies in South America for the South Sea Company, would founder in the end. Nevertheless, the alternative political alliance was a problem often discussed. The remote chance, which had recently emerged, of the Regent assuming the throne of Spain was the objective driving such advisers as the Duke of Saint-Simon toward supporting the return of the throne of England to a Catholic monarchy via the Pretender.

I was always interested to listen to a conversation between Francis and Law, and on the day in question, I managed to slip by and approach that end of the room. It was the Bank of England that they were discussing. Law noticed my approach, and in the most courteous way, sat on the chair behind him while still speaking. Francis hesitated. He was less familiar with my studies than Law, but I saw the tide of doubt leave his face, although he didn't turn towards me. I being more on a level with him now, Law finished by addressing me directly. "Lord Claydon is concerned because I am accusing him of hunting with the hounds at the same time as running with the hare."

"I have bought shares in the South Sea Company, Berthon," Francis said. "Monsieur Law considers it unlikely that the South Sea Company will trade freely enough in Spanish territories in South America after the signing of the Treaty of Utrecht. I am telling him that the Company can compensate by buying the national debt in the form of shares, and then *he* tells me that the Bank of England, to which I also belong, will be reduced if it does."

This very much intrigued me. Law's eye was already on the lease for the territories in the Mississippi, with the idea of trading there in exactly the same manner as the South Sea Company in South America. But his scheme would be in support of the National Bank, rather than in competition with it, since he himself was offering to be the financial backer of the Banque Nationale to the tune of 12 million louis Tournois.

Knowing how complex his intellect was, I could see the danger.

Law said, "I have heard rumours that certain individuals who have information in advance, of the dates on which government debt is to be consolidated, purchase debt in advance and then sell later, very much to their own advantage."

"I think you should sell your shares in the South Sea Company now, Francis."

It was I who said that. Goodness knows why; except that sometimes a part of my brain works faster than I am aware of. I can still vividly remember the sound of my own voice as I had the effrontery to speak so resolutely. Francis looked at me through his teeth. "Climene," he said. Both men now looked at me as one looks at some phenomenon that it would be reckless to ignore. I always hope, when people do that, that they are not influenced by superstition. I am not a dwarf.

Francis said incredulously, "The shares are worth a fortune now. They are high. Climene would be very upset if I got rid of them."

"Maybe sell them then, nevertheless," said Law.

"They will go higher!"

"Nevertheless."

"Is this to save my position with the Bank of England?

It's a private consortium, but I am only a minor contributor. The three who matter are Gibbon, George Caswall and Hoare." I think he was referring to the fact that the premature sale of shares in the South Sea Company, and corresponding call for cash, might embarrass the National Bank.

At this point, if Francis was going to say any more he could not because Climene interrupted us. It was not that my sister lacked interest in our topic, or that she had limited opportunity to gather information, but Madame and several of her ladies had arrived, including the Maréchale de Clérembault.

All rose to their feet and bowed or curtsied very low. And as he did so, Law said discreetly out of the corner of his mouth, to Francis, "No. It is not for that reason, my lord."

Law was aware, as he explained to me later when we were alone, that if the South Sea Company was unable to trade because of Spain's obstruction in its American territories, it would have a disastrous effect on the shares. I now see that this moment was a classic vindication of the wisdom of Christ, who referred to a man's tendency to see a splinter in another's eye, but not his own.

I repeated this conversation to the Maréchale de Clérembault two weeks later. She had dispensed with her velvet mask, as we were in a shaded room of Madame's apartment in the Palais-Royal. She was sitting, and so was I. She no longer kept me standing in her presence, but she continued to be as severe in her demeanour to me as if I was still nothing but a boy. Only rarely did she smile, or even allow any warmth to come into her eye. And then it was only as if a brief exhalation made its way through the surface of a rock.

Nevertheless, I was extremely fond of her, and I think she knew it.

Now, for the moment, the sharp edge of her attention had reverted to her money. She was a calculating and reckless miser, if there is such a thing.

"Are you sure you remembered that correctly, Berthon?" she said. "Because Madame has correspondence with the Princess of Wales, you know. (*Pause.*) That is not for others to be aware of. (*Pause again.*) The Regent finds it helpful that she should do so, while he encourages the government of England to regard France favourably. All sources of friendship are useful."

"You need hardly warn the Princess of Wales to sell shares!" I exclaimed.

I received a chilling glare from her. She said something like, "I am quite astonished, Monsieur de Brisse, that you think that at my age I am capable of such indiscretion."

I had certainly been foolish to forget that the Clérembault had no sense of humour. At which point I had no choice but to take my leave.

CHAPTER TWELVE

LAW'S hands once held the entire economy of France in a steady grip. Law's hands were very strong. I saw him lift a carriage wheel once with them. It was after the issue of shares in the Mississippi venture, when what seemed like the entire population of Paris crowded into the Rue Quincampoix where the centre of the Paris money market functioned, and among those most hysterical to receive audience with M. Law, two carriages collided. Under the twisted wheel of one, a small, ragged street boy was pinned down. John Law had just appeared in the door on his way to visit the Regent, and at first could not move for those who crowded round him, but because of his height he could see over their heads to the child. Without roughness, he yet easily thrust aside everyone in his path, even, as it happened, the Duchess de Maine's sister, and took the wheel in both hands until the boy could be dragged out. Then he got into his own carriage which never stirred from his door, and with his footmen clearing his path, was driven away.

I only heard about this from others, but it added to his fame surprisingly, not because he had saved a peasant boy – that in itself would not particularly recommend anyone to the admiration of the crowd – but for his physical strength which, curiously enough, often is assumed to lend credence to other forms of ability.

This was the time when all who managed to buy shares became rich. This was the time when the Duchess found that the woman whose jewels she had been admiring from her box in the opera was her own cook. To witness the effect of the introduction of paper money a mere two weeks after its adoption, I went with Armand to the Rue Quincampoix. A brisk air of prosperity had begun to animate the trading area as soon as the paper notes had begun to circulate, and well before the issue of shares. Both Armand and I marvelled at the immediate effect the change from metal to paper had upon commerce. A wilting flower given water could not demonstrate more clearly the way in which any conglomerate – whether plant or construct of human ingenuity – flourishes when supplied with the unique conditions it requires to grow.

Some men in their prime are not half the heroes they appeared to be when they were climbing the ladder of their ambitions. John Law was the exception. Long before the Regent forced Parliament to give its consent to the establishment of the Banque Générale, someone who watched and listened to Monsieur Law with care could not fail to notice his presence of mind: an equilibrium that nothing seemed to shake. He had an intelligence, a quality of spirit that was quite remarkable, and is in fact characteristic of those who rise very high in the world, whether they are beneficial or not. When released from the constraint of Parliament's rejections, these qualities in John Law soared. He became a citizen of France under the Regent's own patronage, in order to satisfy Parliament before being, himself, appointed Director of the new National Bank. When the exchange of paper banknotes instead of coin, particularly in commercial trade, began to be successfully carried out, it was extraordinarily impressive to witness the speed with which commerce became enlivened just as Law had predicted. The rapidity with which the money market of Paris responded to the change, by a recovery of rates and an increase in commerce, where before it had been withering, was phenomenal.

Less unusual was the guarded disappointment of Law's opponents. I noticed it particularly. They could not openly deplore a change which showed such signs of serving the national good, but they writhed under the rejection of their own remedy and the resultant loss of influence they themselves suffered. I had seen this before. What else, if not the same dangerously thwarted ambition, had fired the enmity of the Chevalier de Lorraine? Just like the Chevalier, so Law's enemies in the Parliament and elsewhere, despite any appearance of honest relief at the signs of financial recovery, were actually being consumed alive with jealousy. It gave me no pleasure to see, because I knew how dangerous it was. Such frustration must find relief somehow, and I was anxious for John Law, and even more so for my son.

As soon as I focused my mind in this direction, I recognized in a whole train of recent moments, gestures, glances, tones of voice on the part of Law's opponents; the same icily burning passions that had provoked Madame's enemies when they schemed her downfall years ago. Something like a thrill of recognition ran through me. I mentally reviewed the moment I had witnessed when Noailles, hearing Monsieur Law make that curious remark about turning paper into gold, cast a certain glance at the Abbé Dubois which meant something quite different to me now than it had at the time. I wonder whether they actually deplored the fact that Law's device offered a remedy not only for averting bankruptcy but as a secondary effect it offered a means for general prosperity which, for once, the nobles and bourgeoisie would pay for, rather than the peasantry. In France, the nobility do not pay taxes. Meanwhile, the peasants and merchants must bear the whole burden whether the harvests fail or not. The nobility eat and keep warm either way and consider the peasantry merely as animals who can be left to their own devices.

Those men who came to rob us at night when I travelled to Italy with Bonhomme were starving. Even as they fled into the black and deserted fields, I wanted to call them back to question them and find out why their living was so wretched, and perhaps give them some more food. I wonder if one of these days the peasantry will find a way of taking their revenge. Judging by the wretched foster parents with whom my father left me as an infant, and the crude misery of their hovel, they would not be kind if they ever had a chance to stick a hayfork in the backs of their landowners and gain an independence that way.

I privately hoped that Law's reforms would eventually extend to such ingrained problems but did not mention this element to anyone else, Law himself included. But my secret speculation served to sanctify my admiration for so great and strong a man as Law; perhaps even to distort my understanding.

It certainly had an overbearing effect on other aspects of my life, and not least Armand. It was not that I spent less time with him, or had lost an iota of my keen enjoyment of his presence. But I limited our communication to politics and John Law's progress, in the hope of deflecting him from all other concerns. Armand could have dropped dead of his broken heart and I would only have known about it when I saw his corpse laid out on the floor in front of me.

One morning we were studying the fact that John Law had bought almost the whole issue of the discredited *billets d'état*. It will be remembered that the old *billets d'état* issued by the monarch sunk to a discount of 75 per cent after Noailles' insistence on keeping them the previous year at a reduced rate of interest. Armand laughed. I do remember he laughed. He still had reserves of enthusiasm for observing the dexterity with which Law, like an ingenious fox slipping near a hen coop at night, would not miss an opportunity. Law had complete confidence in his own system and foresaw that these old billets would eventually recover part of their value. Indeed, when the moment came for him to personally underwrite the national bank – an extraordinary feat – he was able to use this hoard as a nominal part of the sum of many millions which he had committed himself to supplying as security. In France, he, almost alone, financed and certainly underwrote the risk, of forming a national bank which in England had involved four participants, one of which was already a private bank.

One evening Armand and I amused ourselves with these figures. I was exhilarated to practice, in his company, a skill which we shared. Isabel brought us candles before we had finished. Neither of us looked to the time. Only when Fanette came, dressed for supper and followed by Isabel with a dish of roasted chestnuts, did Armand suddenly realise that he must have missed the Regent's evening. But when asked, he shook his head and declared that he need not attend the Regent this time, but stay with us instead. Even so, I noticed out of the corner of my eye how he bit his lip when thinking he was unobserved. Once the distraction of our mathematical calculations was no longer there to mask it, for once I noticed how livid his skin was, and how restless he became. I remembered it again as I lay in bed that night. But when Fanette stirred in her sleep, and woke and questioned me, I did not want to disturb her with my fears about Armand; and so I substituted a discussion of the speculations of John Law.

In the process of telling my tale, a pattern emerged which displaced my earlier preoccupation. In reminding Fanette of the way in which Madame's enemies had plotted to destroy her, and how they were unaware of how secretly I found out about their treachery, I explained to her how Law's situation now was not dissimilar. He, like Madame, had enemies already planning to destroy him. Armand and I had often discussed the deceitful intentions of Noailles and the inveterate obstructions of parlement. If they once decided to fight, what would their weapon be? A likely trick would be to cause a loss of confidence in the stability of paper money, so that all those who held the new banknotes would panic and cause a run on the bank. No bank would ever be able to withstand such a move. Once the number of banknotes exceeded the availability of coin, or was even suspected of doing so, a loss of confidence – which Noailles, together with his friends, knew how to fan into a flame – could cause a collapse. I happened to know, from the calculations with which Armand and I had amused ourselves, that Law had not still got anything like the millions of livres laid up in cash that he had originally committed as security.

But to carry out an attack, Law's enemies would need secrecy, whereas I had already proved in the past how it was possible for someone like myself to be privy to the real intentions of villains. If I wanted to protect the Regent and my son, and Monsieur Law, I was the one who had the means to do it. I can still be invisible at court. Once out in the wide world – in the streets for example – I tended to attract, rather than repel, attention. But at court, and among those who might conspire against my friends, I could be to all intents and purposes invisible, as when Madame was in great danger. Like a gamekeeper, hidden and unmoving in a nobleman's forest, I could see and hear, however stealthily carried out, the progress of a gang of poachers. For some reason, the thought brought me instant peace of mind. My body relaxed in the warmth beside Fanette and my mind felt renewed, almost as if the prospect of the action which I planned was some kind of holiday for my spirit. In the process, I had once again completely forgotten the danger which Armand was in.

I had scarcely escaped from the attentions of Gaudet and his obsession with neck cloths one morning when Armand brought me some strange news. Apparently, the previous night Law had again attended Madame's drawing room, and after he had left received a message to go to the Regent in his private rooms the following day at 4.30 in the afternoon. His Highness instructed Law to enter by the side door, so as not to be observed, while he himself would return from the Council by the main entrance.

Later the same day, as his carriage crossed the market square, the Regent noticed Armand positioned with his soldiers of the Guards regiment. The carriage stopped and a servant was sent to request Armand to follow His Highness. Armand then passed the baton to his fellow officer and rode alongside the Regent's coach until they reached the Palais-Royal, when he dismounted and followed his Highness. As Armand related all this, he twice interrupted himself to say, "I shall astonish you, Papa." And indeed he did, for as soon as His Highness had disclosed the events which we all now know about – I refer to the edict posted in January commanding, in the King's name, that all commercial contracts should be carried out in the new banknotes – he turned to Armand and enquired about my health, and whether I was still strong enough to undertake a task on his behalf. M. Law had told him of my familiarity with his system, and what he was kind enough to call my expertise in mathematics, and it had reminded His Highness of the tenacity I had displayed in the past when his mother was in danger. I could apparently expect a summons to the Regent's presence in order to be consulted.

I was astonished, and uncertain. It was so long since I had enjoyed that old familiarity with the Duke of Orléans.

Armand was watching me. Not long ago I would have referred to him for his advice, but now I almost always caught a facet in his glance which was both new and less pleasant to me. The realization of it made me sad, and as my spirits cooled, my temper heated.

"His Highness only had to speak to me," I said, rather sharply.

Armand said, "Do you doubt my discretion, Sir?"

I took too long to reply. Because, in fact, the temptation flickered through my mind to take revenge on my son for his unsteadiness before. But I would not have done so if he had still been standing there by the time that I looked up.

The next day His Highness sent for me, with the same instructions about the side entrance, to which Armand showed me the way. I remember my son's coolness and his courtesy in doing so. It cut me to the quick, but just then I felt bereft of the means to speak. The door led to a small private staircase ending in the anteroom of the Regent's office. Naturally, I was a familiar member of the Regent's court, but it was many years since we had had any private conversation and as I waited to be admitted, my mind darted in and out of memories, wondering how His Highness the Regent would greet me. I was overwhelmed with gratitude when, having made my bow, he actually embraced me, and speaking with remarkable ease he mentioned how the formalities of court life never irked him more than in keeping him at a distance from the friend of his childhood, whose making of toys and games he had never forgotten. By which, of course, he could only mean myself.

He invited me to sit, as we were in his private room, and went on to describe a wooden horse which I had made with moving legs, and by degrees, my adventures in the discovery of the guilt of the Chevalier de Lorraine and how I had found the monk from whom he had purchased poison in Italy. At that point, the Regent asked me if it had indeed been Alberoni who had knowledge of the identity of the very monk who traded the poison. The same Giulio

Alberoni, son of an Italian market gardener, who had made great progress in the world since that day when Ernst's young friend had induced him to disclose the monk's name. He has been made a cardinal since, and is now the de facto ruler of Spain, as he has manipulated the King and the queen into habits of complete seclusion. No one is allowed to see them unless Cardinal Alberoni grants the occasion, as everyone who is interested knows.

I was moved, thinking that these recollections were brought to mind by His Highness in order to bind me to him with the reminder of how he cherished the incidence of my having been useful to Madame his mother. But in fact, he was simply drawing near to the theme which he wanted to discuss with me. I had expected him to touch on the subject of M. Law's system, which I was now known to understand well. But I soon realized that this was not to be the subject of our discussion.

The Regent shifted his body in his chair.

He had put on weight since he was a young man but was, and still is handsome nevertheless. And his eye, which he had injured so badly playing tennis and which he refused to care for like he should, no longer needed to be covered. I could not help loving him, even if it were not my duty to do so. What else, when he is Madame's son? I felt a strong impulse to say something to ease his mind but did not dare to try.

He said, "I have an idea that you are the one who may be able to help me, Berthon, with one particular matter."

"I would be honoured, Monseigneur," I said immediately. "I would consider it as a very great favour if there were some way in which I could serve you."

I could feel my blood warm, and a sensation as if the sinews in my throat swelled. I feel it now, remembering that moment.

He stood up quite suddenly and started to pace the

floor to relieve the flow of his mind. He came quickly to the problem of his nephew, the King of Spain, and how he allowed himself to be manipulated, scarcely governing his country at all. When he described the virtual imprisonment which the King of Spain and his wife endured under the controlling influence of Alberoni, he threw out his hand and turned very abruptly towards me. But then, lowering his voice, the tone of which lost in that instant every timbre of generosity or warmth, he described the more confidential details of the conspiracy to make the King of Spain heir to the throne of France if our young King Louis XV should not survive his infancy. On the basis of the King of Spain being the only surviving grandson of Louis XIV, this was an entirely plausible scheme provided that he could be induced to dishonour the contract by which, as the Duke of Anjou, he had forsworn all claim to the throne of France. As I already knew how close was the friendship between Alberoni and the Duc and Duchess du Maine, I was not at all surprised that this treacherous scheme was invented by the Mains. Madame du Maine, particularly, would do almost anything to further their ambition to supplant the Duke d'Orléans as Regent (this being a part of their bargain with the Cardinal), and also to recover their privileges as legitimate descendants of the old King.

Up to this point, I could do no more than listen, although I also felt my own pulse quicken at the realisation of just how angry His Highness had become, in allowing me to witness his rage, when in all public circumstances his habit was to refuse all attempts to discompose him. This moved me very much.

I said, "I had thought, Sire, that you wished me to discuss M. Law's financial scheme. I anticipated..."

His Highness cut me off with an impetuous sweep of his hand and this time he could not avoid oversetting a small lacquer tray on his work table, which crashed to the floor. I was wondering what to do about the pieces on the ground. Should I myself pick them up? But I felt I was too clumsy to risk it.

The Regent looked over my shoulder, making a gesture of dismissal: "Leave it there, Berthon." He put his hand on his face, and turned away. "You will think I have caught an infection of foul temper from the Royal Doll herself."

It was no secret that this was the name by which the Duchess du Maine was referred to at Court, behind her back. In inverse proportion to her size, she was known for the violence of her temper. His Highness was treating me with flattering confidence when he abused a direct descendent of the royal house of Bourbon Conde while we were alone together, but I was bewildered by the turn our interview had taken.

He said, "She craves the position this would give herself at court, as a starving wolf craves food, and I know it. But instead of being able to regard her ambitions with contempt, I am forced to arm myself."

He was only too right to recognize the need for vigilance himself personally, where she was concerned. His own wife is the sister of Mme du Maine, but he dismissed any idea of receiving help from her. I nearly became lost in my own thoughts and caught the tail of the Regent's last words just in time before he turned towards me again in his restless pacing.

To my relief, he spoke calmly.

"Do you remember, Berthon, the day when my uncle the King gave his third son away? He had three sons living and thought that the throne of France was so secure that he could accept the petition of Spain for the nomination of his son's younger son, the Duke of Anjou, to become their King after the death of the childless Charles II. There was great excitement in France about it. My uncle, the King, was so proud. And yet here we are with the Dauphin and his younger brother both dead, and their surviving brother is a virtual prisoner in his own Court as the King of Spain, and incapable of resisting an inducement to attack the security of France led by that villain Alberoni."

At that point, he sat down again, and I was relieved because I could sit again myself.

I did remember, very well, the old King's voice as he announced to the Court, "I present to you the future King of Spain." Louis XIV had confidence in his own advice being a guiding principle for his son when eventually he became the King of Spain. When they heard that the Prince was told to be his own master, and never to let anyone else tell him what to do, Ernst told me that the young men in the schools fell to the ground they laughed so much. But it seemed just as well that the Spanish had him.

And if he now schemed – or Alberoni schemed on his behalf – to dishonour his commitment to renounce all claim to the throne of France, surely all this would only matter if our young King Louis XV should die before attaining his majority. But the Duchess du Maine had apparently devised a means whereby her husband should take over the Regency as well, and before any such eventuality.

The Regent never stopped his pacing to and fro as he debated all this. I could not see my part in all of it. His Highness continued to describe his feelings in connection with the Spanish question, which of course I was aware of. The Duke de Saint-Simon had discussed it at length with John Law, attempting to convince him that France should align herself with Spain rather than England. But what had I to do with all this? I could scarcely be called upon to advise the Regent, or express an opinion of any sort, to do with politics. And yet the Regent's passionate distraction continued, until he stopped suddenly with his back to me, visibly straightened his body, lifted his head which he habitually held down when he paced to and fro, and stood a moment, the tips of the fingers of his right hand on that small table which I had thought at one point he was about to overturn before. He made a graceful gesture, as if to fan away the thoughts which had just now possessed him. I was standing, of course, having risen to my feet when he did.

He looked at me very kindly, and said, "Berthon, you will excuse me, I think. I have wandered away from my point. It is our own parlement which concerns me. Mme du Maine hates me, and would like to injure me. Part of her scheme is the incitement to parlement to obstruct the introduction of M. Law's system. This would throw back our country into bankruptcy, destroy my authority, and clear her path for my displacement. This, even more than Mme du Maine's intrigues in Spain, is what concerns me. The Duke de Saint-Simon and other advisers insist that I should act decisively to curtail this movement, but how can I when conspiracies mature in places that I cannot see? It is not my nature to watch from a hidden place in the hope that my enemy will expose himself – or herself – when my claws are within reach."

The words, "Is it mine, Sire?" were on my lips, but I was silenced by the lack of any opportunity to interrupt him.

"I have noticed that Alberoni is very intimate with Mme du Maine lately. Spain and England are the allies between whom France must choose. Did you ever visit the court of the old King and Queen of England, as we always called James II here? A duller place I never saw. Madame my mother was as fond of them as his Majesty, Louis XIV, was but I have had enough of their conspiracies, and their endless need for French gold. The son is worse than the father." As he said this I believe he had almost forgotten that I was there. His entire gaze was turned elsewhere than in that room, and eventually he said, with some venom,

"The Bois de Boulogne. That was it. That is where he last went begging for money. I heard that the King of England met the Spanish ambassador there in secret only last week, and asked him to procure 1000 ecus for him from the King of Spain. In return for what service, I ask you? He thinks they will help him to recover the throne of England, and then England will combine with Spain against France. Imagine; a man with royal ambitions skulking there under the trees with his begging bowl. And yet Madame du Maine and that scoundrel, Alberoni, want to help him make trouble between England and France. I have stood between her and her ambition in that matter of the old King's will, and now she conspires to stand between me and M. Law and the establishment of the Company of the West, for trading the products of the Mississippi, and the Bank to fund it. This development is essential to the whole of Law's system. Mme du Maine is not only prepared to kill me in order to have all the privileges of royal succession restored to her husband, but she would even sacrifice the economy of France to her own ambition and her revenge."

I was not called upon to say anything, although his Highness paused. When at last he looked up his countenance had cleared enough for him to be able to see me, and even to smile. He gave a short breath almost of laughter, as if to dowse a flame no bigger than a candle. But I had seen him moved, and been moved myself at it.

"Do you see, Berthon? Her passion knows no bounds. *Poupée du sang* they call her. She may resemble a child's doll, and her blood is certainly royal; but she has the dangerous mentality of an angry snake. Oh, she has great friends and influence – and a talent for secrecy, when not brazenly telling all her guests at dinner how willingly she would put a knife in my heart."

I did not know that he had heard of that occasion, although of course it was spoken of at court. Even now he had not finished, but addressed me from the far end of the room before turning again to me, and after a moment of silence, saying with a calmer voice, "Between her personal ambitions, and parlement's willingness to behave like her cat's paw in the pursuit of theirs, my position is dangerous. And yet it is difficult for me to protect myself. Although I can see whatever happens before my own eyes remarkably well, the whole court pays attention to the direction in which I am looking, and acts accordingly. And there are very few of the King's subjects from whom I can expect a totally factual account of matters which happen elsewhere, because any man at court has his own ambitions to consider. Maybe the Duke de Toulouse is an exception, but he is du Maine's brother. And apart from him, I thought of you, Berthon. You might help me."

I pondered this long speech, and there was a pause between us. I found that I could hardly come up with a single name for the role I suspected that His Highness was planning for me. Was he thinking that I could spy for him? Although I have taken advantage of my own invisibility many times, it has been at my own prompting, or rather the prompting of some interest (such as Madame's safety), which I had quite independently adopted. I did not realise that I had, even in presumably the closed circuit of Madame, her son and Clérembault, become identified as an employable expert in deceit.

His Highness the Regent, ruler of France, the Duke of Orléans – the man who had emerged from the chrysalis of a childhood I had shared and been loved by him – had stood silently looking at me for long enough. In spite of my deep sadness, I found the words with which to thank him. And then I left.

CHAPTER THIRTEEN

I SOON persuaded myself to take a different view of the role His Highness had assigned to me, because in fact my spirit thrilled at the prospect of taking an active part in the political scene at such a juncture. Previously I had only noticed de Noailles' constant small barbs aimed at the detail of Law's management, while simultaneously attempting to keep up an appearance of friendship, as a symptom of typical court rivalry. But now it interested me to follow that thread and see whether or not it connected with the Duke of Maine and his appalling wife. With a similar heightened attention, I also scrutinized the apparent friendship between the Abbé Dubois and Law. The new angle of my observation disclosed an unwelcome explanation for how John Law had captured the allegiance of a man whom I knew he despised. He had paid him. Law had paid Dubois 30,000 livres to be exact.

Dubois flourished at court, and his Highness the Regent counted him one of his close advisers. This alone was quite extraordinary, because Dubois was of a very mean intelligence, uncouth-looking and with no discernable talent beyond this quite bizarre facility for secret knowledge and intrigues. In such a capacity, I suppose John Law must be forgiven the bribe he gave Dubois for using his influence to persuade the Regent to support the new financial system. But each fragment of added awareness shifted the pattern of events as I see them now, just as the smallest movement of a kaleidoscope affects the entire pattern of the rest; and too often the result is worsened by it.

As soon as I started to pay him sharper attention than I had before, I realized that the Abbé Dubois also wanted to destroy the Duke of Noailles because Noailles would otherwise compete with him for the desirable post of First Minister when soon it became vacant. To that end also he sided with Law and the Regent to establish the Banking Company of the West (as the new bank was to be called at that time) against Noailles' alternative recommendations.

I found that it was true, as the Regent had implied, that not one single one of the contenders under my scrutiny had the actual merit of Law's system uppermost in their mind. For all of them (to some extent even John Law himself), there were personal and ambitious motives distracting or misdirecting them. Perhaps only the Regent himself analysed the project purely with the concerns of the bankrupt economy of France in view. And myself.

For that integrity alone, I would have agreed to spy for him, since, second only to Madame's, his prosperity and happiness, and that of France, were extremely precious to me.

I needed particularly to penetrate the confidential sessions of the parlement itself, and there I have no doubt at all that the Regent aided me. In order to give credence to his authority, he publicly noticed me in a manner which had before eluded him. He even invited me to his suppers, but it was some time before I had the courage to attend. Those at court who knew my long association with Madame his mother thought they understood his intimacy with me, and no doubt explained to others who did not. But myself, while being joined to these unfamiliar privileges, I experienced a poignant cutting-off from some of those I had enjoyed before; I no longer seemed to know myself. A man who is aware that a piece of his integrity has been lost, like a fragment from a puzzle gone missing, is not so happy. And besides, there was Armand.

To my intense relief, Francis returned to Paris that Winter. Although I had not dared to mention my troubles to Fanette for fear she might speak to Armand – and also, since I could not bring myself to instruct her not to confide in him – I had no friend to share my doubts. These included not only the insult of the Regent's commission on the terms in which he had mentioned it, but also my growing doubts as to the opinion of parlement regarding Law's system. I began to think that they could be in the right. My mind was clogged, like a drain that could not be emptied until I had the stimulus of real debate. I would have been able to discuss all these matters with Armand if he had not given way to that sickness of the mind and the body which had overcome him.

I went to call on Francis as soon as he sent word by one of his servants that he was returned. Unfortunately, his arrival in Paris was a signal for every Englishman in the country to call on him in his new house near the Place des Victoires. I asked him if I might come when he was alone and he sent word that I should come in the afternoon, so I went then and found only Matthew Prior, whose company could disappoint no man sane enough to value poetry, literature and philosophy. Since the years when he had been England's ambassador to Paris, Prior retained the habit of spending at least half the year in France. But now he left soon after I arrived, and I found myself alone with Francis in a room only dimly lit as the candles had not yet been brought in, and the sky outside was already in shadow. But there was a good fire burning and there was no sign of Lord Stair, or Stanhope, or Lady Sandwich, or anyone else likely to want news of how the shooting went in the freezing cold landscapes of Yorkshire and Scotland.

By the flickering light of the fire, Francis appeared older

than I expected, and I wondered if he had been unwell. He had discarded his wig, and his hair, still thick, had become a mixture of bronze and white. I was very surprised to learn that Climene was not with him. When two servants came in with candles, the brighter light momentarily carved hollows, deep and handsome, under his cheekbones and, presumably because I had just said something to amuse him, crevices that laughter had always sketched beside his mouth, and now carved with a sharper tool. One of the servants mended the fire and the other replenished our glasses and then left. Or so I thought. I had asked, half in jest, why Francis was alone in the pleasantness of our comfortable friendship.

"Climene and I cannot agree about something. So I have come alone to make up my mind."

"Has she annoyed you?" I said.

"You always laugh at Climene, Berthon, but her reasoning is not always as frivolous as she likes to make out, as you know."

"But why should that make her quarrel with you?"

"Because she still does not want me to sell my shares in the South Sea Company."

"And you do?"

"I thought so." How interesting, I immediately thought. Very. "So here I am. She made me come to talk to you, Berthon. She says you will know exactly why she is right and I am wrong."

As usual, my sister had shot an arrow right into the very heart of this sensitive matter, threatening to kill stone dead the fluttering pulse of optimism. If I had been in any doubt, I knew in that moment how vivid my sympathies were with John Law, and how passionately I wanted him to succeed in his brave and brilliant adventure.

Francis said of Climene, "She cannot explain for herself what logical arguments may or may not support her convictions, but says you will do it." He looked at me with such an expression: his brow raised in tribute to his own scepticism, his eyes glittering with a pride he couldn't repress in the presence, whether imagined or real, of Climene, and his mouth stern. "Would you say, for example, that John Law's system, which resembles ours closely, has, or has not, your confidence?"

"I would have thought," I replied, "that the position of your parliament and monarchy, being independent of each other as ours are not, would make the whole venture safer."

"So they say. And is it true?" He looked away from me. "After all, your Regent is a man of quite unusual intelligence. I would feel safer if we had him in England."

"I would feel safer too," I said.

That crease on the corner of his mouth deepened.

"He has composed an opera recently, I am told," he said. He had an eye on me that looked as if he was stalking my meaning. "One which the musicians have praised without having to forswear their own principles." This was true. "And Climene says that he has been consulting you, and spends time in your company precisely because of this other question."

"When His Highness was a child," I said, "he was fond of me because I made him toys. That is all." Then I relented, because surely there was no need to take precautions when speaking to Francis, who would never, either with accidental indiscretion or bad faith, betray a friend. "It's true," I said, "that his mind is so fertile that he becomes the master of any subject he chooses quickly enough to make him passionate; by which time he becomes impatient with the facts. Have you anyone in power in England who has parallel characteristics?"

"That describes a dangerously charming fellow," Francis muttered.

"Exactly what the Duke de Saint-Simon says of you English."

Francis looked very surprised. "An admirer, then?"

"No. I'm afraid not." And he laughed, as if I had paid him a compliment. "He considers the example of your financial adventures will tempt us, but that you are skating on solid ice, whereas ours will crack."

But what I also waited to hear was how deeply Francis himself was involved with the South Sea Company. When I spent time, as I had recently, listening with great attention to what was said among our members of the French parlement when they thought they were alone, I had become aware of other risks embedded in Law's system, and no doubt the South Sea Company as well. Uninhibited by the presence of the Regent's Council, members of the parlement like the President – de Mesmes himself – and various others discussed the prospect of profitable trade in North America and pointed out various extreme long-term difficulties. There had been one occasion when a member of the parlement had specifically compared the South Sea Company to Law's Company of the West; what came to be called the Mississippi Venture. He said that there was no chance, while Protestant England was involved on the wrong side of the argument of the Spanish succession, that they would permit the English to trade profitably in Catholic South America where Spain's colonial powers were strongly embedded. If Climene had dreamt of merchants arriving at her door loaded with precious and strange things, and was now disappointed, she would change her mind. I had no need, after I had recounted these thoughts, to remind Francis of how the South Sea Company was holding out the prospect of abundant trade in exotic luxuries in order to tempt investors in the shares.

"And is the same happening here?" said Francis. He turned the tables on me a bit too soon. I wished to goodness I had something in my glass. I picked it up; finding it empty, I put it down again.

Francis made a gesture towards someone who I hadn't realized was standing behind me, and my glass was filled. But grateful as I was, it was out of the question to confess to what I just had in mind, if the servant was still there.

"No," I said. Quite categorically. I got to my feet and moved towards the fire as if I felt the cold. Once there, I chafed my hands, looked sideways towards Francis and said quietly, "But if we were alone it would be easier to talk."

He assumed an expression of such cunning that I hoped the servant, whoever he was, lacked any powers of observation.

When the servant was gone, I looked rather more carefully into the dark places of the room. You would think that someone like myself, who knew so well how a quiet shadow partly obscured by a hanging may have ears, besides having had my own particular leaning in that direction pointed out to me recently by the Regent, would have been naturally cautious.

"Francis, if I confide in you it will be in the expectation that if you repeat my opinions you will do it without giving me credit for them." He agreed. "In which case, not only could it happen here, but I can scarcely sleep at night for the intensity of my feelings at the thought of what we would lose if John Law's plans are unbalanced."

"But trade in the Mississippi has not started yet."

"Has your South Sea Company started trading in South America?"

"They talk about it."

"Exactly. There isn't any; yet, nor ever may be. The Company of the West also faces serious impediments to profitable trade, although in our case they are practical problems rather than political."

Francis said something in English that I didn't understand. From his expression, it might have been a curse.

"When the Regent asked me to make"– I couldn't think of the word for a moment, and then said 'discreet' – "discreet enquiries in parlement I didn't expect to hear anything that would challenge the picture I'd already had presented to me by Law himself."

"And have you since?"

"As you know, Law is a fluent, brave and honest man. Even the Clérembault can't fault his logic. Madame admires him for other reasons, and says that he speaks French better than any other Englishman."

Francis had a way of putting his teeth together and drawing back his lip. It had always reminded me of an occasional gesture of horses, but whereas the horse looks up with a wide stare at the same time, Francis would flex the lid of his gaze and it made me catch my breath. I had always been very glad that Francis was my friend, but when I looked at the man he had become I was particularly glad that he was not my enemy.

"Are you saying you doubt his honesty?"

"I would have said no, and I still would. Absolutely. But I discovered that he has bribed the Abbé Dubois with thirty thousand livres to support him."

"I'll sell," Francis said.

CHAPTER FOURTEEN

I WENT home that night with an unquiet mind. Before we reached the village, I sent the coachman home so that I could walk. I had thought that I had complete confidence in John Law's venture. Not only had I been convinced by my discussions with him and with Armand, but already since the adoption of paper money, trade had recovered like the dead rising from the grave. Law's insistence that commerce would thrive once the money supply was increased had been proved right, beyond question. And I was not forgetting that Law himself had, in my hearing, reassured the parlement that the supply of paper money would always be balanced with specie held by the Bank. Neither was it as if anyone else had a better idea than Law's system. Alternative strategies, beyond such as originally advised by the Duke de Saint-Simon to simply declare the nation bankrupt, were non-existent. And yet I now found myself in a state as if my mind was being haunted by some elusive threat. If I traced my uneasiness, I found only those two shadows: the fact that John Law had bribed the Abbé Dubois so generously, and later, that he had used privately some funds marked as security against the notes issued by the bank, and had even thought it appropriate. But since, he had very much changed his view, finding that the Regent made a profligate use of the same source, and he could not stop him.

Neither action was hard to understand or to defend, given the atmosphere of extreme jubilation which had replaced the former gloom of debt and depressed trade. And yet a worm of fear in my mind, at that point infinitely subtle, owed that particular evening to its existence.

As I made my way home to Fanette, I thought of Francis and his estates in England: the cool stone walls, the fertile, temperate land that knew no Summer storms of ice falling from the sky in June and stripping the harvests, like ours. I seemed to know what it meant to watch the hunt set out in Yorkshire, or in Summer the charm of a farming estate well tended. I knew, from the accounts Francis gave me, how the English aristocracy were expected to make their land productive, and often did; compared with ours, who were encouraged to neglect their estates in favour of being at Court under the King's eye, where they could less easily conspire against him. I had hoped that the South Sea Company would flourish and blaze a trail along which the French Company of the West would follow. And yet Francis had come to Paris to sniff the wind, since he thought a similar financial climate embraced both our lands. And I had been glad when I heard him say that he would sell his shares.

The next day, Climene came to Paris and soon learned that Francis had made a decision which she did not approve of. My beautiful sister made a very uncomfortable companion if she was annoyed. She wore that ring; held it out for me to admire it, and then asked me how I thought Francis was going to pay for such beautiful things if he ran away from the most profitable venture the City of London had ever seen. The Tsar of Russia, who had so recently paid a state visit to us in Paris, had described ice which is capable of penetrating miles below the ground in his own country. Climene's eyes, although they burned, confirmed the existence of such penetrating cold.

My only refuge was to hurry away to the meeting of parlement. I had obtained my passport for these meetings thanks to a certain advocate called Matthieu Moreau. He was – still is – a very steady sort of man. Although it has been my great fortune to have the friendship of Madame and her son the Regent and, by the accident I have described, that of John Law, in general most courtiers ignore me, even if politely. I have heard myself described as one of those curious, and perhaps magically endowed, creatures who figure in children's stories. At the same time, I am not at all wealthy, without being actually poor, which is the outer limit of what is tolerable here. And my appearance has not really improved enough to pass without comment, even with the concealed basket work of our court tailors sewn into the lining of my coat, and wearing my highest shoes. Add to that, it is considered something resembling necromancy that my wife is so beautiful; but then again, she is not strictly at Court, but was a mere actress with the players of Racine and Corneille in Paris, and therefore not a lady to cultivate for the sake of society.

I mention all this only to describe the opposite, who is Matthieu Moreau. He was and is, although much older now, the model of a normal man. If such a thing existed, he would be the template according to which the material of all acceptable men would be cut. Neither tall nor short, he has succeeded in advocacy without being at all brilliant, and in employment in the parlement of Paris without having any claim to aristocracy. The Regent only had to give him a command (and no money), in order to secure his co-operation in accepting the charge of my company whenever I chose. The fact that the Duke of Orléans was aware of this man at all casts one more surprising light on the infinitely facetted personality of the Regent. His Highness gave me a word of caution, which was not to get myself mentioned in the journal that Moreau was known to keep. I am not quite sure whether I succeeded in the latter. It may be some years yet before I find out.

Being seated inconspicuously among the minor advocates whose knowledge of the law was an essential fund for the nobles concerned in ratifying the King's edicts or in attempting to block them, as the case might be, was sometimes tedious. Clerics and judges talked at great length in order to impress an admiration of their own learning on their fellows, or when determined to oppose an edict, to persuade them. I detected the influence of d'Effiat in the passionate bias of de Mesmes, the premier president of the parlement. It must have contributed at least to his opposition to the creation of the national bank. This thought annoyed me very much. Those of us who knew the Regent from his infancy and who loved him shared a common incredulity for his sometimes apparently naive and forgiving nature. His employment of d'Effiat was an example. Admittedly, I had unique knowledge of d'Effiat's crimes in the days when as a member of the Chevalier de Lorraine's *quartette* of friends, he had conspired against Madame. But now everyone knew that he favoured the views of Alberoni and the papal nuncio, Bentivoglio. Why should the Duke of Orléans, whom the Spanish faction would displace as Regent if they could, keep d'Effiat near to him? He must know that from such a position at his very elbow, d'Effiat would give the advantage to de Mesmes in parlement, to oppose edicts likely to strengthen Law's power. The progress of Law's system, with its notable success so far in stemming the financial embarrassment of the State, and the projected establishment of the Western Banking Company, was now the target of the parlement's attack. I had leisure, while attending to their lengthy speeches, to puzzle out a possible solution to the Regent's inclination to use d'Effiat as a friend. I did remember the Regent proclaiming his curious predilection for the company, and even the advice, of villains. He claimed to prefer the company of known criminals to that of supposed men of honour who only wore their reputations as a cloak under which to conceal their motives.

But would he persist in that opinion if he knew what I knew of the past actions of d'Effiat?

I felt bitter. For the Regent's shallow recklessness, a true friend should insist on adding an appropriate measure of the gall of truth, but I thought then that I could not be the one to do it. I could not enlighten him of a past action so utterly corrupt and wicked. I refer, of course, to the murder of Madame's younger son. Even Madame herself, for all her loathing of d'Effiat, would hardly survive such a revelation.

She always hated the man instinctively and opposed him being appointed as her son's tutor, but d'Effiat is a notable classical scholar. He must have been a tutor worth having, since his pupil, now the Regent of France, never lost the taste for his conversation. Is it the case, then, that the person who opens the door to the magnificence of the arts and literature, acquires such status in the eyes of his pupil that almost any villainy is overlooked thereafter?

This atmosphere – this dark night – this solitude – encouraged my mind to wander. I trust such reflections are not as tedious as were those of the members of the parlement.

When she had been in Paris merely two days, Climene began to insist that I accompany her to the Regent's supper. The Regent himself had, as I mentioned a moment ago, declared me welcome, and I knew that my appearance would serve both to ratify the new relations which apparently existed between His Highness and myself and to yield opportunities for observation. But to spend five hours in the company of celebrating roués was not at all inviting to me at any time, and certainly not then.

But if there was one thing more disconcerting about Climene's beauty and her smile as she made a request, it was an awareness – which indeed I had – of her acute intelligence, and her temper if refused. Her temper was not a serious flaw – like that, for example of Lauzun or his nephew, Rions – but more an embellishment that she would put on with the same motivation as she might do up the clasp of a diamond bracelet. And so I agreed to accompany Climene.

I allowed Gaudet to dress me appropriately, which was to say not too well. The Regent did not want court dress at his suppers. But Climene was under no such restraint. Ladies were encouraged to go to extreme lengths in order to amuse and encourage the Regent. Once seated in the carriage with Climene, and rather soothed like a cat on a silken pillow by the billowing of scented silks which my sister allowed to fall over me with instructions that I must not crush them, I remembered the many times that I had travelled similarly with her. But although her enthusiasm for scandalous talk and court gossip was undiminished, mine was not. I thought the Regent's roués would not care for anything except their violent physical appetites, and I would languish in some insignificant recess until liberated by the sun rising on another day.

But there is an alchemical effect in crowds. When we got there I drank wine like everyone else. I was elbowed into position at table, and quite soon, between the conversation that Climene repeatedly dragged me into, and that which I was able to overhear from two gentlemen opposite who were quarrelling about the reputation of the friend of one of them, I found I had been swept into the stream of things like anyone cunningly fooled by a strong current which may drown him in the end. I saw d'Effiat continually circulating close to the Regent, very much as he had clung to the coat-tails of the Regent's father the Duke of Orléans. It almost made me look for Mme de Grancy, who was dead these ten years.

Supper was served in an extraordinary manner. I saw men and women who surprised me; they were not at Court, and neither were they servants. Five of them – apparently members of the Russian court who had arrived in Paris with the Tsar in his recent visit and had not yet gone home – got up from the table and performed some strange but exhilarating music.

There were eight dogs when I counted those I could see at one moment, and a monkey belonging to the newly arrived niece of Mme Guyon de Chinois. Of course, the Duchesse de Berry was there beside her father, and looking constantly to see what Rions was doing, where he, for all his peevish ill-looks, was apparently very successfully entertaining some very pretty women. She was about to get up, but then her father said something and she dropped her head on his shoulder while he stroked her cheek.

This room was the one which is so large, and overlooks the Rue St. Honoré. I had never been in it before. There were musical instruments all stacked at one end, an enormous profusion of paintings hung everywhere, and many tables unusually covered with a mixture of books, silver, food, wine and flowers, from which the servants seemed to be able to recover an inexhaustible supply of delicacies.

We had been there two hours before I saw Armand. When Climene saw him, she immediately stood up. She said she was going to dance, but as I watched her I thought she would be extremely lucky to be able to stand, leave alone anything else.

Inevitably Madame, not to mention Clérembault and Theobon, got wind of my attendance at the suppers. When next I attended on Madame she kept me by her for nearly half an hour with questions about the food, the company, the Regent, the behaviour of Madame de Berry with her father and with her new lover, Rions, and much else. She particularly wanted my observation of John Law, because she had heard of, and even met, his wife. Since he was known to be extremely fond of his wife and always addressing her with such gentleness and respect, Madame wanted to know if he danced and with whom, and other details. I had seen very little of him during the evening. He must have been seated some distance from myself, because when he did stand one noticed him at once as he towered over most other men. I promised Madame to let her know the next time I attended when Law was also there.

Clérembault, on the other hand, was just as pressing, but for news of Law's intentions in business. When I confessed that I had had no up-to-date conversation with Law on the progress of his scheme, she appeared so disapproving that I promised to visit him the next day and make her amends. I had a good enough excuse, even if it was only to congratulate him on becoming a French citizen, which the Regent had insisted on granting, now that the Bank was formed.

In the end, I waited most of the day, and sent Gaudet with a message to find out if Law would be at home that evening. In reply, I received an invitation to dine. It was a small company. Great men like the Duke de Saint-Simon might sit down every day with twenty guests around his table. But John Law and his wife were very domestic. Madame Law was fine-looking provided you saw her right side and not her left. Her figure was splendid, and even beautiful, but her left cheek was stained with a large dark birthmark, which neither she nor her husband seemed to regard at all. She had been married when they met, being then called Lady Catherine Knollys. Whether she had ever divorced her first husband was a mystery, but her living as Law's wife was accepted well enough for her to occasionally cross the dividing line between the Court and those outside it.

I considered her to be exhilarating company. She had a lively, mischievous style in talking but with no ill nature in it, and ordered her household in a calm and happy way. As her husband treated her with such marked respect, other men were tempted not to aim lower than he did, so that her station in life as neither wife nor widow passed without malice at court. It intrigues me that even when her first husband died, she and John Law still did not marry despite having had two children together. I often wondered why. Certainly, it was not from lack of affection.

On that particular evening the company consisted, as far as I remember, of two nieces of the lady, and Samuel Bernard and his wife. When, after we had dined, I mentioned my commission from the Maréchale de Clérembault, Bernard, who rarely smiled, actually laughed. He was occasionally honoured with an invitation to play cards with Clérembault and made a great story of being afraid of her, and of nightmares in which he got up from a table at which they had gambled for many hours, to find himself stripped of his last louis Tournois. A small chrystal of sugar flew out from between his lips onto the table as he exclaimed all this, but he did not notice it, so amused was he by the picture he had described of a man who, having been rich, found himself penniless. And yet this fate was to be his own in time. I do wonder how he survived it.

The house, by now familiar to me, was ingeniously and elegantly set up, and yet quite simple. Considering the wealth Law was accumulating, there was no attempt at ostentation, and yet I knew that he had a taste for treasure. He admired beautiful furniture and fabrics. Perhaps he intended to decorate with more flamboyance the château on the estate he had just bought near Fontainebleau; or the palace he had acquired in Paris that had once belonged to Mazarin. About a week after I dined with them, they moved from that house to one in the Rue Quincampoix in order the be permanently in the financial district of Paris again.

As Madame is so much in my mind as I write this, I believe I could almost hear her voice just then as I remembered her reading out loud from one of her own letters which she was writing, "Today a Duchess kissed Monsieur Law's hands. Who knows what other parts of him the other ladies might salute!" As I mentioned, she often read out to me pieces which amused her, and she certainly thought Law very handsome. So did I. I had fallen as much under his spell as anyone else.

I can see him now, as he looked at one moment that very evening, having left the table and standing by the fire which cast a gleam on his face reminiscent of that of the rose stain on the skin of his wife. On that particular day the national debt had been cut almost by a half, and trade under the influence of the increased supply of paper money, was thriving again in a manner which no one who walked through the financial district of the city could mistake. And certainly, in matters of commerce, the Regent's insistence on the use of paper had triumphed, because the initial superstition in favour of coins had almost totally given way. Law's insistence that money was not, itself, the value for which goods were exchanged, but a concept with no inherent usefulness beyond that of providing a measure by which that exchange can take place, had persuaded a great number of the populace to regard the paper notes with confidence, especially as each was printed with the weight in silver which the bearer could at any time exchange for it. Even so, I myself had not lost sight of the balance of silver he mentioned as currently locked away in the National Bank: 1.3 million of silver livres Tournois was the figure, less than that which Law had initially promised and which featured on the descriptions read out to the King's Council.

But it was a very happy evening and also I had acquired the means of satisfying the curiosity of the Maréchale de Clérembault.

But as I journeyed home, unease reclaimed me. Corruption is one of the worst diseases which can attack either an individual man or a community, or city or country. It is worse in many ways than stealing or plagues, which come and go rather than adopting a parasitic position in the body politic, as corruption can do. They had the plague in the South recently, and some hundreds were killed, whereas corruption can suck the life out of millions, leaving them to live as husks of humanity.

For that reason, the bribe which Law gave to Dubois again stuck in my throat however much I wanted to swallow it. The Regent deferred to the opinion of Dubois in his naïve but sincere pursuit of true prosperity for France. He will have assumed that Dubois shared his ambition, just as a drowning man who sees another swim vigorously through the water can usually assume that he aims at his rescue. But should he be deceived, it may well lead to his death when otherwise he just might have survived through his own efforts. I wondered, and I continued to wonder, how obfuscated the truth might have become for that small item of information to fit so well into the entire complex puzzle of the times.

I had, that night, left behind me a man who was my intimate friend, and who was about to become the richest individual in France; to become richer than the government he served, and even the country. Law's mind, his imagination, had somehow touched a lever in the system of communal existence in France which, for a time at least, guaranteed unlimited license to his ideas. I had assumed that those ideas sprung from Law's conviction that he could do the country a great service. But it would be too much to expect such a motive to be greater than personal ambition; and when personal ambition drives such a man as Law, it may become like an accompanying wolf that has appetites of its own. I am still, all these years later, susceptible to the shadow which looms over my mind when I meditate on some aspects of these recent events.

I hope that nothing in my lifetime will ever occur to dim the light that shone and continues to shine on that place that Fanette presides over; where the very pathways that lead to the village from the palace of Versailles, or from that to Paris, have scents and sounds which foretell of an arrival at the source of all my comfort; a particular sound when the wind stirs in a certain tree; the scent of wood burning which drifts in Autumn as far as a hundred meters from our own chimney, and sometimes Fanette's cat waiting for me at the gate.

Nothing can compare to the quality of the light within the rooms, the scent of lavender burnt on the fires, or in Summer the perfume of warm flowers indoors, laughter from the kitchen, the book which I had half read still open at the page and on the table where I left it, and the unfailing gladness of Fanette at the sight of me.

On the day when I returned from dining with Catherine and John Law, Fanette was more than ever glad to see me. The sun had not yet gone down and laid still warm patches on the floor and furniture in one half of her drawing room. I stood deliberately with my feet in a small square of golden light and while still aware of Fanette having left the room for a moment and waiting for her to return, I felt the dross of my disquiet lose its centre of gravity somewhere round the back of my neck and in my shoulders and my lips. A luxurious sense of restructured ease and innocence flowed through my skin and in my blood. My concern for my friend Law's integrity drifted away, and I felt that all was well and I shall never forget it.

As I stood there, I glanced out of one of the windows, expecting only to see the lime trees shedding their leaves against the evening sky. But just then two mounted guards on horseback came into view and stopped. They were accompanied on foot by a messenger wearing the red coat and livery of his Highness the Regent. Fanette's servant was already at the door by the time I had stepped into the middle of the room. I waited. I had not noticed the coach which also followed the guards because that window had a limited outlook, but when I was called to the door it was there. The messenger handed me a paper signed by the Regent and requesting my presence. No man, unexpectedly and abruptly summoned by his king – or in this case, the Regent – can avoid at least a frisson of apprehension. And then, there were the two guards. What were they for?

Fanette appeared behind me, and I handed her the paper. Then all that I could do was to get into the coach. When I asked where we were going I was told it was to the Bastille. I had brought nothing with me except an absolutely clear conscience. And yet, whose conscience can be clear enough under such circumstances? But if I, even for a moment, dreaded some personal punishment, it was nothing compared with my passionate wish that it was indeed a punishment for myself which was in the offing, and not to do with my son. When we arrived at the prison and I was taken still with no explanation some distance through the building, I was shown at last into a small room instead, and there was Armand.

On the night already recounted, when I came across him by chance drunk, drugged and filthy in the road, he had not looked like this. Now he was neither drunk nor sick, but he had been so badly beaten that I assumed that every bone in his body must have been broken. He was bundled in the corner of the almost bare room. There was so much blood everywhere that I thought he must have been beaten in that very place, but apparently he had been carried from somewhere else. I called at once for water and cloths with which to clean his wounds, and the guard brought them to me. Armand could not lift his head but when I took his hand he pressed mine. Unaware of the tears which poured from my own eyes, I very gently wiped his face, lifting it with my other hand. I had money on me – a purse which Fanette had put into my hand as I left – and with it paid the guard to fetch some wine and a comb. There was one chair in the room, and a bed. When the guard returned he helped me to move Armand. It was a lesson to me to discover afterwards, when I recalled all this, that under the extreme distress of the moment I myself had been able to move unaware of my usual clumsiness and inability. It was I who half carried Armand onto the bed; who knelt on the floor in front of him to comb his hair, and who wrapped him in a horse rug. The guard also fetched wood and lit the fire. I held the wine for Armand to drink, and broke off the softer pieces of the bread, but it became soaked with blood even as he ate it. He had several teeth broken.

Little by little my son was able to whisper an explanation to me. It was necessarily very brief. And yet even now there is little point in elaborating on it because the story was so plain.

Armand, maddened by his passionate love of the Duchesse de Berry and unable to bear the cruel treatment which Rions accorded her, waylaid the wretched lover and tried to kill him. The finer points of this story I heard later from the servants. Rions at once complained to Mme de Berry and even slapped her by way of demonstrating his fury, whereupon she called her guards and had Armand beaten in front of her. When the guards stopped, she forced them to continue. She made them use iron bars. When he could no longer move she kicked him herself. Rions started to laugh. He caught her arm in midair as she prepared to attack Armand with a knife when he could no longer move out of her way, and as if to reward her, kissed her full on the mouth, so that she changed from a wild animal into extreme gentleness in an instant, and went with her lover into an adjoining room.

The next day I presented myself at Court in attendance of Madame at an early hour. I told her all that had happened. Although I mastered myself as well as I possibly could, my distress was evident. For the second time in my life I wept, and for the second time Madame comforted me. She got up from her chair and standing before me took my hand in one of hers, and with the other, wiped tears from her own eyes. Clérembault and one of Madame's ladies of honour heard and saw all this, and Madame then asked for paper and ink and sat down to write to her son the Regent. She read out to me what she had written and finished by ordering him to see me that day.

And so I did see him. I expected His Highness to be ashamed, but either he was not, or he pretended not to be. If before I had marvelled at the affection he showed his daughter, I now saw evidence of how profound an affliction – if that is the correct word, and I think it is – he suffered under for the sake of his infatuation. If I framed my complaint to him in terms which implied any criticism of the Duchess de Berry whatsoever, he would not countenance it. Armand had been nearly killed, and might still die. He had been beaten, and arrested by the archers like a common peasant, as no noble man's son should be, and thrown into prison like a thief. Was I to plead for his life to this man who dared not cross his own daughter, even as she was, so reduced by her sickly passions? My own passions were within a hair's breadth of hers. I no longer recognized His Highness as a great man but saw only a complete stranger. A fool, if I dare say so, even on this dark night so many months later and with no witness. For the first time in the Regent's presence, I saw only a man. My fury, which I held somehow in check, seemed to turn my bodily waters to gall. I have seen sandworms when dug up by the fishermen for bait, cast up their own entrails, and such a violent repudiation of one's own existence was very nearly mine. Even so, the Regent refused to offer any pardon on his own behalf to my son. His only concession was to say that he would try to persuade his daughter to see me. In this at least he succeeded.

I was led to her room that very evening. I was not familiar with her house. I had never had occasion to visit her in her palace of the Luxembourg. When I called it was already late in the evening. I had the impression that the Princess was rising for the first time that day. The house was ill-lit. On arriving in her own apartment, there was a curious smell as of warm linen not unpleasantly – or not entirely unpleasantly – mixed with scented herbs and bergamot. The room was lit by the fire in the grate. There were also candles, but too few, and I was in no mood to count them. Only two maids were attending to her while she dressed. One was pinning jewels in her hair while I paused in embarrassment, not knowing how to begin. She seemed to see my reflection in her glass because she half-turned, stared at me, gave something like a half-smile and made to rise. But she had not the strength to get up. In the end, she could not resist the wayward inertia of her limbs and abandoned the attempt.

I approached her, bowing. She looked at me as if she had no idea who or what I was. Her maid whispered something to her, and she cast me a look of immediate hatred which lit the angelic features of her sick and beautiful face with an unwholesome incandescence. I would have pitied her if the circumstances had been different. After staring at me in silence while I expressed my regret that my son had offended her, she shifted her gaze to a footman who approached and announced the arrival of M. Rions. She rose at once, as if she had never faltered, but before leaving the room, paused and told me that I might go.

"And may my son be released?" I managed to say.

"Of course," she said in the same tone as an impatient woman might shake off the attention of an importunate beggar or a lapdog – which was what she thought I was. In the time that it took me to make my bow, she had already hastened from the room. I never saw her alive again.

CHAPTER FIFTEEN

IN the morning Fanette accompanied me to the Bastille. Armand had been moved into one of the rooms kept for members of the nobility, but although the fire was lit and his bed was a comfortable one, he had lapsed again into unconsciousness, and even if he had been conscious, he could not have walked. He was carried in a litter to our coach where with several cushions, and with Gaudet to hold him from falling, we made our way home.

A very high fever had overtaken him by the time he was settled at home. He had regained consciousness, but only of a sort. His speech was rambling, like a man with live dreams who speaks and acts according to a narrative that no one else can see or hear. I sent to request Fagon, the former doctor of the old King, to come from his garden where he now spent all his time, but Isabel and Shemshir Khan insisted that Armand should not be bled, but bathed with cold water and given a distillation of herbs. There could be no harm in such remedies, and Fanette and I were too distraught to be as useful as we should have been. The bone in his leg and his right arm needed setting, but it seemed that Shemshir Khan had experience of such things, and while Armand was barely conscious was a good time to do it. I could not bear to watch it being done. Such excellent legs the boy had, so unmarked by crippling diseases, that scarred so many and particularly myself, to be so broken and likely to mend askew. I could not bear it. His face was wet and grey but with a dark inward light of fever; his eyes turned up so that the iris almost disappeared under the upper lids. Thinking he was about to die, I could not bear it. My own physique seemed to be exploding in cross-currents of fury and despair, which I struggled with all my might to control. I should have been comforting Fanette, but it was beyond me; and also she was so quiet that I only thought of it later.

When the boy was at last lying with one leg bound with strips of linen to a splint of wood, and his right arm likewise, we piled warm covers on him because the fever still made him shiver, and when he suddenly said, in a voice that we could recognize as his, that he was very cold, his mother and I were too overjoyed to respond and only Isabel came forward with a warm brick wrapped in wool, while at the same time Shemshir Khan still rested the cold cloth on his head and face and wrists. At about five o'clock in the morning, he fell asleep. He was not unconscious, but sleeping. His skin was still grey except for livid patches under his eyes. He looked twenty years older than he had the previous day, and it was by no means certain yet that he would live.

Neither I nor Fanette dared to go to sleep, for fear of finding him dead when we should wake. The hours trudged past with unfamiliar tread. Intermittent scuttles of mice marked the silence. Sometimes Armand's breathing was so quiet that Fanette once held glass before his mouth to make sure that he was still alive. The day began to creep into the fields, under the crack of the door, and formed a sliver of shadow on one sill. A cock crowed. There was a sound of wheels on the lane. How old and clumsy that cart sounded, I thought to myself. The boards were starting from their fixings with every variation of the surface, and a loose part was intermittently dragging on the stones. Poor man, whoever was using it: too old or too hard-pressed to be able to repair it. It seemed to me that the entire world needed my pity, if not my despair. I even remembered the Duchess de Berry with dismay and some compassion. Isabel had returned while I was lost in thought and came now with warm milk and bread for Armand, but seeing him still asleep she gave it to me. I shared it with Fanette. The hours indefatigably moved on and on. From time to time I got up to look more closely at the boy's face. His skin was a little less discoloured on one side of the face, with deep bruises on his brow and cuts on the other cheek. But he breathed evenly. He was no longer sweating. Isabel returned, and this time put a little food against his lips, which he sipped like a cat. And then I fell asleep.

Armand survived, or I would not be writing this.

But for everyone else, at that very time – perhaps brought about by some movement of the planets in that huge void of eternity which stretches above our heads night and day – a cataclysm also occurred. It is no longer strange to my mind that the very small and the great have so much in common; that both are caught in violent currents which rip through nature, indiscriminate of the affairs of men. I could even see the near-killing of Armand as the unidentified precursor of the moment when the Regent's naïve and stubborn patronage of evil men snapped through the brittle covering of apparent control and wreaked havoc in the whole of Paris.

For a start, the sense of security which I had always had with regard to the Regent, his intelligence and goodwill, was destroyed on a personal level. And with regard to the management of the King's affairs, the Regent simply would not recognize the duplicity of d'Effiat. You might as well set a poisonous snake to guard a child's cradle as try to use that man to negotiate rational and well-intentioned government between the King's Regent and parlement. The parlement had President de Mesmes at its head, who was poor, extravagant, ambitious and unprincipled, and he was d'Effiat's creature, just as d'Effiat himself was a creature of the Duc and Duchesse du Maine. They played the Regent between them almost at will, d'Effiat convincing him that his own closeness to the Maines was merely a device to know their business and in order to be able to keep the Regent informed. He also convinced him that de Mesmes was a trustworthy accomplice. All three of them wanted only to destroy and eventually overthrow the Regent.

Carrying out the Regent's demand that I should position myself at court to learn the secrets of others, I was already aware of this situation. It is a relief for me to record on this page, when remembered anger and frustration can at least do me the good of keeping me warm, how little I was able to do about it myself. It was my misfortune to be given the opportunity to serve the Regent at the very moment when my affections towards him as a man were diminished. If I had started to uncover the situations which he had himself created and which now promised to confound all his ambitions; if I had made these discoveries in the ordinary way before the two incidents of his treatment of myself which shocked my confidence in him enough to unravel some of my affection had occurred, it would have been less painful. Or would it? Given that he would never act upon the knowledge of the plots which I alerted him to, perhaps even the patience of a still-devoted friend would have worn thin. Even here and now, in this dark night and this solitude, I still struggle with the conflict between my disappointment in the man and my lifelong affection for him. It is as well he had a mother whose love could not be shaken by anything he did, since I know my own affections to be strong and faithful and yet they have not withstood such a test.

But to return to the actual possibilities which troubled the Regent, they centred at the time around Spain, as I already said, and the fact that the King of Spain was a grandson of Louis XIV. The Dauphin, Louis XIV's only son with the Queen, had three sons who survived childhood and were healthy young men. When the King of Spain died childless and Louis XIV was invited to allow one of his grandsons, the Duke d'Anjou, to inherit the throne of Spain, it seemed appropriate to him and he was very proud of it. At the time a contract was sworn under which the young Duke d'Anjou, on becoming King of Spain, resigned forever any pretensions to the throne of France. But when first the Dauphin died, and then the new Dauphin, Louis' last grandson, also died, the picture was very much altered.

This was part of the situation which caused the Regent to fear the hatred of M. and Mme du Maine.

I had already had strong suspicions of a plot in the making, even before the Regent mentioned it to me. I now knew that under the guidance of that villain Alberoni, whose influence over the King of Spain was quite scandalous, and with the connivance of d'Effiat, de Mesmes and the Maines, a conspiracy had been entered into, which, if it should succeed, would displace the Duke of Orléans as Regent, in favour of the bastard Duke of Maine. I made up my mind to confront the Regent with these conspiracies with more openness than I had considered before. I even planned to tell him what I knew of the past wickedness of d'Effiat. I no longer wished to spare him from the mortification of knowing the truth.

At about the time when Armand was on the way to recovery, I presented myself for my weekly meeting with the Regent in his cabinet to make my report on whatever news I had been able to glean. This had, since the Regent's ignominious response to his daughter's criminal attack on my son, become difficult. He received me courteously, but without any warmth, and my own feelings were similar. When he had cast aside his wig, which he usually did in his private cabinet, instead of persuading my eyes not to see that his hair was now so thin, I noticed it. On this occasion, I began by mentioning Cellamare, who was the ambassador in Paris at the time, sent there by Alberoni, and his hope that the King of Spain would take the throne of France if Louis XV of France did not survive. The Duke and Duchess du Maine would at last have their royal prerogatives returned to them, and the title of bastard discarded forever.

At that point I then interrupted my narrative, noticing that I had His Highness' full attention. I had worked out the form of words with which to introduce my disclosure about d'Effiat, and began, "Monseigneur, if you will permit me, I need to warn your Highness about Monsieur d'Effiat." He looked up, startled, and said something which I now forget. "Monsieur d'Effiat is not to be trusted," I said. "He is more friendly with M and Mme du Maine than you are aware of, and so also is Monsieur Dubois."

The Regent became very still and attentive, but with a coldness that should have warned me. I then proceeded to tell His Highness the story of the poisoning of his baby brother. He was astounded; and extremely angry. I expected that, and as I related details of the scene I had witnessed I became, rather gradually, aware that the main target of his anger was, absurdly, myself. He leapt to his feet, and shouted at me, "Where do you say you were? What were you doing there? I am well aware that you do not like Monsieur d'Effiat. If this were true you would have mentioned it before."

I explained why I had not done so, and as I recount this I am even more aware, than I was at the time, that the Regent had turned the tables on me completely and I was defending myself. I stood as rigidly as I could, and wished that there was a high-backed chair or a table nearby, to rest a hand upon as my legs were unsteady. The Regent charged across the room as if he were looking for something to throw at me. A servant entered in response to the Regent shouting, and he became calm again, but said, "Take this man away. I have no wish to speak with him."

It is a matter of interest that the wicked men of one's childhood remain, and provided that they do not succumb to illness or accidents, find matter to work on as vile when they are old as they used when young. D'Effiat, whose malign presence was the bane of Madame's life when he was involved in the plots with Lorraine and the two women to ruin her, would destroy her remaining son now if he could. And he would do it while seeming to be his friend. I had watched him. He was not as tall as the Chevalier de Lorraine, but very thin. He always wore dark colours. If it was a green, it would be very dark, like a jewel. He had such a green coat which he wore often in the week following the murder of the little prince, with black hose and a green enamelled buckle on his shoe.

The Chevalier de Lorraine had never been able to recover his ruined character with Madame's son after the evidence I brought back from Italy. But d'Effiat had been his tutor, and unless I had disclosed what I knew of the murder of the little Duke of Valois, I would not be able to convince the Regent to look on d'Effiat as an enemy. Despite the fact that the Regent had personally commissioned me to find out such things, he would dismiss any attempt of mine to dislodge d'Effiat.

I was, of course, temporarily destroyed by the way in which my efforts had been received. I had no idea what to do other than to leave His Highness on that dreadful day. In trying to decide I was hampered by this new ingredient in my own mind, which was an unaccustomed sensation: utter shame. It stifled the fire of activity which had always cleared the way for me when I perceived an objective which called for action. I could not turn to Fanette for consolation nor Madame. Francis was in England again.

I noticed Fanette inventing new small matters for my comfort, but she was wrong in thinking that my spirits were only affected by Armand's troubles; this other cause played a part. While Armand continued to recover, it was not the initial shock of his near-death that sickened me, but this later scene, and the manner of the Regent's refusal to help either Armand or myself when he had been so viciously attacked. Neither was it only that, but it was also the way in which he had thought it necessary to manipulate me into spying for him. As an inferior in rank, and very much so in my case when considered in conjunction with the greatest Prince in France as the Regent now was, I had nevertheless felt a kindred spirit with him which was born of my supposed knowledge of his true qualities from childhood; a bond which underpinned my loyalty as a subject. He had now demonstrated to me that he did not value that bond, or deserve it. This was not an event, which, like Armand's physical injuries might with time be forgotten. It was a discovery of a truth, if truth it was, which would always be painful.

And yet, for Madame's sake if for no other, I would not let harm come to the Regent. I spent many hours looking for a solution, and eventually decided to talk about it to John Law. Law himself could not speak to the Regent on such a matter. He had not the entrée for that. But given that on every Tuesday morning of the week he conferred in private with the Duke of Saint-Simon I asked Law if he would inform the Duke of the true nature of d'Effiat and persuade him to warn the Regent.

Law, also on his own account, needed to get rid of de Mesmes, who was set on leading the parlement in obstructing the introduction of his financial reforms. While de Memes was there, the parlement's ambition to alter the balance of power between themselves and the monarchy was going to be a serious problem. To have the parlement at war with the King, and determined to acquire power over the government and finances as well as their limited role as a legal chamber would be nothing new for those familiar with the history of England. All that I heard, when accompanying the lawyer M. Moreau in his duties in parlement, confirmed this. Fortunately, the parlement decided to make the trial of strength against the Regent now, when His Highness' blood was up, and for once resolution positively altered the air around him and gave him an unaccustomed determination.

Curiously, looking back on that moment, I cannot help smiling and I wish that Law was still here to share with me the memory of the Regent's firmness of resolution, since this frame of mind in him was so rare. Once equipped for battle, the Regent showed the same talent for arms as had his father. I happened to be in Paris on the day when the premier President, de Memes, with all the pomp and self-importance of councillors of State in attendance, marched through the streets to the Palais-Royal to confront the Regent.

Their immediate demand was that he should consult parlement before issuing any edict in future, and rescind that which he had already passed concerning the mint. The entire membership, dressed absurdly in their bright red official gowns, expected to impress the crowds who were there to see them. A mob of peasantry can sometimes be surprisingly perceptive and on that morning, to a man, they laughed at the members of parliament with noisy ribaldry, shouting 'lobsters' at them. My man Gaudet was also there and joined in the laughter. He said the skin on their faces soon matched their clothes from sheer embarrassment. The Regent, on behalf of the King, saw to it that his own

Regency Council summarily cancelled the demand of parlement. This was a clear declaration of war.

It was at this time – perhaps the next morning – that following my established routine I went to the parlement in attendance on the lawyer, M. Moreau. Among the papers presented on the previous evening was an edict, not yet published, but submitted for M. Moreau's consideration. It was a legal warrant to have John Law arrested by the bailiffs and taken under guard to the Palais de Justice. By the time I found this paper, Moreau had gone away from his desk to exchange opinions with another lawyer, or to gossip and obtain material for his journal. I had to wait for his return. The Regent's wisdom in securing my help and attaching me to Moreau became very clear when I reflected that if this edict had been published the parlement could have had John Law taken inside the Palais de Justice and then they would have been within their rights to refuse to give him up, even if the King demanded it. Even now, there was no time to waste. The purpose of such a move was deeply sinister. The members would be entitled to give Law a three-hour trial and hang him there and then, inside the Palais de Justice. Even if the maison du Roi were armed and sent to save him, Law could be killed before the guards could break in. The indictment was that he had embezzled state funds and acted unlawfully in the conduct of the King's finances.

I dared not wait for Moreau to return but left at once myself. Neither could I take the edict with me. The guards might arrest me as I left. But unobtrusively I made my escape. My carriage was not waiting for me. I had to make my way on foot to the Palais-Royal, and as I did so I thought with wry philosophy of the crippled leg of the Duke of Maine.

I presented myself at the small side door which gave access to the staircase leading to the private cabinet, but this was not my accustomed time and the guard had to be persuaded to send a messenger to Monseigneur. He did not hurry. Knowing as I did that as soon as Moreau took up that edict he would have no choice but to publish it, upon which there were probably the officials all in waiting to seize Law, I chafed at the delay. As soon as the messenger returned, I made the best speed that I possibly could to the door of the cabinet. To this day I sometimes wake in the morning knowing that I have dreamed of that cold, ungainly climb, with the chill of the stone and the desperate, clumsy shortness of my breath. When I finally arrived I was told that the Regent was on his closed chair, and I must wait. I knew how his bowels gave him very little peace on waking, and that his condition after each night of revelry was a protracted struggle. So much so that news, if urgent enough, could be presented to him where he was, but I held back and was relieved when soon enough His Highness appeared, although only half-dressed.

I lost no time in giving him news of the plan of the members of parlement, and the extreme urgency of it. He said at once, "Give me the edict," but of course I had to explain why I had had to leave it where I found it. He wasted no time with anger at that point, but sent at once for the captain of the musketeers, with immediate instructions to arrest John Law and bring him under guard to the Palais-Royal, where he might be kept safe. If he had been already taken to the Palais de Justice, his fate was probably sealed. The Palais de Justice is more a fortress than an ordinary building, and once the doors were locked only the King himself could gain entry.

I saw John Law myself at this juncture. When he appeared he was accompanied by the Duke of Saint-Simon who seemed to have been forewarned. What astonished me was the condition of John Law, and to see how terribly he was affected by this threat. No one wants to die, or above all to be summarily hanged in such an awful way; but Law had shown such imperturbable courage in the face of all the other accidents of his amazing career – such cool presence of mind and strength that his complete collapse when physically threatened now was not expected. He paced the floor, which by this time was littered with torn papers and discarded bits of clothing. I thought from the way he staggered that he would faint. It was a shock to see so strong a man weeping.

The Regent showed great kindness to him, and I left.

When, later, I went home to Fanette, she was not so surprised as I had been by my account of Law's distress. Above all, she said that she was certain that the Regent would save him, as otherwise His Highness himself would be destroyed. It was an historic trial of strength between the King of France and parlement, with Law himself as the prize.

Finding Law already under the Regent's protection in the Palais-Royal, parlement decided to go even further. They declared their intention not only to charge Law with the crime of defrauding the state and, if possible, execute him, but they intended also to rescind all the measures which he and the Regent had taken to rescue the finances. They would return the economy to the use of coin, burn the paper money, and in fact do everything they could to imitate the English parliament in its seizure of executive power from the throne, short of executing the King.

There was only one solution to this conspiracy, and that was for the Regent to declare a *lit de justice* and give no warning of it, but make all the prior arrangements in the most complete secrecy. Even parlement would not dare to flout the authority of the King himself. I myself was kept informed because the Regent stood by the plan he had earlier formed, of making use of my inconspicuous omnipresence. I would enter the Regent's cabinet by the private stairs as I described before, and sit with my back to the company where the light was not good, taking notes and not being introduced. Monsieur the Duke, at Law's request, was included in the small number who knew about the Regent's plan, and La Vrilliere and Fontanieu, and Fagon, the son of the old King's doctor, and of course Saint-Simon – who, in all encounters where I was overtly included, gave the best possible proof of the fact that I was insignificant enough to be not noticed at all.

Nevertheless, I kept him in sight. For example, he went from his own house by the private door to Mass at the Dominicans' church on, I think, it was the fourth day, and it was there that I overheard a rumour which was being discussed by two members of the congregation near me. They were whispering but I was able to make out that the Duke of Maine and some members of the parlement intended to declare the King to be of age, which they had the power to do. This would make it legal for them immediately after to form a Council with du Maine at its head, to rule in the King's name.

When the service was over I followed the Duke de Saint-Simon and intercepted him before he entered his private door. He would have entered and allowed the door to be closed in my face, but I said quietly that I had news on the Regent's business and he let me in. It was just as well, because he was called to a meeting at the Palais-Royal immediately after, and there recounted this story, which served to add to the prevailing urgency with which the *lit de justice* was being prepared.

Those who do not live in Paris will have no idea of the startling splendour and overbearing sense of power and apprehension attending a *lit de justice*. It is a ceremony precipitated by a crisis of some sort, when powerful contenders are summoned by the King to state their case before him in his private rooms. The assembly of all the great men of parlement, the clergy and the aristocracy, all dressed in their ceremonial robes and under the protection of the guards and the household cavalry (the Maison du Roi), involves such a mastery of heraldic tradition, precedence, organization of routes and seating plans, as can hardly be conveyed to someone who has never lived through such an event.

In this case, all the preparations, which took five whole days, were carried out with the utmost secrecy. The Duke de Saint-Simon did not even warn Law, and therefore he knew nothing of it. But on the day itself the sound of drums being beaten all over the city at dawn aroused the populace with a sense of dread and fear.

The peers were summoned, each individually, with no prior warning, by servants of the Regent in their scarlet coats, and commanded to present themselves at the Tuileries. I can only imagine with what a premonition of disaster the Duke of Maine must have been hurried from his bed and made to don his most formal robes. All those with feelings of enmity, whether secret or declared, towards the Regent surely must have felt their hearts beating very fast.

The populace began very soon to mass as near as the guards would allow, around the gates of the Tuileries to watch the Dukes and the senior peers arrive, and later to scoff at the members of parlement all done up in red like lobsters again, as the vulgar crowds had decided to name them.

Assembled inside the great hall there will have been the King's ushers, with their silver maces, grouped near his throne, the Grand Chamberlain nearby, while all the peers were seated, as bishop-peers and officers of the crown stood. When eventually I heard more details from various sources, I was filled with wonder at the account of the firmness and determination of the Regent. He was never known for those qualities but was very much praised for his dignity and purposeful conduct on that day by the Duke de Saint-Simon who described the scene later to John Law, and particularly the meeting which preceded the *lit de justice*.

Before the King was brought into the hall, the Regent read out a proclamation nullifying all the parlement's recent decrees, and also – to what incredulous alarm to some, and horror to others – the demotion of the bastards to their ordinary status as peers. The Duke of Maine, thus deprived of all his ambitions and his royal prerogatives, became as pale as a corpse and limped, accompanied by his brother the Duke de Toulouse, to the door. They left the building. I felt it in my heart to pity him when I heard this. I know he is considered to be a coward and a dangerous man at the same time, and that the Duchess du Maine plotted unceasingly, always hoping to substitute her husband for the Duke d'Orléans as Regent. But the thought of that old man, always lame and now utterly defeated, making his way the full length of the hall before the crowded throng of his peers and inferiors, moved me, and not least because of the overwhelming satisfaction of Saint-Simon, who would have rubbed as much salt into the wound as he possibly could.

CHAPTER SIXTEEN

FROM that moment the Duke of Maine was no longer in charge of overseeing the King's education, as he had been, and neither would he retain his precedence in the order of peers. Even there, he would rank after men whom he would formerly have scarcely felt obliged to notice. To him, and particularly to the Duchess, this loss of precedence would be like a severe physical amputation, and one for which no healing process could likely mitigate the pain. I know this frame of mind, although I do not share it. Having been brought up as I was, and in my condition, the futility of cultivating this obsession – overwhelmingly important though it was to all others at court – was from the first quite still-born in me; and yet, I intimately, and instinctively, knew about it.

Madame, for example, knew and insisted upon every smallest variation of precedence and courtly tradition. If a lady should sit in a chair with arms when her rank only allowed her to have a stool or tabouret, she would be severely punished. If she had formerly been invited by Louis XIV to Marly, those invitations would stop, along with many other privileges. The Duke de Saint-Simon himself carries in his mind an inexhaustible awareness of every nuance of precedence, to the extent that he even told John Law, after the event I was describing, how he, on entering the great hall at the Tuileries, insisted that the footmen open both the double doors for him to enter, since as a Duke and peer of the realm it was his right to have the two doors opened before him, where two existed, and not be expected to make use of just one. I mention this to make absolutely clear the depth of the humiliation that was inflicted on the Duke of Maine, who had been legitimized by his father King Louis, and was now relegated to the status of a bastard once more.

No one could deny the Regent this power when the King himself confirmed it. In its proper sequence in the ceremony, the King that day did confirm it, and at a *lit de justice*, when the keeper of the seals first mounts the steps to the King's throne where he is now sitting, hears his order, descends again and announces 'Le Roy le veult' (the King wishes) a current of air, like a streak of silent lightening, passes over everyone who hears it.

In this way, the Regent successfully won his battle with the parlement. De Memes and his cabal of plotters were utterly demolished, and the Regent also rid himself – or so I presume he thought – of the Duke and Duchess du Maine and their constant schemes to promote their own ambitions.

From that day the financial systems of John Law progressed at a faster pace, but I was less concerned in it. I had reason to be far too anxious on account of Fanette and Armand. Our son's recovery would seem imminent one day and snatched back the next. Fevers of various kinds, some with terrible sweating, some with marks all over the skin and bouts of sickness when he retched as if his vitals would be dragged out of his mouth, afflicted him. And us. Fanette did no better than I did myself. We both mimicked the condition of Armand as if our bodies were stitched to his. At moments the only ones in the household still able to walk were Isabel and Shemshir Khan.

After six weeks, Armand's condition began to stabilise. I first knew it when I realized that a certain patch of sunlight which lay on the floor of Armand's room and which I noticed on the good days, was there for me to look at two days running. When he was struck with the return of his illness, the curtains always remained drawn. On the third day, the sun did not shine there, but it was because clouds had been draped across the sun, not our own.

I began to return to court, and there I heard the more detailed descriptions of the *lit de justice* and the events there, which had circulated by then. John Law had now left the Palais-Royal and established himself in the palace which he had bought, and which had once belonged to Mazarin. I often dined with him, joining a considerable number, among whom would be Francis and occasionally Climene, when they were both in Paris. Also present was a certain Cantillon in whom Law often confided, and occasionally the Abbé Dubois, and on several occasions a Mme d'Albret.

Several weeks after the *lit de justice*, this lady approached me in order to confide, as I presumed from her conspiratorial manner, some sensational secret. Since her tone of voice rarely altered, I had become familiar enough with it to be able to make some sense of her remarks. She favoured truncated sentences, phrases muttered as if to herself, and a general air of conspiracy. In this present case, although I had the advantage of familiarity, I was disadvantaged by my own assumptions, since she used exactly the same enigmatic style to discuss a slice of mutton, or the next visit of André-Hercule de Fleury, the Bishop of Fréjus, a blameless and rather boring cleric. But this time she seemed so much in earnest when describing her own anxiety for the Regent that I snatched back the part of my attention which was still deployed in overhearing what I could of Law's description of M. du Maine's retreat from the Council chamber, and listened only to her.

For several minutes after I signalled my real interest, she held her silence. I thought perhaps she regretted an indiscretion; in which case I might have missed my opportunity. But after a long and enigmatic pause, she resumed; and here I will describe the plot she unfolded, without insisting on verisimilitude, since her manner would involve me writing about nothing else for the rest of this night.

M. and Mme du Maine had been closely involved in a plot of that villainous fellow, Cardinal Alberoni, even before they suffered the shock of the *lit de justice*. Alberoni had always seen an opportunity for himself in the Maines' vindictive jealousy of the Regent. To somehow unseat the Regent and have her husband take his place was the obsession of Mme du Maine. And Alberoni had further plans, once that had been achieved. Between the three of them – or the four, as we must include Cellamere, the Spanish ambassador in Paris – they conspired to raise a revolt in France against the rule of the Duke of Orléans as Regent and substitute the Duke of Maine, on the understanding that if Louis XV did not survive infancy, the King of Spain would take over the throne of France. It must be remembered that he was the great-grandchild of Maria Theresa, Louis XIV's Queen, Spain having been her native land.

As soon as I had the whole story more or less clear in my mind after this conversation with Mme d'Albret, I was able to disclose the affair to the Regent the following day. I had difficulty persuading him to take it seriously. But matters took a turn which left him no choice. Two young diplomats from Spain were arrested at Poitiers on their way to the frontier with the Netherlands and found to have papers with descriptions, in full, of the plans the du Maines had formed with Alberoni. The men had somehow aroused the suspicions of the Abbé Dubois. The papers they carried disclosed the whole Spanish plot, including the undoubted involvement of d'Effiat, and also the Spanish ambassador to Paris, the prince Cellamare.

This was a mere two months after my disastrous quarrel

with the Regent. The news from me of yet more treachery seemed to have exhausted him, because he took no action at all in response to this disclosure. In the end, the Abbé Dubois assumed all the responsibility for arresting the du Maines, deciding where to imprison them and negotiating the complicated diplomatic formalities of imposing house arrest on prince Cellamare. As ambassador, there was a certain embarrassment to do with detaining him, but a detachment of musketeers remained with him in his house. I have no doubt that he hated it.

I thought, with a painful spasm of my heart, of how the Regent had had no hesitation in accusing me when I told him about d'Effiat and wondered how it made him feel when d'Effiat, realising that he had nowhere to hide, confessed to the Duke of Orléans and resigned his post. Even so, the Regent could not bring himself to punish d'Effiat. One can only assume that the bond formed in his youth when d'Effiat was his tutor was too strong.

The Regent gradually seemed to have recovered his usual equilibrium. His ripostes to the parlement, and his counter-attacks, eventually entertained everyone. He even demonstrated a rare appetite for cruelty, because on the day when he allowed the Duke of Maine an audience (in essence, an opportunity to speak in his own defence), the Regent positioned himself at the furthest end of the great room, which was empty except for some servants, and du Maine was obliged to enter by the opposite door. I was in the anteroom with Monsieur Moreau and was able to witness the terror of the Duke of Maine, since it would have been legally permissible for the Regent to have his old enemy executed, and du Maine knew it and was bitterly afraid. At the time he was over sixty, and having been lame all his life could now scarcely walk. He made his way very painfully, sweating with exertion but also fear that His Highness would condemn him. It must have involved all his endurance to drag his useless leg and bent back the entire length of the room. I myself was more in a position to pity him than most, but even I felt he deserved the punishment that he was getting. The time had come to separate the Regent from those men whose ill-intentions towards himself his Highness was usually incapable of assessing.

If I had imagined that the Regent would not have paid me any attention were I to discuss my suspicions, I was amply justified by the way in which he had brushed aside even the Abbé Dubois when he gave evidence of this additional Spanish plot. Admittedly he was just leaving for the Opera when Dubois appeared with a handful of papers, but he would not spare the time to listen to him either then or later that same evening. He told Dubois to make use of the time to study the papers himself.

Dubois did so, and discovered the involvement of Argenson along with all the others. Argenson was made to give up the seals of office immediately, and at last the Regent himself became properly aware of the outrage planned against the crown.

At an urgently convened meeting of the Regency Council, the entire situation was described by the Regent to all other members of the Council. The Duke of Saint-Simon was present, and relayed every detail to John Law, who immediately told me. The members of the council were left in no doubt of the conspiracy as being principally between Alberoni, the Prince Cellamere, the Spanish ambassador in Paris and the Duc and Duchesse du Maine. His description of the conversation between Saint-Simon, the Regent and Monsieur the Duke, as to an appropriate prison for Mme du Maine, made me smile. That she should be sent to the Château de Dijon, the property of her own nephew, Monsieur the Duke, who hated her, was what they called poetic justice.

The Regent was now set on a path which, for once, I hoped, he would follow to its end, without becoming weary of it, or being seduced by a new argument. I watched him as he arrived at Madame's drawing room in the Palais-Royal on the afternoon following the completion of the sentences. He looked very much as usual, except that perhaps there was more than the usual brightness in his step. Undoubtedly, although the very outrage of the plot must have made him angry, there was the satisfaction of knowing that Mme du Maine had set her foot in a trap whose teeth had now closed firmly over the royal doll's ankles. The Regent bowed to his mother and kissed her hand before embracing her. I very much hoped that they would turn to the Regent's left in order to talk privately, because I might be able to overhear them if they did. My prayers were answered, as they often were, but Madame had already chosen the subject she wished to discuss which was the parlement's decision to oppose the minting of the new coins; which was none of their business. She was being forthright in impressing on her son that he should not countenance the interference of parlement in his decisions. This, of course, had been the main burden of the conflict, as Clérembault would have pointed out if she had been present. I presume Clérembault would not have dared to mention her other bone of contention with his Highness, which was that in her opinion – as she had emphatically explained to me two days ago – Law's system would not survive the interventions of the French monarchy in the finances. The Regent was known to have given shares as gifts to anyone who asked him, and the reminting of coin, which parlement was opposing, was only one result of his own actions.

But now that de Memes, the President of parlement, and his great friends the Duc and Duchesse du Maine had been caught in a scandalously treacherous plot, the Regent seemed to actually enjoy his mother's indignation. I heard him say Francis and M. Law had been warning him that de Memes and the du Maines wished to follow the example of the English parliament in seizing legislative powers, but he had not been able to see his way to doing anything about it. Whereas they had now conveniently indulged in such disloyal conspiracies as left no alternative other than severe punishment.

The Regent held a Council meeting in the Tuileries, the next day, at which two of the letters written by Cellamere and seized at Poitiers were read out. You would have thought that some poison had been released into the air in Paris in the week succeeding these discoveries. People were less raucous on the Pont Neuf; no songs were yet pinned up there, and every move of the scarlet-robed footmen of the Duke d'Orléans was watched and commented upon.

Subsequently, Fanette would hardly let me rest at home for five minutes, for sending me to Madame, and to Versailles and to the Palais-Royal for news of these events. The number of arrests multiplied, to include Pompadour and two others, who were all sent to the Bastille.

Did I remember to mention that Cellamere's house was searched from floor to attic by Dubois and his men?

It was suddenly, one evening when at home, that I was confronted with the fact that far from having recovered, Armand's health had undergone an appalling reversal. Immediately, I realized that Fanette had conspired to keep me away deliberately, to hide this fact from me. Alas, I was so disappointed that I was enraged with my wife. I accused Fanette and tore my own clothes in my fury. I must have caused the very tumult that she had striven to avoid. Eventually, when she could no longer hide it from me, Armand had not only the appearance of a starving man, but a mad one. I was now told – several days later than the event – that twice without my having been allowed to know of it, he had climbed out of his window in the dead of night, and walked barefoot to Paris where he had been arrested by the night watchman trying to get into the palace of the Luxembourg to see Mme de Berry. The second time he only got halfway to the city before being brought back by Shemshir Khan who was fortunately strong enough to carry him bodily home.

Fanette had deceived me. I had taken for granted the profound mutual dependency and trust between us, and the ingenuity with which she had betrayed me removed all kindness from my heart as if I had had it extracted like a tooth. It did not matter to me that she might have been trying to save me from suffering; the trickery of it enraged me.

As for Armand, I could now see for myself just how grossly damaged he was. He had been so splendid until he entered the service of the Regent and became one of his roués. Even then, if only he had not fallen in love with Mme de Berry, he might have weathered the storm. He had had a quick intelligence and a presence of mind which served him well during the period of his military training and schooling at court. His entire bearing had marked him out with distinction. And above all, he had been my friend. My most beloved friend, and my son. I was heartbroken to have somehow let his well-being slip through my fingers.

When I first made this discovery he attempted to reassure me, but it was utterly beyond him. I saw, to my mortification and despair, how he tried to assume the bearing and expression of a sane and sober man. It was like seeing someone with a mask fitted on his face with the features upside down. And he did not even know it. He imagined, as I could tell, that he was able to convince me. He smiled at me, and I wept. It was ludicrous. I think all four of us – Fanette, Isabel and Shemshir Khan and I – wept, and only Armand stood, attempting not to waver or fall; and smiling with that terrible way that a child on the brink of hell tries to reassure onlookers.

As soon as I was able to do so, I consulted with Shemshir Khan and demanded to know if he had given my son potions from the store of drugs from his native country, which I knew he kept and added to and studied. Many people who knew of him consulted him for remedies, and he also knew the drugs indulged in by the roués. Armand himself must have known what a desperate longing for peace of mind had prompted Mme de Barry to drink the poison which was even now killing her. He might have talked to Shemshir Khan. Had he deliberately, with the intention of accompanying her, found a store for himself?

By the time I summoned Shemshir Khan to speak to me I had mastered myself. But even so, I heard my own voice sounding sharp enough to cut a man's skin. I was only really brought to my senses when I saw how firmly he received my questions, and when I became calm enough, to realise how much he pitied me. His kindness, given the recent roughness of my outraged anger, brought tears back to my eyes, but this time I suppressed them. I learned that Shemshir Khan knew the drug Armand had taken. He would, if permitted by my wife and me, search Armand's room and any other likely place in the house to find the store he must be keeping. He intimately knew how to manage such a thing. He was familiar with the ingenuity of addicts. I asked him why he had not told my wife of these things, and he said that he could not bring himself to speak of them to a lady. He said that he had often advised Armand against the influence of certain potions, but if Mme de Berry took them he could not be stopped.

I must pause here and listen to the night. I need to let the cold air wash against the fever aroused by these memories. If possible, I must hear the ripple of moonlight, or just air, which stirs the long grass and those seeds still clinging to the trees. I must look at the covering inside my coach to remind myself of the courage of my one-time friend and servant, Bonhomme, who was killed in my service and that of Madame. I have to remember these things before I will be able to relate, with the clarity of an unmoved man, how the restraint of Armand in his fury was managed. Also how Fanette and I tended him in his wretched sickness when his body, like a split wine skin, could not hold the life which belonged to it. In those days and nights, I often needed to promise myself that if he died I also would take my leave of this world. Only that bargain sustained me enough to live; that and the return of my love for Fanette. Before my very eyes her youth left her, and like the petals of a dying rose her skin took on a certain frailty and wilted grace which scourged my heart as nothing else would have done. Such sadness needs no dwelling on, particularly at night. Our son recovered.

CHAPTER SEVENTEEN

IT was while all this was going on that John Law made the rapid progress he had so longed for. Supported by the Regent and with the parlement now docile, the reminting of the currency had taken place almost unnoticed. This device brought the desired balance of paper money and coin back to parity. Then the Company of the West was formed to manage the development of the huge area of land now held by France in America, since the lease was bought along the whole length of the Mississippi. Law had also been made a citizen of France and had formed the Banque Royal, of which he was the Director. He had bought houses. He had become rich, and now, with the issuing of shares in the Company of the West, which was renamed the Company of the Mississippi, riches scarcely imagined seemed to rain down on the whole land. France, which together with her economy had so recently been stranded like some huge galleon on a rocky shore, was washed back out to sea on this irresistible flood tide of prosperity.

When at last I was able to venture to Paris again, I visited the site of the new Bank (now called the Banque Royal) in the Rue Quincompoix, but could not keep my footing among the crowds of people fighting each other to buy the limited number of shares being offered in the Mississippi venture. Just as the South Sea Company in England had acquired land in South America where they planned to carry out trade to support the sale of shares in London, so John Law and the Regent intended to develop the newly leased French land in North America. Although it had not yet started to trade, great things were expected from it. The Regent and Law had a fleet of ships built to carry prospectors, explorers, artisans and labourers out to the new colony, and to return laden with cotton, tobacco, minerals and gold. I stood for some time, buffeted by the crowd which milled with near-frantic urgency in the street. At one point John Law came out onto the balcony, to shouts of enthusiasm from the crowd, and yells demanding shares. Once a person had a piece of paper as proof of ownership, they might not leave, but could continue to try to get more. I was astounded.

Given my recent experience with Armand, I could recognize a collective fever of the mind when I saw it. And yet, here was Law, now one of the richest, if not the richest, man in France, and riding an apparent crest of fortune which seemed to enrich the whole country. But that delirium, that raucous greed at the same time, greatly disconcerted me. A man beside me, his face a bluish red, collapsed even as I caught sight of him. The nearest in the crowd tried to lift him up while still knocked on every side by new petitioners. I really have no idea if he was dead or not.

I had planned to visit John Law in his place of work, but it was obviously not possible. He was now no longer standing on the balcony. He must have gone in while I was distracted by the man who fell. He was probably now sitting as I had often seen him, writing at his desk while the noise of the crowd surged behind the walls like the sea hitting against rocks.

It was time that I should visit Madame, and so I went to the Palais-Royal. I entered her drawing room at midday, when she would be likely to be drinking chocolate with her ladies. But to my confusion, I realized, as I crossed the floor to make my bow, that an unaccustomed frisson of attention had silenced the company. I looked behind myself, to see who might be following me, but finding no explanation and reaching Madame I lifted my head to see her regarding me with astonishment. When I say astonishment, I do not mean admiration of any kind; nor yet quite horror. But certainly she was moved, and even rose and took a step toward me with her hand extended. I bowed again and kissed the hand which so rarely was offered to an undistinguished courtier like myself.

"My dear goblin," said Madame, as if I was still a child. "You are so altered! I was afraid you might die, and have sent word often enough for news of you. Now I can see you have escaped only by the skin of your teeth."

It was true. My hair had started to go white. But when you see yourself in the glass daily, other details escape your notice; and I never did dwell very much on my face. Of course, Gaudet shaved it. This unaccustomed attention was yet another trial I had to bear, but one that I soon delighted in. Theobon spoke to me with a tone of entire sweetness, and the Maréchale de Clérembault, coming into the room, actually smiled in my direction. I think. She had her velvet mask on her face as usual, but I read the shape of her eyes. When the chocolate was served she took off her mask and asked me to come beside her in order to answer questions about my health and about Armand, and to tell me how much the shares in the Mississippi Company bought last week had multiplied in value.

To show how rapidly news travels at court, that very afternoon John Law sent me word to take supper with him in the evening, saying that he would send his coach for me. Knowing that he would allow me to be accompanied by Fanette, I accepted. We left Armand in the care of Isabel and Shemshir Khan, having very carefully prepared ourselves and our manner of dress in order to repair the impression I had made at court in the morning.

This supper was no longer a small and quiet affair as in the days so recently when John Law lived simply. At least thirty were seated at the table, and of course the surroundings were magnificent. Law had paid one million livres for this house which had formerly belonged to Mazarin; and also, it could be argued by his Protestant forbears, allowed his soul to be added to the bargain – since he had had to convert to Catholicism in order to become a citizen of France and to have the right to buy property. Having done so, he then bought the house of the Comte de Tesse for 500,000 livres as well as this one of Mazarin, and more.

You would expect these actions to presage an onset of the disease most associated with riches: an affliction of the spirit of some sort, or a bilious eruption of pride like boils on the inner skin of a man. But for Law this was entirely not so. He was the same person. But a great deal richer. He wore similar clothes, and only when you were close to him did you realise that they were his old ones copied by the best tailors at court and using the finest silks and wools. These replacements enhanced his appearance, which had always been very good.

Fanette had been anxious about this evening, since she was not accepted at Court; but it turned out that even some individuals who had formerly pretended not to know who she was altered their demeanour now that they saw how courteously and respectfully Law greeted her, and placed her at the table when we came to be seated. He had many liveried servants now. I recall that Samuel Bernard was present on that particular evening. How strange to reflect now, years later and unhampered by any distraction in this quiet and dark place, that, as he sat down at that table and turned to hear something murmured in his ear by his neighbour, Mme de la Manche, he had very little time left to live.

I happened to be near him, and I never could see him

without remembering the day that he had spent at Marly when the old King encountered him ostensibly by chance when visiting a courtier who occupied a permanent lodging there. This arrangement was necessary because the King himself could not issue an invitation to a man of Bernard's low rank. But if the King happened to visit that courtier when M. Bernard was with him, Bernard could be presented. Louis XIV then walked with the delighted man of finance in the garden and condescended to show him many of the glorious arrangements there. And in return M. Bernard lent the bankrupt King six million livres Tournois.

At M. Law's dinner table there was some talk of the theatre and I saw Fanette blush when mention was made of Racine and Corneille, with comparisons of the various actresses who had played leading parts. I of course would never forget the time when I first saw her acting the part of Aricie; how exquisite she was. How beautiful she still is. Even so, I was grateful when John Law changed the conversation with the skill of a fish in water, able to turn without appearing to disturb the very element he swims in.

When late that night Fanette and I were driven home, I remember we seemed to carry with us a radiant banquet of high spirits equal to the fare that we had left behind: the table, the rooms, the hundreds of candles and the apparently invincible achievement of John Law himself. At that point, he had risen to the very height of prosperity and had lifted proportionately the fortunes of France from bankruptcy. Was it possible that anyone in the land could fail to feel gratitude to him?

I myself had not yet bought any shares, I was not quite sure why. When my friend Law had first been permitted, by royal decree, to establish his private bank of Law et Cie two years ago the capital was six million livres and I could have bought then. Later, when it became a joint stock company called the Banque Générale, the same applied. John Law had explained the vital importance of the discipline of retaining parity between the printed money and the gold and silver which backed it, and as long as he himself was the only holder of the power to do otherwise it was a safe investment. Then.

In December 1717 a half-yearly dividend was paid to stockholders of $7\frac{1}{2}$ per cent, and Law's banknotes were exchanged in the money markets at a premium of 15 per cent. The next step –to develop a commercial project in the whole length of the Mississippi – all that was proportionately easy to achieve since the Regent was convinced of success. He had now renamed the Banque Générale the Banque Royale, under the crown of France. The obstructions of parlement were at an end, but the change to the bank meant, of course, that John Law was no longer the sole power able to manipulate the currency.

That evening, talking in our coach, Fanette and I recalled a very early conversation that I had had when M. Law was still only a private foreigner in France. He and I used to meet nearly every day in the library, and either talk there or go to court, and he would unwind his plans before me, as if laying a conversational trail which his own critical mind would follow. On one occasion I specifically remember that, having emphasized the vital importance of the discipline of keeping parity between paper money and specie, he checked himself and was silent for a full two minutes. I watched him, fascinated. His profile, remarkably strong, with a long, chiselled nose, lips pale but full, and eyelashes – I particularly remember noticing his eyelashes– long straight and thick. All this was so noticeable because the sun was behind him where he sat. He remained absolutely still, stalking his own thought until, suddenly, he said, "Land." He put his teeth together, and was silent again for only a moment, but then turned back to me and said, "Land, Berthon! That must be the answer. In order to maintain prosperity, there must be growth. Nothing in this world is static." I was about to disagree. After all, look at a chair... But he carried on: "If a bank can govern the supply of money so that commerce increases, there will come a time when commerce itself needs new fuel, and that must come from the land."

At the time I merely stored his words in my mind, waiting for the moment when I should understand them. And of course, when Francis next visited Paris and described the South Sea Company, and how the English designed to use it to trade in new and fertile places where the extra funds needed could be generated, I recognized Law's lesson in this other context. This was at least six months before the incident when I advised Francis to sell his shares!

An event such as that which we had all had to endure with Armand so disrupts the normal train of life and thought that I had never before put these two events, the South Sea Company and the Mississippi together. Later, however, I wondered if perhaps my inner mind – that fleeting phantasmagorical companion of our conscious thoughts – had reanimated the moment in response to some hint.

Not during the immediate aftermath of that evening I just described, when Fanette and I travelled home in such high spirits, but later, I found my thoughts veering in this direction again without any prompting from me. When was it that the Regent, having now renamed the bank as the Royal Bank of France, insisted on a new printing of paper to the value of one thousand million livres? That is one thousand million livres for which the Bank would be answerable. Law did not like it by any means but could not stop the Regent now that the bank belonged to France. He tried. Whether that had happened while Armand's life still hung in the balance or later, I cannot now say. And yet surely it was no mean accident that an essential lever of equilibrium should snap in so many directions at once.

As in a natural catastrophe rocks collapse in a sort of sequence, flood water breaches one barrier after another, and so it happened with us. Armand somehow heard about Mme de Berry's confinement and the child she carried fathered by Rions. It was useless trying to keep all knowledge of these events from our son.

Mme de Berry, meanwhile, was not expected to live, and yet in the frenzy of her undiminished passion for Rions she clung to life if for no better purpose but to see him. She died without his having accorded her that satisfaction. In the last frenzy of her sickness, she had somehow managed to go with all her servants and her ladies to La Meute. This was near enough for me to come and go once, and I kept Fanette informed, without Armand suspecting the truth, or so we thought. But in that belief we were mistaken.

Of all the horrific stories, I now have to confess to his last desperate visit, when he forced his way, by a combination of cunning and, where necessary, naked threats, into the presence of the dead body of this terrible woman whom he had so much loved. Fanette and I were unaware that he had left our house. The princess died at midnight, and Armand must have climbed out of the window of his bedroom, and walked there in the dark, compelled and led by some appalling instinct as yet not understood by human beings. He arrived at La Meute when the opening of her body was in progress. Mme de Saint-Simon was standing with her hands extended. That task, namely to accept the heart in her naked hands and place it in the urn, was a truly horrific honour which only Mme de Saint-Simon's great sense of duty enforced on her. The sudden arrival of Armand, closely followed by a member of the guard who seized one of his feet and would not let it go, was quite incredible. Nothing more undignified, and yet crudely appropriate to Mme de Berry's dreadful depravity while she had yet lived, could possibly have been dreamt of, leave alone occur.

Armand was taken by the guards to the Bastille, and I myself summoned peremptorily to the Palais-Royal, where to my shame the Duke d'Orléans refused to reproach me, but despite being himself so distraught with grief for the death of his most beloved daughter, had pity on me for my son's sake. He wept very bitterly with me for the intolerable suffering caused to fathers by their children. He took me in his arms, and I him in mine. I have never seen a man weep more copiously or longer or more fiercely than His Highness the Duke of Orléans on that occasion. I think that in the end I was attempting to console him and my presence was solely for that purpose. When eventually I returned to my house and to poor Fanette, I was driven there in the Regent's own coach, with one of his servants in attendance, charged with the duty of doing whatever he could to help me and to return to Paris only when I gave him leave.

I think Armand must have died following this dreadful relapse, but for a certain Joseph Garus. I knew this name from a previous incident when the elixir which he was famous for – a distillation of strong herbs inherited from an account of Paracelsus – had restored Villars to health when he was dying. I was reminded of it by the rumour that Mme de Berry had demanded his attendance on her. Apparently, she was showing remarkable signs of recovery over several days but Chirac insisted on purging her, with the result that she died.

Without hesitation, I immediately sent Gaudet to find this Joseph Garus, and to promise him whatever he asked if only he would come and treat Armand, who was once more at home. Garus came. He took up lodgings in the house of my steward and agreed to stay there until Armand was well enough. In return, he asked me to procure for him the famous diamond which the Regent had bought from the Tsar. I had to explain that although I would make the request if he insisted, it was not possible that the Regent would agree, and that even if I sold everything I possessed I would not be able to pay for it. Having listened to me, this man went to speak to Shemshir Khan in his kitchen. After half an hour he returned and said that he had been paid and would now commence the treatment. I asked no further questions.

After one day, Armand was minutely better, which is to say that he was calmer and would accept the medication when it was given him. After three days he was unrecognizable as the violent and feverish invalid of the days before, and after a week he seemed cured. Fanette would not trust to this good fortune. She begged Garus to give her the recipe in order to have it to hand in case of another relapse, but Garus would only give her enough to continue the cure for another week. What was equally important was the instruction he gave, to keep Armand well away from any alternative medical advice and allow no doctor to bleed or physic him regardless of how eminent. It must have been a very terrible event for Garus when, in his absence, Chirac had bribed the woman in attendance, and allowed him to purge Mme de Berry, even though Garus had warned everyone that to do so would be fatal. It is a wonder that merely because he held the title of the King's doctor not only was Chirac able to do such a thing, but he was not even punished for it. In effect, he murdered Mme de Berry. And what is more, Chirac knew that the elixir prescribed by Garus had restored Villars to health when he was dying. It is no wonder that this elixir became so famous, but the secret of it was never disclosed. Garus was prematurely killed by his coach being overturned one night on the road to Dijon, and he had given no one else the recipe.

In the weeks following, Fanette and Isabel and Shemshir Khan nursed Armand back to strength, but I took to wandering among my friends at court and spent much time with John Law. I waited almost daily on Madame when she had returned to St. Cloud, and I dined with Francis at the Pont Neuf, and heard about the Regent's suppers from His Highness himself, and even attended some.

At this time John Law was sending groups of pioneers, labourers and artisans to the new territory of the Mississippi, and I went with him to the harbour to see them load. It was an amazing sight, and Law was very proud of it. He said he loved the sea. He seemed to think that if his mother had not been English this attraction to the ocean would not have been born in him. I saw suppressed laughter in Francis's eye when hearing this claim for the umpteenth time and nodding his head in agreement. It is apparently true that the English are particularly fond of boats and ships, but if ever a man was a Scot, that man, according to Francis, was John Law.

But perhaps the vital piece in the jigsaw was not in his blood, but in the huge commercial adventure with which those ships were loaded. If the English could trade in South America and make a great success of it (which at the time was talked of but may never have actually happened), we, the French, should certainly be able to thrive in the Mississippi. As Francis had said, it was a considerable threat to the English venture that the Spanish might obstruct the South Sea Company's attempts to trade in that territory which Spain virtually ruled over. Law would not agree and was most anxious to reassure him. If Law was to trade successfully in the Mississippi, he did not want to see another country fail in an endeavour that could be called in any way similar. Even the fury of Spain over the failure of their ambition to re-establish the Old Pretender on the English throne could not be seen as a cause of political vengeance. He was within an ace of calling Francis a coward for even having the idea. I had not seen Law so moved since the night when he was nearly captured by parlement. But fortunately, at that moment he was called away to examine something on one of the ships.

Francis said to me, his gaze fixed on Law's back as he strode away, that it was as well that it was not generally known that he, Francis, had sold his shares in the English venture. And then, with that dry humour which was never far from him, he looked carefully at me and said, "But there is no reason why I should not mention your advice, Berthon." He was referring to my having recommended the sale. But I was used to his sense of humour and did not take fright, even for an instant.

Was that the occasion when it first occurred to me to ask Law if Armand should take part in this adventure? I must have been influenced by the weather, which was very bright and fresh; the sort of day when the shackles of routine life are loosened, and the wind worries the reefed sails of a ship in harbour so that they stir like sleeping giants. The sort of day when Bonhomme and I set out to Italy from Versailles, and I sat on my proud horse Maud and felt that the world belonged to us.

I returned that evening to Fanette. I dared not mention my idea for Armand to join the expedition to the Mississippi. But I had it in my mind the whole evening. He dined with us, and I watched him most carefully. If someone is sick and wishes to conceal it, I recommend paying attention to detail. When they stand, is the body symmetrical; do they walk easily, without self-conscious care; does the hand tremble when drinking or eating; are the eyelids well flexed but not too much, and so on. Armand responded well to all these examinations. And eventually I also noticed a wary glint in his eye which, when Fanette was absent briefly, he allowed me to see face to face.

He had noticed my scrutiny and I had to explain myself. I believe he was laughing at me. So I told him of my visit to the shipyards, and the idea I had had. He seized upon it. And just as a beloved person who has been very sick delights a friend who sees their appetite for food return, so did I feel a thrill at seeing such a sign of Armand's returned appetite for life. I described the ships to him as I had seen them in the morning, and the fact that John Law was seeking men and women who would sail in them and establish industries and mines in the Mississippi. The idea seemed to blow the cobwebs from his mind just as the sea wind would blow the sails of a ship. His eyes lit up, and I almost think that if he could have stood and left for the harbour as he was, without waiting to change his clothes or even say goodbye to his mother, he might have done so. It made me laugh to see him.

A laugh which changed to something else when the next morning, with the fumes of wine cleared from my head, I contemplated the prospect of him leaving France. Then I think I might have stopped him, if it were not for his mother. Contrary to what one would expect, Fanette was certain that Armand needed this adventure, and for the dregs of his tragic obsessions to be swept away by the sea. It was she who reassured me.

I am tempted now to take this uninterrupted moment to reflect on Armand's mother for the extraordinary woman that she is. Except for the aggressive claims of such as *les précieuses* made in my youth, surely a woman has limits delicately placed by divine will to shelter her from the heats and tempests of intellectual responsibilities which men have to bear? The very freedom of those ills exacerbates the frivolity which seemed, initially, to deserve protection. This state of affairs was accepted by me, until I loved Fanette.

Only then did I find I had been mistaken. And that most other men were mistaken. This was because her mind was at least as strong as mine, and by what means she had been educated I have never quite fathomed, but she possesses the knowledge and the range of any well-schooled man I have ever encountered. And as for the idea that this would detract from her feminine charm, I had better be silent.

As a mother, she might have opposed the very notion of Armand leaving on a perilous voyage at that – or any other – time. But from the very first she applauded the idea. She took my hand and kissed it. "It is exactly what he needs," she said.

Armand had to have leave granted from the Regent. When I answered His Highness' summons myself, I could see that he doubted the wisdom of my plan for Armand. He was still haunted by the death of his daughter, and distrusted Fate in any form. But his nature being so gregarious, grief only impinged on his natural diet of solitude without lengthening it. Within the week he had resumed his suppers, and seemed to have fallen in love again.

CHAPTER EIGHTEEN

I CANNOT pretend that it was not painful to say goodbye to Armand. The unspoken question of whether we should ever see him again took all my powers of self-delusion and discipline to suppress. When I looked at Fanette, her profile pale and even, as the inside of a shell, while she fixed her gaze on the ship, and Armand boarding it, I marvelled at her strength. But it was obvious from our son's manner, his stride, his expression, that this was exactly what he needed to complete his recovery, and so how could we regret that?

After all, I had travelled, when I was much younger than Armand was now, with only one servant to help me, from Paris to Italy. We also made ourselves at home wherever we could, be it an open field with darkness falling, or the house of a stranger. Although preceded by a journey crossing the greatest ocean, Armand when he arrived would have the same challenges which had seemed nothing but adventures to myself and Bonhomme. And he would have the company of several hundred of his fellow countrymen although very few of them would be gentlemen. Above all, Rions would be nowhere near to reactivate the fever of Armand's extraordinary obsession and fury. So long as that wretched nephew of Lauzun lived in the same city as Armand, my son might murder him. I looked with renewed irony at John Law next time I saw him, because he had murdered his rival for the love of a woman, and had been condemned to death for it too. Perhaps the English let such men escape on purpose. Surely they have prisons built of stone like ours. I never have understood quite how John Law made his escape, but he was lucky that it had not been in France that he was arrested.

Once Armand had left, Fanette and I were fortunate that we had distractions of every kind only waiting for us, the chief among them being Francis and Climene who at that very time came back to Paris. Francis invariably brings a number of interesting things with him when he visits us: books, music – and this time it was a striking sketch by the Italian painter Pellegrini, who was competing for the commission to paint the vault of St. Paul's in London. Francis had had his entry copied, and a vast sheet had been unfolded, over which he and Law were bent in admiration when I visited the latter soon after the departure of Armand. It was a brilliant evocation of Christian themes entirely suitable for a cathedral; but John Law set his heart upon having it copied in the entrance hall of the Compagnie de l'Occident.

There was no point in attempting to dissuade him.

Neither did I want to. Such a tide of exultation had swept over the city that it was difficult for those of us who did not oppose it to remember any difference between magnificence and success. The Regent himself in those days seemed to have recovered. I noticed that he looked physically strong; a quality more often confined to his brain and his emotions than his body. It was not exactly that any need for defence had been obliterated, since it was in that interval that the Duke de Noailles persuaded the chancellor Daguesseau to conspire with him to create a run on the Bank. Had they succeeded in presenting a demand for coin in exchange for paper money at that moment, and to the extent they would have liked, the ruin of Law's scheme would have taken place then.

Personally, I also found reports of the Duke and Duchess

du Maine entertaining, each separately imprisoned, she in Dijon and I forget for the moment where the Duke was kept. The Duchess had a truly magnificent temper. She could shout insults and threats loud enough to clear the foxes from all the henhouses in France. Her jailors were afraid of her, although she was so small. At this distance in time I can find it in my heart to pity her husband, because although the dangerous venom of ambition and jealousy ran in his veins instead of blood, he was a frightened man. A coward, and always known for it.

But to return to Monsieur Law, these were the days of his glory. The Regent was not the only person who delighted in them. Fifty thousand new shares at a yearly dividend of 200 livres per 500 were issued by the Compagnie de l'Occident when, in January, it had also been granted the monopoly of all French possessions of the East India Company established by Colbert. Since the shares were paid for in banknotes at their normal value but worth only 100 livres, that was at a rate of about 120%. There were 300,000 applications for these shares and Law's premises in the Rue Quincampoix were besieged so that there were accidents caused by crowding, as I already related, and fights among the jobbers. Any house in the street available for sale went at 200% more than its normal value, since the occupants could take advantage of being nearby. There was a cobbler I knew about, who had always had a stall in it; and now, to his astonishment, he could earn 200 livres a day by renting it out. A hunchback made money letting people use his hump as a writing desk, to add to the flood of petitions pressed through the door of the bank. Soon Law moved to the Place Vendôme, and at once tents sprung up and booths everywhere for doing business, or gambling and even food.

Share transfers could not be carried out through other means than by Law himself and his small group of employees. The premises were moved yet again to the Hotel Soissons, and in the garden behind about 500 small tents and pavilions appeared in no time at all among the trees and statues. To these jobbers attached their colours – ribbons and flags – and with the noise, people and music it was an astonishing sight. I took Fanette to see it several times, and Isabel and Shemshir Khan both managed to buy some shares. The volatility of the shares was such that a servant, sent out by his master to sell at a certain figure, might find that by the time he reached the market, the price had gone up, and he might keep the difference.

Each tent was rented out for 500 livres a month payable to the Prince de Carignan, who still owned the garden. Law told me that the Prince had already made 250,000 livres. Francis and Climene, when they saw it all, could hardly believe their eyes, and Climene exclaimed again and again at the festive beauty of it all.

It delights me to have the opportunity to remember all that now. I swear that I can almost see those banners and flags, and hear the sound of the drums and trumpets which were used to signal the opening of the market at dawn, and at dusk, its closure.

But in the fragment of a second, my imagination fails my inner eye, and this dark night and its chill breezes shuffling the dead leaves reasserts itself. I am here, after all, for a funeral rite and not a wedding. And as if dogging the steps of my mind as he once haunted Madame, my thoughts have turned now to the Abbé Dubois. The Regent has always been fond of him. He recently appointed him to the Regency's council, and last year Dubois achieved his life's ambition and become a cardinal. Madame was mortified and did her best to dissuade her son; but once Dubois had been appointed to the post of being his governer when the Regent was still a child, her battle was already lost. Dubois knew well, and still knows, how to make himself liked, and he made sure that the child who was the Duke de Chartres should love him and continue to love him when he became the Duke of Orléans, and subsequently Regent.

When Law needed a cleric to prepare him for his conversion to Catholicism – a conversion without which his ambitions in France would inevitably be curtailed – the Regent depended on the advice given him by the Abbé Dubois. And when Dubois himself needed a sponsor for his own induction into Holy orders (a prelude for his reaching for the archbishopric), the Abbé du Tencin was chosen for the task. I wondered at the time, and still cannot help the twist of a smile catching my lip, at the fact that Tencin was the grandson, just as Law is the son, of a goldsmith. This is exactly the sort of sophisticated joke which endears Dubois to men like the Regent. Individuals with wit and charm but entirely without innocence are dangerous, in my opinion. But likeable. I even quite like Dubois myself.

CHAPTER NINETEEN

I REMEMBER that I have now, in my pocket, the latest letter that we have received from Armand. I am going to transcribe it in its entirety, as it gives such fascinating information of a life that could hardly be more different from that we know in France. On arrival in Louisiana, he was sent North to prepare the ground for another settlement, and this is how he described his life there. Like us in parts of France, wolves are a great problem.

"I have been sent further North in company with a French pioneer who is famous here for his remarkable strength and height. I felt, when I first met him, as if I must have shrunk during the night myself, whereas the true explanation is that he is head and shoulders taller than most other men. At the same time, he is a gentle and kind man, as those who have naturally no need to fear others tend to be. His name is Jacques Michaud, and I am lucky to be with him.

"We went for an expedition to find wood for building the new settlement. We left the only rifle we possessed to the leader of the group who would follow after us, as Jacques had two pistols and thought, in this season, that no animal would be likely to attack us. Also, the river which we needed to follow was frozen, which makes it difficult for a wolf to use his normal speed, whereas we were going to use our ice skates.

It was a delightful beginning. The air was calm although very cold and we found our Indian friend, Kapenau, who I described to you before, encamped further up so that we were able to stop for a short time and take our mid-day meal with him. When we resumed our journey Jacques carried my wolf skin sack on his shoulders as well as his own, as the weight meant nothing to him, and we made thrilling and peaceful speed until we came to a place where we paused a moment to get our breath. And in that moment a wolf's howl reached our ears coming from the very direction in which we were going. We stopped. In the sharp air and the declining light we stood absolutely still; and heard another howl, and another, until the full chorus of a whole pack could be heard, and we caught sight of the dark spots of many against the white snow in the distance still far from our frozen highway of the river.

"Jacques said that we would have no chance to get past them, and all we had to worry about was that they might have already got our scent. We would have to turn around and race for dear life in the direction from which we had come.

"It was thrilling at first. I felt the excitement of being strong and fast and able to outstrip the pack, whose howls were getting louder every second, so that we knew that they had now scented us. There was a chance that if we could go fast enough they would lose our scent and turn off towards the forest. But they came on so very fast that they were catching up with us on the hard-packed snow. But when they reached the smooth ice they were no longer able to run quite so fast.

"Forward we went, faster than I ever hope to skate again, but they were still gradually gaining on us. Jacques shouted encouragement to me, saying that our pistols could kill the two leaders and that the rest of the pack might stop to devour the corpses. But when next I glanced behind me I saw, to my horror, that they were but twenty metres away.

"At that point, we had to try a desperate manoeuvre.

We waited until the wolves were almost on us, and then spun round on our skates and dashed away. As expected, the pack fell headlong over their own leaders, and could not stop themselves on the ice, as we could. We got away; but not for long. We did this several times, until the wolves had learned our trick and no longer tried to turn themselves, at which point Jacques, as he skated in a wide curve, drew his pistols and shot the leading wolf, and that behind it, dead. Their followers started tearing away at the dead bodies, and we got away again, but not far enough. Most of the pack had recovered their vicious intent and were only just behind us. Jacques reloaded his pistols as he skated, and shouted to me, 'Don't flag. Keep on. Keep on. They will tire eventually,' and certainly they began to draw out in a longer line. But if only one wolf should catch one of us by the heels it would be death. Two huge brutes were less than three metres away from us, when we heard shouts ahead, but not very near.

"'Come on. Come on Armand,' shouted Jacques. 'Use all your strength.' And at last, faintly ahead, there appeared Kapenau and a number of Indians rushing forward with sticks and rifles. Kapenau yelled for us to turn on the side and enable him to fire at the wolves. Four of the howling brutes rolled over, dead, and the rest of the pack veered off to the bank and scattered away into the unbroken snow.

"We stayed with the Indians for some while. They gave us warm broth, and their squaws rubbed our ankles and legs and bathed our feet in water.

"I must leave off now, as there is work to do here – mainly the felling of trees and clearing of the land, but also the search for gold. I will be a stronger man when I eventually return to France!"

And there follow his farewells to his mother and myself.

On a later afternoon, when I was returning home alone

from having enjoyed dinner with Francis and Climene at their house, one of the two horses on my carriage became suddenly lame. My servant asked if I would let him see to it, and I decided to dismount from the carriage and walk part of the way. I started to walk a small distance toward the river from which our road branches off North toward the village of Versailles. After perhaps five minutes I noticed a figure ahead of me which I thought I recognized, and indeed it was John Law, who rather than walking purposefully, was standing with one hand on a piece of iron railing beside the path, and deep in thought. He seemed startled to see me, and I think he was reluctant to be called on. But what could I do? I could hardly walk past a friend such as himself without stopping. We exchanged the obvious greetings and I explained why I was walking. He said that when he felt cramped by too much sitting at work, he would often take exercise by walking from the Hotel de Soissons to his own house. I was surprised that he could do that without being mobbed by the crowds, but he explained that he escaped in his carriage, but got his coachman to stop and let him out halfway, and as often as not he wasn't recognized. Tall and strong as he was, I could well understand his need to stride out on his great legs.

"A man's body and his thoughts," he said, "have to be harnessed together. You can't have one utterly outstripping the other."

I suppose he must momentarily have forgotten to whom he was talking! I gave no hint. "Climene would agree with you," I said. "I dined with them today, and she complains that whenever Francis spends any time in the City he goes back to the country like a man who simply cannot sit still."

"I thought he'd sold his shares in the South Sea Company," said Law. Francis must eventually have told him.

"There are other matters that can make a man restless," I said, "besides money and risk."

"I have never lived a quiet life," said Law.

Neither would I call a life like his quiet. Starting with that duel in which he killed a man and his subsequent sentence of execution in England, his career has certainly continued to be tumultuous. "But now," I said, "surely your financial scheme is vindicated and triumphant. No one can harm you now."

He left too long a pause before he nodded. The light was fading in the way it does in early Spring; a more fragile distillation of colour than Autumn, and a delicate settling of the currents of air in the face of night's cool approach; but I could still see clearly enough to make out the disturbance of his expression.

"Are you teasing me, Berthon?" he said. "Are you deliberately describing a peace of mind that you doubt my having?"

I kept silent because of my extreme reluctance to offend him. But I knew that the Regent, since the Bank had been liberated from the restraint of parlement and also renamed the Banque Royale of France, had been giving shares to anyone who came to him. The Regent's delight in being able to please even his enemies rather astonished me. He seemed not to realise himself that this was not mere paper that he was distributing, but state promises of gold and silver to individual citizens, who, if they called for coins too fast, could break the bank. And at the same time, so like the man I knew; so like the Regent. Unless Law had greater resources to back the balance sheets than I was aware of, he might well have doubts. I wished, and this time for a different reason than usual, that Armand had never become entangled in the feverish scandals of court life and was still merely working with Law and able to tell me how things stood.

"I assure you, Berthon, that I have sufficient funds," Law said. It had not actually occurred to me that the funds used to underwrite the bank might be inadequate. How often it is that when one is unexpectedly reassured by a man in some way that you would not have dreamt of needing as reassurance, the reason behind his words is the deep knowledge of what, in spite of his own preferences, he knows he will allow. As a thief who you took for an honest man may say, "I will not rob you."

At the time I instinctively reassured him; but he carried on. The lines on his face seemed to get deeper, especially the long sometimes sardonic fold that crossed the corner of his mouth. "Enough!" he said, referring to his underwriting of the shares. "There is plenty provided His Highness will stop this excess, but will he? Today we have had to address a problem with the paper mills because there is not enough paper for the Regent to spend. Not enough paper!"

He gripped the iron rail again, set his teeth and I think he would have stamped like an angry colossus. At this point, my man came running to tell me that the horses were ready. Law looked at the man with such a dark and startled glance that he immediately stopped short and turned back to the coach. Law then transferred his attention back to me without in any way modifying the intensity of his glare. He was clearly very determined to make his point when he then said,

"Any hint of uncertainty could be fatal, Berthon. Please accept my word that I have sufficient funds, and say nothing to anyone to the contrary."

I reassured him. But I could see that he still regretted having confided in me.

"I have sufficient funds," he reiterated more calmly, "if only Monsieur le Duke of Orléans can be persuaded to restrain himself."

We parted then. He declined my offer of supper at home

with Fanette but was calm again. He gathered the scattered elements of his confidence around himself as a man who despises the cold may retrieve a torn cloak. From his great height, he looked down at me and gave me a bitter smile which I remember. I walked away, aware of the fact that I loved this man; and was very much afraid for him.

The next day I waited upon Madame at St. Cloud. This entailed a very early start in the morning, but as well as the call of duty, I simply experienced that odd sensation that has accompanied me all my life: namely, the need to speak to Madame whenever my spirits were disturbed.

As usual, the palace at St. Cloud was deliciously light and airy. Madame's ladies were almost always in high spirits, and since the sun was shining and the flowers of early Spring beginning to burst open their buds and not only scent the air but seem to invade, with their reflections, the rooms of the palace, the atmosphere was delightful. Nor must I forget the fact that Madame, as she very soon reminded me, had been given an increase of her pension, by the Regent, of 150,000 livres. Having never had any great income of her own to dispose of, she was as pleased as a child on its birthday, and had distributed all sorts of favours and treats to her household.

No doubt, I thought, her son inherited from her his generous delight in giving gifts. When I presented myself to Madame on this particular morning, she received me very kindly, but was distracted at first by some medals which she scrutinized with a magnifying glass, and kept consulting the Clérembault about their relative values and other details. She eventually had them returned to the box in which they had come and suggested a walk in the garden. I was to accompany her.

All her little dogs scampered ahead, one being rolled over when she stood up and it was dislodged from where it had been lying on the bundle of her skirt. The Maréchale de Clérembault and Theobon followed us, but her other ladies in waiting remained. I was hoping that I might have some private conversation with Madame, but there was a danger that if Law's name came up, the Clérembault would become too interested.

I need not have worried. Madame, when she had repeated her delight at her son's generosity, had another matter to discuss with me. She did not seem interested in His Highness's other distributions of wealth, which I now knew to amount to more than a million livres. In addition, there was the debt for the military, debt from the last war, the shipyards, and the Regent had printed paper to the value of 1,000,000,000 livres.

"Have you heard about this, Berthon?" she demanded, but it was on a very different theme from the one I had in mind. "I want to know what my son thinks of this arrangement for the Abbé Dubois, and I shall not be able to ask him myself because he may not visit me for several days yet."

I guessed that she meant the matter of the Abbé's request to be made the Archbishop of Cambrai.

"Of course, I also know the gentleman who is to officiate. It is M. d'Entragues," she said, expressively. Every now and then she stopped and leaned on a small stick. She had never done so before. I think it was the first time I had noticed it. "Who doesn't know the Abbé d'Entragues? As if a man who can't even decide if he is a man or a woman is a fit choice to sponsor anyone who wishes to take holy orders! Even one like the Abbé Dubois."

"Your Highness knows that the Cardinal de Noailles was first applied to, but refused," I said. "The Abbé Dubois is so determined to be made the Archbishop of Cambrai that he is willing to make use of d'Entrangues, who is the only cleric who will help him."

"I must speak to my son," Madame said. The tone of her

voice reminded me of a previous occasion when she was so angry with her son that she boxed his ears, and that in the presence of the old King. "Listen, Berthon. I have been told that that man, d'Entrangues, is to be found at midday sitting up in his bed doing tapestry work, and dressed like a harlot, in a room decorated like a harlot's room. I was told that he was wearing a lady's cap with a very elegant lace frill, and a number of silk ribbons securing it in various colours. In addition, he wore a frilled bed jacket, and three or even four elaborate necklaces of diamonds and other precious stones as well as his favourite pearls; that his face was painted and patched and the entire ensemble as well as being very surprising was actually elegant." And with that, Madame laughed and laughed so much that the Maréchale de Clérembault came forward with a small glass vial which she held so that Madame breathed from it.

I was laughing myself. D'Entrangues is much loved at court for his wit and charm. But Dubois was making a joke at his own expense in being prepared to make use of him for such a serious matter as preparing him for Holy Orders; and simply making it quite clear that no one else would do it.

"That man!" Madame said, when she was recovered, and by her tone I presumed that she was again referring to Dubois. "What can my son be thinking of to appoint him Archbishop of Cambrai?"

"I do not think it was M. le Duke of Orléans' idea, Madame," I said. "He was taken by surprise." As it happened I was there when the subject was broached, although the Abbé Dubois did not notice me because I was discretely seated in a corner where His Highness had been talking to me. "His Highness spoke in a manner that would have shamed any other man. He burst out with the conviction that no one would be willing to consecrate Dubois, and said so to his face. But Dubois deliberately made out to understand that His Highness would grant his wish if that difficulty could be overcome. And when did the Abbé Dubois ever fail to overcome difficulties put in the path of his ambitions, however devious and charming he had to be to do so, or however low he needed to stoop? To be consecrated by the Abbé d'Estrangues suits him very well, in my opinion."

I was thinking, at the same time, and with regret, that M. Law was involved with Dubois on many levels. Dubois had a genius – one must admit the use of that word – for ingratiating himself and actually being useful in that manner which passes for usefulness at court. But there is a danger in using unworthy friends who offer to help you. Madame approved of my last remark to her.

"Dubois thinks he will, in the end, be made a Cardinal," she said gloomily. "I must remember in my prayers to remind the Good Lord that we need better shepherds than Dubois if we are ever going to get to heaven."

After this conversation, I did not think it right to mention the concerns that had been on my own mind in connection with Monsieur Law. It seemed to me to be more important to allow Madame to relish the apparent prosperity of France today, undisturbed by any task to do with reining back the generosity of the Regent tomorrow.

I knew where to find Law in order to have a private conversation with him and went to his house, where his wife received me when others would have been sent away.

The house contained a fine library, with an excellent number of books in both French and English. I was standing a few paces into the room, and Madame Law had left me.

I looked to find a place to sit, and saw, to my astonishment, at the far end of the room, a man who looked remarkably like Law himself sitting at a desk writing. As soon as I began to approach, he stood up. It *was* Law himself.

"Forgive me," I exclaimed. "I must have misunderstood. I thought you were from home and I was to await you."

"I'm glad to see you, Berthon," he said, "and I apologise for the trick, but the person whom everyone thinks is myself is currently working in the Bank, whereas I –who would never these days be allowed to come back to my own house to work in peace – can do that very thing so long as my double is dressed in my clothes and is taken for myself being at the Bank."

I immediately wondered how that could be managed, since the person who seemed to be Law would be expected to give orders and so forth, but apparently that had all been thought of, and Law's actual deputy managed everything, including frustrating any attempt to confront the figure, whose back, as he was sitting, was to the room. "As you saw," he said somewhat sadly, "even in my own house we are very quiet about this arrangement, my wife and I."

"It is the price of your amazing success and fame," I said. I knew that that remark would shake his doubts out of hiding, if he still planned to deny me. But he did not. He smiled grudgingly at me, his eyes kindly but his mouth bitter.

"I think you may have realized that that is not the whole story, my friend." As we both sat, he sighed but blocked his mouth with his fist to cut his breath short. That end of the room was somewhat shady but there was a small shuttered window in the panelling, and he had already opened it. A discouraging afternoon light liquidated some of the shadows.

"It is exactly as my critics – or at least some of them; the Maréchale de Clérembault, the Duke of Saint-Simon, my old friend Matthew Prior, and those in parlement who opposed me with intelligence rather than just jealousy – it is exactly as they all originally said. The constitution of

France did not allow me to create a barrier between the monarchy and the bank."

"How bad has it become?" I asked, feeling my pulse race. "You mentioned the Regent having used up all the paper in the paper mills."

"I was not joking," he said. "And any further paper presented from this very day on will be worthless. If the Regent gives away all he already has, leave alone his future plans, my only hope is if the people retain absolute confidence that their paper money will be worth what is printed on it. Once even the faintest suspicion emerges, I will be as helpless..." He simply lifted his arms in a gesture of eloquent submission, and then, after a pause, said, "I saw a man in the distance once who happened to be standing on a mountain in the Savoy in Spring. He was a peasant looking for a lost animal, I think. High above him, as I looked, a vast section of what looked like rock but was in fact snow and ice all balanced in a terrific mound, came crashing down. The speed was terrible. The man began to run away but he might as well have stood quite still. When the air had settled, there was no sign of him. You would think that in all decency the snow should have arranged itself to show something; some acknowledgement of what it had buried."

If he had intended to bury my spirit in as much cold loss as the man he described he could not have better succeeded. But I knew better than to show it.

He was silent.

I said," Who have you confided in so far as to the situation of the Bank?"

"No one," he cried. "Not a soul."

"Not the Abbé Dubois?"

He hesitated. He looked as if he had his tongue pressed against one of his teeth. "Why do you say that?"

"Because he is a dangerously insinuating man."

"Well – if you are right; yes, you are right. I had it in mind to consult with him this evening but now I will not."

"Does he then suspect something? Why were you going to speak to him?"

"Because he is a 'dangerously insinuating' man," he quipped back at me. "He also has the Regent in his power. His Highness dare not cross him, in which case if he suggested that all extractions from the bank to pay for state debt and largesse must stop, the Regent would at least hear what he said."

"But when you say that to the Regent yourself?"

"Why. He agrees with me. He says that he understands the problem. He actually reminds me of the rules which we set in the first place at his own and my instigation, to say that paper must not exceed the value of specie held. But you and I know how susceptible to new influences he invariably is. He seems to agree one action but then, with no intention of deceiving anyone, does another. As far as this particular problem is concerned, each new avenue of expenditure seems to him to be unique, and to fall outside our agreement. And since he is a director of the Bank and of the trading companies, he cannot be stopped."

We each were silent for a long moment.

I was wondering if it would be possible to steal the Regent's store of paper money and share certificates. But I waited, in case there might be a less dangerous suggestion from Law. He was very deep in thought. One great strong hand kneaded his jaw as if he was trying to get the bone out.

"I think we will have to steal all this paper from His Highness," he finally said. And after a pause, "Are you smiling, Berthon? Does the task appeal to you?"

Alas, it certainly did not.

If I carry on like this, I will be dead before there is any danger of this story being discovered by anyone else, and so it may not matter who is incriminated by it. Those fellows who drove me here have fallen asleep in the bushes. They made themselves drunk enough to do it, and perhaps I should have done the same. But I thought Madame's funeral cortege would cross the river some time before this, and I wanted to witness her passing with an unencumbered mind.

A moment ago I opened the carriage door and got out onto the ground to look further than my view could reach from within. I regretted it the moment both my feet were down. The twigs and small branches blown off by the wind made balancing upright absurd, while the longer grasses bit into my stockings spikes of ice. But once there, I could not waste the effort by not taking at least one step toward the edge. I stood, leaning on my stick, and glaring at the river and that ill-favoured bridge and the two flares which had been lit from the start. I screwed up my eyes and looked far toward the right bank. At once a sliver of frozen air slipped between my skin and the collar of my coat and my neckcloth.

The road was still empty. I do not mean entirely, but it was too dark to see. For all I knew, there might be a man as parched with cold as myself down there, and with no house to ever warm him when this night's mission should be accomplished, whatever it was. Perhaps such a wretch kept these dreadful hours in order to steal something; or to attempt to keep warm by walking with the prospect of sleeping during the day. I wished him luck, if he was there at all. But certainly, no funeral cortege was yet in view. Even at the furthest limit of my view, there was no glimpse of any light. However self-denying Madame's last rites were to be, there would be at least eight guards with flares accompanying her, and so far there were none. After a few minutes, I turned to get back into the coach. With difficulty I avoided falling. When I gripped the side of the coach in order to pull myself up onto the step the wood was so cold my skin was not immediately loosed when I undid my grip, as ice will stick to your hand. It is no mean task for one such as myself to get in and out of coaches at the best of times. Alone on a night such as this, the least said about it the better.

I may as well return to my writing, which keeps my mind entertained even enough to forget the cold and the sadness of my heart. This matter of depriving the Regent of his store of paper, whether in the form of shares or banknotes, will warm my blood as it certainly did at the time. It was my intention to insist that Monsieur Law himself should undertake the task of unlocking the case in which he had last seen His Highness put away his store. But I have devoted so much time and so many words to describing my own insignificance – my own tendency to be seen and yet not seen – that clearly it was I myself whose fate it was to act the thief.

It might happen from time to time that when I went to make my weekly report to His Highness at the appointed hour, another might come and distract his attention when I was about to leave. In that case, the Regent would precede me, and his footman, having closed the door, would remain. But I had noticed that on the small staircase there was a point at which some previous intention of the builders of this part had resulted in a small unused recess which was quite dark. If I settled myself within that, both Law and I agreed that the footman must return to the bottom of the stairs after an interval of time without seeing me. Because of the way the wall kept its angle, and because of the disposition of only two small windows, he could pass without catching sight of me as long as I did not move. And if he did see me, I would make as if I had been overcome with a sickness on my way down. Clearly, a great big tall man like Law could not take that part.

The plan was that I should then remount the stairs and enter the Regent's cabinet, taking care not to be seen by anyone coming from the other side where it gave onto his bedroom.

M. Law meanwhile would have secured a copy of the key, and also, in addition to his role of distracting the Regent from his inquisition of myself, would leave a folded bag made of dark cloth on the floor of the cabinet. He would be able to hand me the key easily without being observed to do so. The three of us – the Regent, Law and myself – would then leave, but I would be unnoticed if I disappeared en route, as it were, down that narrow twisting stone stair. It would be up to Law to keep His Highness too interested to notice me, or to make excuses for me saying something like, "He left, Sire, seeing we were engaged in serious discussion," if I were actually missed.

I very much disliked this plot, but could not think of a better. It went according to plan until when, toward the end of my interview, the servant arrived with a request from M. Law to be permitted to ascend to the room. His Highness denied him and sent the servant down with a refusal, but Law managed to write a note mentioning a possible emergency of the valuation of banknotes and paid the servant to represent it. By this time Law was so prominent a man – a hero of the state even – that such a move was not impossible. At the second request, the Regent assented and soon M. Law appeared. He had the bearing of a relaxed and eminently successful man, and His Highness, profoundly pleased as he was with the way he thought matters were established, was at pains to minimize his own inconvenience although he had an appointment to visit his mother. I soon found myself descending the stairs behind the two of them as they engaged in rapid conversation, and slipped unnoticed into the recess. From my hiding place, I could hear Law's voice continuing. He had found a great deal to speak to the Regent about, and His Highness was become restive, until without noticing my own absence he dismissed Law. It was then, for me, but a matter of waiting until the footman descended. I cannot imagine what kept the fellow so long, but at last he did go down. I emerged, entered the room and was leaving with the papers in the bag which was larger than I thought and in which not all the papers would fit, when I realized that unless Law found some way of rescuing me I would have to wait in the recess until the following week.

That was the point at which, for the first time in my life, I realized what detail and attention to a variety of circumstances burglars and members of the bourgeoisie, and politicians, must have to pay to the plans they put forward for execution. They might bankrupt a nation, for example, by overlooking one thing.

I decided to brazen it out, and simply descended the stairs and opened the outside door. The two guards were surprised to see me, that is true, but I made out that I had had to stop to relieve myself, and that M. le Duke of Orléans and M. Law had left without remembering me. They accepted that explanation. With my heart beating fast, and also feigning to carry that heavy bag with ease, I got into my waiting coach and was driven home.

That afternoon John Law dined in private with Fanette and myself, and left with that sack of papers. It seemed to have relieved his mind a great deal that we should have carried out this simple remedy to the problem, and particularly as I explained that I had not been able to take all the papers. The residue would be enough to make the Regent think that he had given away more than he remembered, and had fewer left than he had supposed, whereas an empty chest would have only one explanation.

Even so, for several days after this escapade I could not set eyes on a piece of red cloth without my heart bounding within me at the thought of the Regent's guard in their familiar scarlet livery being on my track. But soon I was reassured well enough, and besides, the tide of disaster was not so easily turned as to expose my actions to any peaceful scrutiny.

CHAPTER TWENTY

WHO would have thought that two men born of the same name could be so utterly different in temperament as the Cardinal de Noailles and the Duke of Noailles, his brother? Whereas the former was a kind man with unquestionable integrity – for example, he had been the first applied to by Dubois in his search for a sponsor of his ecclesiastical ambitions and he had refused absolutely, despite attempts to bribe him. The Duc, on the other hand, was unscrupulous and prepared to lie until he was blue in the face in order to destroy John Law. I became aware of this situation originally during the chancellorship of D'Aguesseau and through my association with the advocate Mathieu Marais. In all this time, from the inception of Law's system to this moment at the height of its apparent success, the Duke of Noailles still harboured the most virulent opposition to the man Law himself, as well as to his financial system.

Francis and Climene were again in Paris, so that both Law and I dined there almost every day, and I particularly was in a position to know the extraordinary dilemma in which Law hung, like a bird caught in a wire, between success and incipient catastrophe.

On perhaps the second week of their return, Law and I arrived at the same time at Francis and Climene's house near the Luxembourg. I had brought Gaudet with me, and he was standing on the steps, the door behind him held open by Francis' footman, waiting patiently while I limped my crooked way across the paving. I paused for breath, and in that moment Law's carriage appeared and stopped, and he leapt from the step as if he was in the middle of a quarrel with the vehicle itself, or the trees outside or the stones on which he landed. His complexion was darkened with the anger which had possession of him, but it softened on sight of myself standing still, half turned toward his arrival. And although he cast aside his expression of rage and tumult with the impatience of a man snatching a mask off his face and throwing it away, it was too late to deceive me.

We went into the house together, where Climene came racing down the stairs into the hall with her silks caught up in the air behind her and calling out, "Oh Berthon, how clever you have been. I always knew that you would save us and look what you have done!"

I was too startled to know what to reply, but Francis was on her heels. He laughed at my obvious bemusement.

"You made me sell my shares in the South Sea Company, Berthon!" Good heavens. Was that all?

"And if I did?" I said.

"If you had not, I would have lost my inheritance; my house; our land."

Law was standing, agape. He said nothing.

"Climene," Francis said, appealing to her, and observing Law, "it is not a cause for joy, when others are so badly hit. Have a care."

And in that split second we were all three transformed, silenced, turned toward Law. He stood a moment. Then, as if with one inward breath he took into his body all the blood and vitality he seemed to have lost, his limbs seemed to harden. But in that moment he knew the South Sea Company had gone down, and that the Mississippi would follow unless he could somehow hold it up, like Atlas supporting the world.

At least, that is what he told me later.

On the evening in question, with a mighty effort he recovered his usual composure and said, "What news do you have, Francis? I am already on my guard, having encountered that wretched fellow Argenson with a great sheaf of paper sticking out of his pocket which the Regent had just given him."

"What?" I said, startled. But Law gave me a look to silence me. I waited, only taking a glass of wine as it was presented to me, and being very glad to have it.

"Simply this," said Francis. "The South Sea Company is bankrupt, and all those who invested in it have lost their money."

I began to say, "But surely..." I had to wait again.

Climene began to exclaim at the same time as Law, and their voices collided, before the gentleman gave way, and the lady insisted that he should not do so, but then allowed him.

"Then let me congratulate you," Law said, saluting Francis and Climene with his glass, "on having a constitutional monarchy in England. Because here the Banque Royale is what it says it is. It 'belongs' to His Royal Highness."

"But *our* problem is the South Sea Company itself," said Francis. "Our problem is that Spain has frustrated all our efforts to trade in South America. And who with any understanding would have thought they would do otherwise, when we have refused to allow his Catholic majesty James the Second *or* his son to sit upon our throne?"

"And *our* problem," countered Law, "is that if in England you had our French constitution, your King would simply take all the money needed to pay the debts of the South Sea Company from the bank. And I doubt if your bank would survive it. But fortunately for you, your king cannot do that."

Francis was no longer laughing. Indeed, there was

complete silence in the room. As I remember, not one of us even moved a limb or a foot or a hand. Then Francis silently made a gesture to the servants to leave the room, and when they had gone he stepped over himself to take up the wine and began to circulate each glass.

When he got to Law, he first filled his glass, and then looking him squarely in the eye, he said, "Have they yet traded in the Mississippi advantageously?"

Law simply said, "How quickly can seven shiploads of working men uncover gold and grow crops where before there was none?"

"But you must have known that from the start."

"We did. But the time needed for the maturity of such trade was to be counterbalanced by money in the bank. In our case, our king has had need of it –" and he paused, giving the phrase as if in a toast: " The Banque Royale." Having said that, he drank all that was in his glass, and Francis filled it up again.

It is quite extraordinary how words – mere words – can apparently drain the blood out of a human body. I felt myself as if my flesh and bone had become like sand. All I could do was wait, and meanwhile my thoughts flashed over a number of possibilities, but I knew all along that we had not thought in time of our scheme to denude the Regent of his paper. He had already given away more than Law had been aware of.

"Who knows about this?" said Francis. "We had the impression that your venture, your entire financial scheme, was a great success. Surely, the debts of France have all been paid – the wars past and present, the ships."

The complete quiet which greeted his words was unsettling. Finally, Law said, "Yes", took a few steps across the room, and put down his glass. "Yes," he said again. "For now, at this moment no one except myself knows about this. France is on the crest of a wave. We are prosperous.

Bankruptcy stared us in the face and we have put his eyes out. But don't expect the same fortune next week. At this moment no one knows, but Noailles and Argenson suspect, and if they see their chance they will act. Unfortunately, the Regent has put it beyond my power to protect the people of France from the consequences if Noailles and Argenson organize a run on the bank. If some rumour causes the people to lose confidence in the credibility of paper money – that the paper they hold will mean cash when they are ready to exchange it – the Banque Royale will not survive. I have not been able to stop the printing of paper money far beyond the capacity of the bank to deliver on the promises of gold and silver."

"Everyone knows," Francis said awkwardly, "that confidence is important to your scheme. How much cover have you got in the bank?"

But Law was not going to tell us that; and for a moment Francis looked curiously like a boy who has just accidentally spilt his wine.

"I have enough!" Law said. "I have gold and silver. And add to it the other metal which is even more precious, and that is enough." By 'the other metal' he meant courage. The English use the same word.

It is easy to love a person who has courage. I think that courage was one of Madame's great charms, and without doubt I thought my friend Law to be a prime exponent of it. On that evening which I just mentioned, he seemed to recover his good humour in such a way that one could have thought his previous disquiet a brief example of the token superstition of a man who insures against the threat of his own overconfidence by arriving at the possibility of failure ahead of his enemies. Who among us all does not imagine that some power beyond our ability to perceive, maintains an equilibrium between high and low? We all pay homage to it.

I must have been the only one during the time spent that evening, apart from Law, who was aware of what the future held. I rather watched him like an astronomer watching for the predicted movement of a star. How astonishing it was that he ate so well; that with such verve he discussed with Francis the just completed treaty of Stockholm between Sweden and Prussia; that he had the energy to describe and to mourn the death of the English essayist, Joseph Addison; that he should have delighted Climene by agreeing with her that Handel's latest harpsichord suite was the best he had written, and promising to send her the name of a maker of musical instruments.

And yet, no sooner had we together set foot on the path that led from that house to our waiting coaches than he stopped and held my arm to delay me.

"Feel the night air, Berthon."

In my obedient way I paid it great attention. It was cool; silken, like river water. It was not that the streets outside were uninhabited, or that others were not hurrying on their usual ways, but a stillness settled over us. That moment, like a seal, like a benediction, is even now part of the furniture of my soul. Any time I seek it, it is still there.

CHAPTER TWENTY-ONE

WHEN next I attended a meeting of the parlement with M. Marais, I contrived to be within hearing of some of his colleagues when shares in the Mississippi venture were being discussed. An individual not known to me was making a great story of the value of his holding until his audience began to weary of it. Finally, he was challenged by them to make an experiment; he was to take payment in paper from the jobbers, and then to go to the bank, and see if they would give him coin up to the value printed on his paper. He refused, saying that he would not agree to 'lose' – as he put it – the treasure he had amassed and which he had hopes of for the future. But as his companions persisted, he grew uneasy, and finally made an excuse to leave them. In following him with my eye, I saw the approach of an advocate who would have business with M. Marais. I very much wanted to hear what the remaining group of gossips might say now that the shareholder was out of hearing, and fortunately they did not waste time, but began at once speculating on the likelihood that M. Mathan (the man himself) would privately sell only a part, in order to test the credibility of his papers as they had suggested. Whether from malice or fear, I had the impression that they expected him to fail.

I remained in attendance in parlement for the rest of that morning but heard no more rumours. The conversation that I had already heard was enough to depress my spirits, since it bore witness to the emergence of the very doubts that Law feared. Some men love the sensation of standing so close to the edge of a cliff that they experience a sort of elation, but I am not one of them; especially when it is not myself but those whom I care for most who are nearest to the edge.

About three weeks later, on my way to Francis and Climene's house for dinner, I was engrossed in a plan to test the market for myself. Clearly, I could not personally go into the Bank and present paper for encashment, but I would give that task to Gaudet in the evening. With that in mind, and paying not a great deal of attention to the direction we travelled in, I was surprised when my coach was stopped. We had apparently encountered a great crowd of people. They pressed against the coach, and my servant protested to some of them, and they shouted back. As we turned a corner, I saw that the crowd was even more packed ahead. My coachmen could only make way by pushing the nearest people aside, which they did not like, and protested. I could see that at any minute we would be forced to a standstill. I looked about me more carefully and saw that we were just two streets away from the Hotel Soissons. Several men in the crowd were waving papers, and impotently shouting to be allowed past. Then, from further up, some fellow must have got hold of a trumpet of some kind, because he blew it loudly, and could just be heard screaming his message in the intervals of his making that infernal noise. I have been writing as if only men were there, but many peasant women and merchants were also in the crowd. I saw not far off only one lady attended by two footmen, but she was not doing well. She spied me at the same time as I saw her, and began, like a weak swimmer in a heavy sea, to struggle towards my coach. Her footmen, whose livery I could not recognize, fought to keep the way open for her, but were buffeted by wave upon wave of people, some of them now frightened, others despairing and intense. Almost all shouting.

She reached the door of my carriage and one of my men helped, or rather threw her in. Her hair was all terribly disarranged and parts of her raiment torn, including a piece of lace still attached to one sleeve at either end, but with the gathering between unravelled so that it looped every time she lifted her arms to struggle with her hair.

It was then that I recognized her. She was Francoise Marie D'Aubignay, one of the younger daughters of the Duke of Noailles.

"Oh," she exclaimed, "Monsieur de Brisse, I should not have come. Please do not mention it to Mama." But she laughed at the same time, just as Climene would have done, and added, "I simply wanted to see if my father's plan would work. And it has, hasn't it!"

"I believe it has," I said.

"It is called a run on the Bank," she explained. "If you get enough people to ask for cash in exchange for paper all at the same time, this is..." and she carried on, thinking it a great game, and mentioning how clever her father was to have thought of it. I was scarcely listening to her. Someone was hammering on the coach with, I think, a shoe. My coachman shouted out: "Maison du Roi. Maison du Roi."

The King's household cavalry had an extraordinary effect on the crowd. I could have sworn that nothing on earth could have disentangled such a milling throng, and yet, like some magical slipknot becoming disengaged, they flowed aside to allow the horses through. My coachman attached us neatly to their wake and in such a way we escaped at last.

When, some time later, I descended from the coach and entered Francis and Climene's house I found that my legs, which were bad enough in the first place, had started to tremble. I am used to my own deformities. Inside the shambolic arrangements of my body, I always feel strong; much stronger than observers are apt to think I can be. But for once I was too weak to disguise the fact that for me the ground beneath my feet is always arranged as if an earthquake has recently broken it up. Francis was fortunately waiting for me and saved me from falling, but I could not pretend to be unmoved by what I had seen. And when I described it to Francis and Climene, they looked as dismayed as myself. The question now was whether John Law would be murdered by the people if the run on the bank had been organized well enough to make the situation clear to the masses.

A servant was sent to his house, to find out if he had returned or not, and while we were still waiting in the drawing room, he himself walked in. I think, when I look back at that moment, that the fact that he was accompanied by his wife explains his seeming confidence, when I knew that he could have none; none at all. And because I knew how terror had overcome him when the guards of parlement were threatening to seize and hang him, I feared that he would be similarly overcome that evening. But he was accompanied by his wife, and would have been too proud to let her see that he was afraid, whether he was or not. Both of them were elegant, calm and smiling. When we discussed the scene I had witnessed, Law himself was eager to hear my account. He explained, with some panache, that the crowds were deceived into thinking that he was in the banking offices, while he himself was working at his desk at home, but he was nonetheless curious to learn more.

I found it difficult to match his mood, which so successfully simulated one almost of mischief as well as confidence. He must have known that many in that crowd were not the usual men and women who had so recently formed the daily press of those anxious to buy share certificates, but layabouts and thieves, paid by Noailles to be there.

I even dared to say so.

The news did not seem to unsettle Law. He stood there – and I see him still in my mind's eye – very tall, his right arm hanging with the fingers quite relaxed, and his left hand raised to his neckcloth in which a small diamond was pinned, the fingers loosely cupped except for the index finger, with which he stroked about an inch of his neck as if deciding something.

The very dark green cloth of his coat, superbly cut, emphasized his physique, and he was wearing his brown hair tied without a wig since he knew that he was coming to dine intimately with friends. The line that cut attractively around the corner of his mouth whenever he smiled was more deeply engrained now than it had been, but to look at him was to see a strong and healthy man with nothing to fear. I will never forget how deeply I loved and admired him at that moment.

Even now, when I reanimate this form in my imagination, I can feel my heart as if it will turn over in my chest. I know how intense his emotions actually were. I know that I would not have believed, without having been made aware beforehand, that the burden of the entire prosperity of the greatest country in Europe rested on his shoulders at that moment. I saw him master himself, knowing that to instil confidence in others was at the root of his own chance of survival. I feared, nevertheless. At the apex of any political structure there is a point at which the people will not allow any one man the privilege of saving them. I had been reading about Aristides in ancient Greece and how at the summit of his strength and benevolence the people voted to ostracize him. The very same fate could easily fall upon this hero of the French nation.

Afterwards, that evening we discussed only ways in

which the Regent might be persuaded to abstain from any further raids upon the bank. But fate had an even more compelling weapon with which to pursue Law's ruin, and I will now make a record of it, for what it is worth.

Some days later Argenson, entirely on his own authority, published an edict via the council of State declaring that the remaining stock in the Mississippi Company and the paper money issued by the bank were to be reduced in value month by month until halved by the end of the year. This was to plunge a dagger into the very heart of the finances, and so clearly an act of malice that when I heard of it I had no doubt that the chancellor would be sent to the bastille, and Law himself would like to see him executed. But it is notoriously futile to attempt to kill a cat which has already been let out of a bag.

Even so, the Regent, infuriated, commanded Argenson to come to him, and dismissed him immediately. The next day someone had hung a verse on the Pont Neuf saying: "Twenty thousand livres reward. A large black dog with a red collar has been lost in the Faubourg St. Antoine. Anyone who finds it has only to tell the Abbess of Trainel, and she will give them 20,000 livres." Everyone knew that M. d'Argenson wore the red collar belonging to the chancellor of the order of St. Louis, and also that he was very fond indeed of the Abbess de Trainel, in whose convent he very often spent the night, and now had hidden himself.

He said that he had intended to resign anyway, but considering the Parthian shot with which he crippled Law's system, my thought was always that he took his revenge out of malice.

Given the damage it caused, the Regent should have imprisoned him. Someone must have persuaded His Highness that Argenson's action was intended to help the economy of France to survive the rack on which it was being stretched, and that the chancellor himself was stupid but not evil. It was always possible for the Regent to be persuaded by an argument which was the latest that he heard, and so he took the seals of office from Argenson but left him with his body.

At that time, from day to day, I myself spent most of the hours I had at my disposal in John Law's company. He was convinced that order could be restored if the people could be persuaded to resume their optimism and confidence in the value of printed money. If they could not be persuaded, then he urged that we should look for other means to make it impossible for them to do otherwise. The Regent was as determined as was Law. He demanded, at the meeting of a parliamentary deputation at the Palais-Royal, that Law should be given six more days in which to produce an answer to this crisis; that those who had been most enriched by the shares in the Mississippi should be taxed; that it should be made illegal for anyone to hold more than a certain very small fund of gold or silver coins. And each one of these remedies precipitated a more desperate sickness in the economy.

I read once, many years ago, in the days when I spent so many hours in the King's library, a description of starving peasants who invaded the field of battle after there had been a huge slaughter in order to search through the dead bodies heaped on the ground. I cannot remember where or when the battle had taken place; but I do remember the awful image conveyed of many emaciated hands urgently shuffling the abandoned cloth and skin and bone in search of the means of their own survival.

That memory surfaced unwillingly in my dreams at the time. There were also consultations with various representatives who met daily to gather the results of the count, at towns outside Paris where coin was minted. The purpose of this was to lock up as much gold and silver as possible, in order to remove the option for the public to use, or not to use, paper money.

I woke in the mornings counting the green leaves of the tree outside my window as they struggled out of the bark, as if some figure existed which could defuse the unbearable suspense of another day. On about the fifth day I could tolerate it no longer and left at dawn to present myself at Madame's court in St. Cloud. I had Gaudet dress me with great care, and wore my best wig and was shaved freshly and very well. Having sent a message to Law saying that I would be gone, I sat down in my coach and experienced the luxury of a small breeze through the window and the brief sensation of escape which belongs simply to movement even when on a track leading to death itself – as all men know.

I presented myself at Madame's levee. There I saw Theobon for the first time for many weeks among her ladies in waiting. Madame displayed a flattering eagerness to hear all my news. She was most particularly shocked at the event of the household cavalry having been called to the riot outside the bank, and later, walking in the garden, and sitting in the shade, Clérembault had some past copies of the *Mercure de France* which contained anonymous letters which she claimed to know were by Law himself. I had thought they were by the Abbé Terrasson, because the language was elaborate and somewhat polemical, which was not Law's style. But we agreed that the climate of triumphant delight and confidence, which had gripped the populace and the country since the beginning of the year, had changed. The fact that Law's enemies had worked hard to produce this reversal was a bitter pill to swallow. I could not trust myself to speak of de Noailles or Argenson. I had not felt such enmity for any men since the days when the Chevalier de Lorraine and d'Effiat plotted against Madame.

As a means of delaying the moment when I should have to speak of them, I broached the subject of the Cellamare's conspiracy, which Madame could always be diverted by. I said that it was high time the treason of some of those who benefitted from the Regent's confidence was brought to light, just as had the treachery of the Spanish ambassador Cellamere.

Madame immediately spoke to revile Cellamere and his accomplice, Alberoni. She would recount a favourite piece of news or gossip with as much fervour as if none of her company had ever heard of it, and she did so now.

"Did I tell you that the letter which was intercepted from Alberoni to the Lame Bastard" (by whom she referred, of course, to the Duke of Maine) "advised the Duc to destroy our mines as soon as the war, which they were trying to foment with Spain, should be declared? And this unspeakable treachery is still denied by my daughter-in-law. She will not believe that her sister, the Duchesse du Maine, had any part in it. The most lazy woman in the whole of France, and yet she can find the energy to deny that obvious truth every time it is mentioned. She, who was merely one of the old King's many bastard daughters, and had the great good fortune to be married to my son, who is now the Regent of France, and yet she can make excuses for a man who conspired with foreigners to assassinate her husband and replace him as Regent. When she visits me, I find various topics which give me the opportunity for me to remind her of it. I simply cannot feel any pity for that lady; not even when Clérembault told me about how her husband was received by the Regent."

But the recollection of du Maine's humiliation put her in a better humour. "Did you hear Clérembault's account of it, Berthon?"

I prepared to hear it again.

"Clérembault was there. My son sat on the throne in

the great hall of the Palais-Royal and had the 'prisoner' brought in at the door at the other end. He had to walk the whole length of the room, and you know what a wretched mess he makes of that, limping frantically, nearly dead with fright because he was aware that his crime was punishable by sentence of death. Clérembault said that it took him at least ten minutes to do it. Everyone says that he is such a miserable coward but for once I can almost take his part, since if he had had to deal with any man other than my son, he would have faced death – and not a polite one either." I wished, in my heart, that de Noailles could be sent to join Mme the Duchess du Maine in her prison, or even better, in the Bastille like Mademoiselle de Launay.

The sun, which had become very bright, began to shine on the end of the bench on which Madame was sitting. She would move in a moment. She would walk now on the shady side of the path toward the little pavilion, where she might invite the three of us to sit on the stone benches, and the servants would bring chocolate to drink. I no longer knew all the names of Madame's little dogs, but one of them was the great-great-granddaughter of Charmille.

As we walked, Clérembault managed to say quietly to me that she wished to hear about Monsieur Law, and would I please not attempt to divert Madame again, but give them the news they wanted to hear about events in the Bank, and about the confiscation of coinage and the reprinting of paper with the promise to pay the bearer not gold or silver, but only shares in the Mississippi? I looked up at her. I was walking on her right, she being more in the shade and of course wearing her velvet mask as always. Considering how beautiful her complexion was despite her age, I reflected that it was surprising that all the young ladies of the court did not copy her. I said so.

"M de Brisse," she snapped, "you know me well; far

better than you have any right to know a lady of my birth, and I would thank you to remember that."

I was tempted to reply that yes, and in view of that I would talk about matters which really concerned her, such as money and gambling. But of course I held my tongue.

The moment we were seated in the pavilion, the Maréchale de Clérembault said, "Madame would like to hear about M. Law; is that correct, your Royal Highness?"

Madame was not yet settled in her chair. Her skirts had caught on the stone, and she half-raised herself, pulling a handful of silk one way and gently pushing an eager little dog another.

"Certainly I should," she said. "My son did not visit me yesterday nor the day before. What is this about gold and silver coins being no longer used at all? It will be very inconvenient. I buy my medals from the North and Germany. What will those people say to French paper?"

"And our own people," said Theobon. "I was told that there was an argument in our kitchens last week when some of the farmers refused paper."

"The Regent says that they will get used to it."

"Will that be enough, Berthon? Is it just a matter of habit and confidence? Because if it is I might as well say here and now that the gravel on our garden paths could be declared to count as pieces of silver!"

"Pieces of gravel would be more difficult to mark than paper," I replied with mock gravity. "It is a question of what is promised in writing which is to the point. You will agree, Madame, that writing on gravel would be a problem."

"And you could say there is too much of it."

"Monsieur Law's point exactly."

Clérembault did not enjoy this silliness. Madame noticed it and would tease her no longer. She said, "The Maréchale is getting impatient, Berthon, so please tell us more about the riot. What of the Maison du Roi?"

"Monsieur Law," I said, "cannot run his system if the people turn against it. The household cavalry are very fine and impressive, but they can't be available all the time to stand outside the Bank. His Highness is very perturbed to have had to use them."

"What else can be done?"

"Or not done," I said. "There are those who have been scheming to undermine the public's confidence. All that Law needs is for the people to believe what is printed on the paper."

This was too much for Clérembault. She could not leave while Madame was still sitting, but she stood so abruptly that she nearly knocked over one of the footmen who had just appeared behind her with the tray of chocolate. "You know very well, M. de Brisse," she snapped, "that the paper may *not* be worth its stated value if there is not enough coin in the vaults to pay it out when demanded. And *that* is what the people are saying. Where are the riches that should be pouring in from the Mississippi? And if it is too soon for them, how can this latest deluge of paper be justified?"

It was quite impossible to reply to this while the servants remained within hearing, since the answer was to strictly limit the issue of paper, and the reason why that was a problem was that the Regent regarded the very Bank itself and all the paper it issued as a royal perquisite. But when the footmen had gone, I did explain this. And I had to describe Law's bearing when last I saw him, which was on the very day of the riots; how unmoved he was.

Madame was silent when I had finished this recital, but Clérembault said at once, "Tell me, Berthon –" and she raised her hand with one finger outstretched, appearing almost to touch the air between her face and mine as if there was a point in it which she knew exactly how to identify – "what precisely is the value of specie against paper at the moment?"

"I cannot tell you," I said. "It is more than five minutes since I last spoke to M. Law."

Clerambault's eyes glared at me, but Madame intervened.

"Oh Clérembault, you want us to suffer. Now you have gone and annoyed her, Berthon, you will have to go away together into some other part of the garden and talk arithmetic for as long as you like. Even if our situation is unstable, I say that M. Law has achieved a miracle already." She paused to see the effect of her words, but not long enough to imply that she had finished speaking. "Look at how the late King's terrible debts have been paid. Wood costs half the price it did, and all those import duties on wine and meat and everything consumed in Paris have been abolished. This situation now has more to do with jealousy than anything else if such a polite and brilliant man is criticized by those who had not one good idea themselves for how to avoid the shame of bankruptcy. He is not secretive like they were, either. If there is a problem, everyone knows about it."

"But that is exactly what I was asking for, Madame," exclaimed Clérembault. "And you see what sort of a reply I got!."

"Then if there is really not enough coinage to match the paper money down to the last cent, the bank will have to insist that only paper money is used until the coffers have filled up again. They can compel them," she reiterated, as people so often do repeat a statement which they know to be rather fallible. "They can make it law." And she laughed heartily at her own wit.

I could see, to my dismay, that Clérembault would take advantage of Madame's permission to grill me, however.

Whether or not the gullible poor had been made very happy recently, she would insist on unmasking their benefactor. She would know already that the survival of Law's system would depend on the confidence of the people, which could not be tampered with in quite the way Madame seemed to think.

CHAPTER TWENTY-TWO

WHEN eventually I escaped, I felt like a rat who had got out of one trap only to be caught in another. I told my coachman to drive me to the Hotel Mazarin, because I wanted very much to see John Law. I felt sure that the previous day's riot had been managed from start to finish by de Noailles and Argenson, and needed to consult privately with him as to what I should discuss in my next day's appointment with the Regent. But when I got there, to my surprise I found not only Law, but also Fanette.

My wife held a letter in her hand and John Law was standing beside her. When the footman opened the door, he did not announce me, so that for a moment they were not aware of my entrance, and I saw with surprise he had his hand on her shoulder. What was more, they looked so well together, she so delicate and he so tall and strong, that I swear my heart gave me a small pinch as if momentarily trapped in a narrow space. They were both reading the letter, but when I took a step forward they heard me at last and turned, Fanette showing an excited face and holding out the letter.

"This is from Armand," she said, "but you must read it at once, Berthon. He should come home. M. Law agrees with me."

It was a long letter. He had before described how the pioneers lived and built themselves whole towns and villages but rough and practical places to live in. I could well imagine Armand, with his court dress replaced with things called trousers and the remnants of his fine shirts with the sleeves rolled, cutting wood with an axe for hours on end, or dragging timber from the forest with a group of men in harness when horses could not be had. And there were the natives – a most curious and fascinating splinter from the great tree of mankind. He described them as having skin the colour of new chestnuts, and living an itinerant life, with no fixed houses. Some were very dangerous, and others befriended the settlers; but the burden of this letter had to do with a spate of sickness and an Indian girl called Ashatea. Interesting though it was, this news did not sweep all other matters from my mind, as it did for Armand's mother. I said what Fanette needed me to say, but turned fairly quickly to Law, who in his usual way had returned to his open books and papers.

At the mention of the name of Argenson, he looked very scornful, and laid down his pen, saying, "The Regent has refused his request to be forgiven, and has promised to take back the seals in addition."

"Surely he will do more than that," I exclaimed, "and I thought he had already done it!"

He paused for quite a while before saying, "What sort of punishment would you recommend, Berthon?"

"Don't tempt me," I said. "I want to sleep at night."

"Well. I sleep at night," he said.

I was shocked. I thought of that young man being broken on the wheel at Law's insistence, and I experienced, just for a moment, like a man attempting to balance on an unstable rock in the middle of a deep river. The image came to me because if I lost my trust in Law, I would be losing a friendship as important to me as my life.

"We shall have Dagesseau back," Law now said.

I didn't believe him, but the next time I went to work with Mathieu Marais I sounded him on this matter, and he said that the Regent had, in the last few days, considered every magistrate in parlement and refused to appoint a single one of them. According to him, the Regent was trying, and trying again, to persuade M. le Duke of Saint-Simon to accept the seals but, as a noble man, he absolutely refused. And in the end, indeed, that wretched fellow Daguesseau was disinterred from his exile in Fresnes; but it was generally admitted that three years of boredom had immensely improved him.

On that evening, from the account of which I allowed myself to be diverted just now, Fanette and I stayed for supper with John Law and his wife. Monsieur the Duke also appeared with the Duchess and Monsieur d'Antin and several other guests. Lady Catherine was now very much liked at Court, and Madame had mentioned to me before that her house was full of duchesses. With such excellent food, wine and company, the limited yield of goods for trade from the Mississippi, or the haggling over the balance of gold and paper, lost their power to monopolise our attention and we only left when the candles had burnt very low. I believe we even solved various problems of the economy. And before I left I reminded John Law, to his great amusement, that we had been introduced to each other by Pythagoras. And of course, Pythagoras believed that it was not the case that for the gods, some things were possible and some impossible, as rationalists tend to assume. But that all things are possible.

The following morning the same radiance was still in my blood. It was in the air and the sunshine, and in Fanette who woke with joy at the thought of Armand's return. I looked at the prospect of seeing Armand again with delight, and included in it the Spring morning, and a vigorous expectation that such an amazing feat as that which Law had already achieved could not be shattered. I was to set out for the shipping office as soon as we had breakfasted to gather information of returning ships. Isabel and Shemshir Khan and Gaudet all knew about the letter. Gaudet accompanied me to the docks. As I often did when my clumsy body didn't actually trip me up, I felt wonderfully strong.

I arrived at about eleven o'clock. I think this was in the last week of May. I expected to perhaps find Law there. Again, the scene of the water, the sunlight glancing off the disturbed surface in the wake of boats, the birds calling and swooping, the general activity of men and nature, thrilled me. I began to wonder if I myself might ever put to sea. I need not go far. Just because Armand had sailed for America there was no reason why I myself should not put out for Brittany, or Amsterdam. I wondered what it must feel like to know that water was beneath one's feet; what it must be like to look to right and left, before and behind you, and see nothing but water. I stood there dreaming for quite a while before turning toward the offices where Law might be found.

I was not disturbed when he was absent. I collected what information I needed and then was driven to his house. I was actually getting out of the carriage before I noticed two Swiss guards were there. A friend – Jean Victor, Baron de Besenval – was at that time a major in the Swiss guard, and he was also there, but it was not just his presence that alarmed me.

Now that I looked about me with more care, I saw several more of his men with him.

De Besenval himself was standing at the entrance with two men of his regiment on either side. There were more soldiers at the gate leading to the garden, I immediately feared that some disaster had struck John Law; a thief, or an assassin.

"What is this?" I asked de Besenval. "What has happened? Has M. Law been harmed?"

To my relief he said not at all, but that His Highness the

Regent had perceived a need to protect M. Law, against that very possibility, and that there were sixteen men of his regiment stationed indefinitely on guard. We were standing in the hall by that time, and to my relief Law himself appeared, evidently about to go on some mission of his own because he was dressed for the open air, and carried a portfolio with him.

On seeing me he stopped to explain that he was on his way to go to the Palais-Royal and would I like to accompany him. Before I could reply, de Besenval stepped forward, and said with the utmost courtesy, that his Highness had requested M. Law to remain indoors.

"In that case," said Law, without a moment's hesitation, "let us go into my study, Berthon, and we shall have a cup of chocolate and talk."

I followed him. I had seen no disturbance in the streets during my short journey to his house. It was true that these were fractious times, but the previous months had seen Law besieged on many occasions – in the street, in his carriage, wherever the excited crowds could get at him. A boy had successfully cut off a piece of Law's hair by standing on a wall as he passed only a few days ago, and sold it strand by strand for a small fortune to devotees of his trade. Law was used to it. He had even had his coat torn almost off his back, and the Regent had not worried for him then.

I carried these thoughts with me in silence, noticing as we went, how every door was guarded by soldiers. I half-expected to find at least one in Law's study but there, to my relief, we were left alone.

"Where is Lady Catherine?" I said. "It must be very disturbing for her to have this immense bodyguard in the house."

"My wife is upset," he admitted. "The Regent has dismissed me from my position as Controller-general of the finances, which, as you know, was a very great honour for me. Don't, please, be too alarmed, Berthon. Nothing new has happened."

"Do you not call this new?" I said. I could hardly believe my eyes, that he stood there so phlegmatically unconcerned in the centre of an event which I now recognized as entirely hostile, and not at all one for his comfort.

"New? Admittedly yes; but only in a sense. His Highness has never before deserted my cause, but there is no new development in the affairs of the Bank. Except," he corrected himself, "I must admit that La Houssaye, in his role as head of the Regency Council, has called there, accompanied by the merchant's provost. I imagine they are still there."

I could not emulate his extraordinary calm. Clearly, he was under house arrest. I took a step forward and knocked into a small table, which nearly fell over. Before I could excuse myself, I lost my cane and it fell with a crash. Law actually laughed.

"Sit down," he said, "before you smash all my furniture." I did so, and for the rest of that morning he talked to me more about his personal life than he ever had done before.

It did not calm me. It sounded to me like the valedictory conversation of a condemned man. He told me about how he had met his wife in Amsterdam, when her husband was stationed there, and how he had immediately felt as if a violent form of physical magnetism actually pulled him towards her. Since his career in life had already been so drastically manipulated by his attachment to one lady, he had subsequently decided that his heart owed him a huge dividend which he chose to take in the form of a great many lovers. But his attraction towards Lady Catherine was such that it stopped him in his tracks. I thought to myself that I had never known a more whole man; one whose body, character and talents were so integrated. It simply remained to see how he would repair his current situation. There was no doubt that, as he said, if only the movement of money could be absolutely controlled for so little as a few months, the entire economy of France might outlive this present danger, and thrive. I knew very well, when I left, what a terrible reckoning he faced if that was his aim.

The following day I and the Duke of la Force called at Law's house and drove him to the Regent's front door, but here Law was denied access. The humiliation of that moment was painful and I believe that for a while I felt sheer hatred for His Highness, the Regent. To deny Law, and at a moment when his need of friends was so dire! I visited Law that evening, and of course found him feigning indifference to the situation in which he found himself. I felt certain that the Regent's frame of mind could not be actually so altered. Although we all know that he vacillates and still does, his entire character is not malicious or lacking in courage. I suggested to Law that he should let Sassenage know, and arrange to be let in by the back staircase.

He took my advice the next day, and indeed once Law appeared in secret the Regent was happy to see him, and apparently he actually embraced him. Whether some casual remark of his had been misunderstood by the footman, or he had deliberately ordered for Law to be refused entry before, the Regent was in no position himself to manage without Law as his friend, any more than Law could thrive without him. From then onwards Law worked every day with the Regent for all the world as if nothing had happened. That extraordinary man made no complaint, and neither did His Highness offer an apology. Both of them cut from such unusual cloth, they simply applied themselves to the mending of the wreckage of their plans. Loving both of them as I did, I simply could not imitate their *sang froid*. I felt profoundly miserable. The situation they were in was a shock to my entire understanding of the natural balance of good and evil in the world. I was far too debilitated by my emotions to be of any use.

The Regent was determined to limit the circulation of all forms of wealth other than paper, and that meant all coins, and soon after gold objects, jewellery and precious stones. I couldn't see such a simplistic move as winning the game they were committed to, with parlement as a hostile opponent and the people a volatile mass of unpredictable loyalties. When even Madame regretted the idea of the disappearance of coinage entirely, saying she had always been used to keep some gold louis about her and liked the feel of it in her hand, what would the poor say to such a challenge to their habits? Coins, even copper, were valuable to them too.

To my surprise, this edict, when it was made certain, was better tolerated by the people in general than could have been expected. There were no riots. Perhaps after the demotion of Argenson and d'Effiat, Noailles would need time to mend his opposing forces.

But the days of Law's popularity were at an end. It had become a question of endurance. And when in July it was considered necessary to extend the ban to jewellery so that people might not hoard precious stones, nor sell them other than to foreigners, the very atmosphere of Paris began to seem suffocating as if some component part of air itself had been extracted. To complete that story, if a family sold their jewels abroad and received coin for them, those coins could not be regarded as their own property, but belonged in the bank, which would issue paper in exchange. I need not labour the point of all this. It was a situation which closely resembled the old King's melting of the solid silver benches from the Palace of Versailles, and the plate of his court. Ordinary people could see that it was not tenable, and the potential vigour of the mass reaction hovered over our very heads, like a yellow-grey sky full of thunder.

I spent as much time as I could with John Law and with his son, who was now nearly a grown man. But Law was no longer the companion I had become so used to. His character had survived the acquisition of great wealth, as few can do. He possessed five magnificent estates, two in Paris and three in the country, and yet his manners had remained as humorous, modest and calm as they had been before. He had still loved his wife and treated her with unfailing warmth and respect, and as I have already described, his houses, whether in the Rue Quicompoix or Mazarin, although exquisite were without opulence.

Now, however, to my distress I saw his features settle in new lines. It is extraordinary how a man's skin can actually harden in as short a time as a few weeks, and lose its capacity to reflect sunlight. His eyes took on an opaque hardness which would be dispelled if I spoke to him of certain matters and in a certain way for perhaps five minutes. Then, like a man remembering a previous existence, or one rising to the surface from a noxious dream, he might regain for a short while his previous manner.

The Regent complained of Law's short temper when speaking to the Duke of Saint-Simon one day when I overheard them conversing. It was like hearing a man being sentenced to death to hear that. The Regent loved comfort and an easy life even more than most men, and although his kindness was often (or so I had thought) a distinguishing quality, I feared how long it would last if Law lost his charm. In fact, to live through those days was to be aware of the sensation of a man who treads on the unstable boards of a hastily constructed platform of execution.

I can easily recall the misery I myself lived in for those days. Fanette was so taken with the return of Armand that she did not notice the change in me, as she would have done. I was unable to share her joy at the prospect of Armand's return. My spirit was so overcome with fear for this extraordinary man, Law, who had achieved such an exotic feat of mathematical invention, who had saved France from bankruptcy and who needed so little an adjustment of confidence, to make him and the country safe. Was he not entitled to expect the people to be willing to exert themselves to the very utmost endurance in order to bridge the gap between economic success and failure? I was intolerably aware of how brief an interval of time and confidence would suffice to knit the frayed edges of the economy together. Viewed from one angle, France looked like a ship in full sail, but viewed less favourably the water under the ship of state was seen to be full of monsters.

If only the people were to unite in support of the new system, and maintain their faith in the bank and the currency which Law had invented even just for a few months, they might all be safe.

When I was attending Mattieu Marais one morning, I saw the Duke of Noailles and felt such a rage flood my heart at the very sight of him, I could swear it nearly stopped. To know that he and Argenson had manipulated the public to create this situation made me blind to any other cause, and I literally lost the ability of my eyes to see my physical surroundings so drastic was the fury that ran through my system. I had half risen from my chair, and M. Marais, having just said something to me which I didn't hear, had assumed an air of alarm.

He put his hand flat on mine but I shook it off. I was on my feet. The benches and floorboards of the building seemed to flow under my legs like a river moving of its own free will. I was by now standing before Noailles, and looked up into his face with rage and shouted, "Sir. Any bank would be exposed to a shortfall in the circumstances you have deliberately caused, regardless of its integrity and strength, or the genius of the controller general of the finances. For reasons of mere jealousy and spite, you are prepared to destroy France." He was the culpable villain of this piece, and I hated him.

However, many of the men in that room did not even know who I was, but they all knew the Duke of Noailles. My voice, which had sounded so loud in my own ears, may not have been loud enough. It did not help that he was such a tall man. I was stranded; becalmed in the middle of a silence. It crossed my mind to strike the man, but such an outrageous offence against the manners of court, although it might have altered the calm dismissal with which the Duc turned his back on me, would have disgraced myself. I was disgraced enough already.

As I turned to walk back to my place of work, one young man muttered as I passed, "Well said, Sir." I had to be content with that.

CHAPTER TWENTY-THREE

FANETTE and I dined often with Law and Lady Catherine after Francis and Climene had returned to England. After the event I have just described, I found myself rather tired and planned to spend the evening writing to Francis and urging him to return to us. I would stress the fact that John Law needed the armed support of anyone strong enough to protect him. But since the scene I had caused was immediately talked of everywhere, John Law forestalled me by sending his own coach to fetch myself and Fanette for supper that evening. So my letter to Francis, for the moment, remained undone.

When Fanette and I arrived, we soon both noticed that that delectable harmony running between Law and his wife was now strained, as if disagreements already arrived at, in private, still affected them. It became more noticeable after a few days.

As we returned to our house one night, Fanette said to me, "Berthon, would it perhaps be better for you to see less of your friend?"

I barely closed my teeth in time to hold back a reckless protest against what she said. She only noticed my suffering. She was not admitting mean thoughts. I gripped her hand so hard I may have hurt her. She said nothing more.

I had already written to Francis and begged him to come back to Paris. I also had the effrontery to attend the Regent's supper, with the sole intention of pleading the case for John Law, but that was not what was expected of the roués. It was so clear to see how utterly the Regent divested himself of all cares of state, once he had entered his own rooms with his close friends, that I gave up the idea. He even shed all sorrow for the daughter whose presence had been the light of his own life while she lived. He was always open to the attractions of lust, and between the pleasures of eating and drinking and being surrounded by so many beautiful women he was able to distract himself. I saw that, and what could I do?

Later on in July, the Regent and Law published a measure establishing the Indies Bank (as it was now called) as a trading company. The Indies Trading Company was to replace the Bank of the Mississippi, but even with the tobacco monopoly and other vast sources of revenue assigned to it, it could not match the guarantees which it had to undertake. The claim that it was capable of guaranteeing the exchange of six million livres in banknotes at the rate of fifty million a month was simply not believed by anybody who stood more than three or four paces distant from the Regent or Law. The ineradicable curse of Argenson's edict of May 22nd persisted. Once frightened, the mass of the people can't easily be lulled back into confidence. The paper money had already been lowered in value to the ruination of many, and yet the Bank was still unable to meet the demand for payment of its notes. I saw inspectors with search warrants entering the home of M. Bernard one day to remove jewellery or gold, of which I have no doubt he kept a store. To lose all his money and suffer such indignity was his fate, and the fate of many others. He was ruined, by the end of all this. He died in a cottage in the provinces.

And yet in all his trouble I simply could not detach myself from the infinitely tenuous possibility of Law's survival. Despite all that Fanette could say to me, and despite the return of Armand, I was unable to turn my mind from an obsessive attention to this one view of all life: the concentrated microcosm of a vast expenditure of brilliance and courage being crushed by the very people it had been sent to save.

While Law still worked with the Regent in his cabinet there was usually one day in the week when I also was in attendance on my particular duties, although I worked at a small table in an alcove where I could not always hear what was said. Similarly, I was occasionally there when the Regent went into the adjoining room to work with the Duke of Saint-Simon. Since the Bank was now converted into a trading company, and one with a monopoly of all French trade, I and many others became like shepherds in the wastes of the Auvergne when the wolves are most active and the law of the land forbids a peasant to bear arms and shoot them. With just as much anxiety as they listened for wolves, we listened for any noise from the streets of Paris foretelling revolution. In any city there are occasional bursts of sound – a group who gather around a musician, or a cart heavily laden with many attendants, or young men driving their carriages with shouts of triumph and warning at the people they threaten to crush. But I remember at that time how, in a serious expectation of rioting on the part of the people who were so recklessly being harassed by these restrictions, any unexpected noise would cause a man working on papers within doors to raise his head, and look anxiously towards the window. I must exclude the Regent from that assumption. His dauntless and enduring temper would not allow him to fear the French men and women in the street. His grasp of reality seemed to stop short of revolution. But I feared it on his behalf, and on that of John Law.

I now remember that several citizens were extremely harshly punished for attempting to frustrate the new laws regarding valuables which they kept hidden. I could not shake from my mind the memory of the wretched young Comte de Horn broken on the wheel so recently, and that at Law's and the Abbé Dubois' behest. It tormented me.

And yet, if I wavered in my courage I had only to study the bearing of Law and His Highness to recover some hope. They seemed so convinced of the ultimate success of all these disconnected and futile measures, and so determined to drive the bolt of their defences home in defiance of the resistance of fortune and the will of the people.

parlement was still unwavering in their opposition. When I accompanied M. Marais, he confided his opinions to me and I could not but report back to the Regent the conclusion that parlement would still maintain the fiercest opposition that it could. They showed their metal in the middle of the following week by refusing to register the new decree regarding replacing the Bank of the Mississippi with the Bank of the Indies, with all the monopolies included in the Regent's edict. This was the seventeenth of July.

When I returned that night to Fanette, I found that she had spent the day with Lady Caroline, whose suffering was intense, given the danger for her husband but also her mortification at the outcome of his plans in so far as this affected so many innocent people. She regarded it as a personal debt that she and M. Law would have to defray, no matter how long it took, but I could not help realizing the futility of such a gross scheme – in the same style, indeed, as the Regent's unrealistic confrontation against his own people and against parliament. As I wearily consigned myself to the task of preparing for bed, I mentioned to Gaudet how tired I was, and how deeply the tranquil scented warmth of our own house soothed my mind. He took advantage of the opportunity to ask me if I intended to go to Paris the following day, and to put forward some disquieting ideas of his own, but I decided not to listen to them and dismissed him for the night.

Madame had so far remained at St. Cloud and would not come into the town but sent word to me to attend her. I was at my wit's end to know how I could absent myself from Paris, when events were so threatening. I sent a letter to her, explaining my position since this was a day when the Regent expected me. I set off after dawn toward the Palais-Royal, intending to go past the Bank, now situated in the Place Vendôme. Long before arriving I heard the roaring of a great crowd coming from that direction. I have heard something like it before when a loaded ship crashed against the harbour in a storm, with the howling of the wind and the cry of sea birds.

But this was a huge mass of people gathered in the Place Vendôme, with whistles and clubs and the chaotic mass of their interrupted trades being stumbled over, with shrieks of abuse and some fellow with a pipe, whose wild tune flew up into the air. Initially, the crowd had only gathered in front of the Bank in the Hotel Soissons, and in the nearby streets to demand money for their marketing. How else were they to live? La Vrillière was trying to harangue the crowd. Intermittently his voice could be heard, but never a complete sentence before the yelling of the populace drowned him.

I would have driven off, but within moments my carriage was hemmed in and to force a passage would risk crushing men and women and children on foot. In fact, several people had already been suffocated by the crowd, and I saw, over the heads of the seething masses around me, bodies being carried by men of the watch, directed by the lieutenant of police. Gradually, and not before at least half an hour had passed, mounted horsemen of the Maison du Roi appeared yet again, and the crush of people dwindled. And then largely persuaded by Le Blanc, who succeeded

La Vrilliere and spoke with far softer words, the crowd began to disperse. The King's Household Cavalry then returned to the Tuileries. I hesitated, uncertain whether to go forward and seek out Law or retreat as I was now expected at the Palais-Royal. At that moment Law himself appeared. My coachman had advanced a little with the intention of turning the horses, but seeing Law struggling through the remnants of the crowd, who reviled him as he went, I called out to him and he was able to climb in beside me, while men hammered on the sides of the coach and my man flicked his whip in the air. There was the sound of glass being broken from the direction of his house. The crowd threw stones at the windows and smashed them. There was nothing to do but escape. Law attempted to thank me, but the crowd were still following and their screams drowned his words. They pursued us right up to the Palais-Royal, where the footmen slammed the gates against those behind. But some more determined men, full of vengeance, had crammed past beside the horses, which were stamping and jumping in their traces so that one of my coachmen leapt down to steady them, and was immediately hit in the face by one of the ruffians who drew back his fist covered in blood before he fled. John Law's face was in a sweat and he trembled visibly. When at last we gained entrance to the Palais-Royal and were in the presence of the Regent, the extraordinary calmness of his Highness's demeanour made it clear that what he expected from us was a similar composure. But I remember the great difficulty of controlling my breath which clattered in and out of my ribs with a sound which to my ears was offensive; but Law assured me later that he could hear nothing.

In reality, the Regent was extremely angry. His calm manner was deceptive. He had received a deputation from the parlement that morning which had put him in a rage which was all the more dangerous for being cold. When

John Law offered to leave, he would not hear of it but instructed his servants to prepare a room, in which Law could safely be lodged in the palace and remain there.

The Regent commanded me to follow him, and we went into his Council chamber where he sat with the manner of an infuriated general on the field of battle. With all the grace and discipline of his habitual bodily movements, rage seemed to seep out through the weave of his clothes, so that I thought at the time that if a lighted candle came near him he would go up in flames. I was more alarmed than I had been by the rioting crowds. I kept silent.

For a few moments, in that combustible atmosphere, the sound of his pen scratching on paper was all I could hear. The result was a royal proclamation which was posted immediately around the streets of Paris and particularly in the Place Vendôme, announcing that owing to the disturbances, the Bank would be closed until further notice.

The following morning we waited some time to hear of rioting such as would exceed the chaos of the recent past. But to everyone's surprise, the people showed a mildness and obedience which was the last thing to be expected. Even so, when I set out for Paris in the afternoon, troops were everywhere, both cavalry and the Swiss Guard. Some had been brought into Paris from Charenton. The musketeers were ordered to remain in barracks but to keep their horses saddled and bridled in case of an immediate need, and the general clatter and preparedness could be heard and seen in passing. There is no sound, in my opinion, more exciting than that of a horse whinnying when it senses adventure, and to a degree the atmosphere thrilled me that day. I do believe that if I had been born straight and whole I would have enjoyed war. It is, after all, the field in which young men contest with all their strength and either win or lose, as opposed to this political tedium and hypocrisy.

When I was young and too lame for the military training

of the schools in the palace of Versailles, I used sometimes to imagine the delight of being fit, and racing down the stone steps into the courtyard as I saw other boys of my age do. The old King once arranged for me to be included with the company for the Autumn manoeuvres in the Low Countries. That was one of the years when Madame de Maintenon went with the King and insisted she could not be parted from the young Duchess de Bourgogne who, being such a favourite at Court, was allowed to go with her in addition to some of her ladies. His Majesty could never bear to be parted from the ladies he loved, whether La Valliere or Mme de Montespan, or finally the Maintenon, and he particularly doted on the childish Duchess de Bourgogne who had come to Court when she was twelve and affianced to the Dauphin. Both Louis XIV and Mme de Maintenon allowed her to do whatever she wanted, and on the occasion I am remembering they were all three grouped on a knoll, where their carriage was drawn up overlooking the troops on the plain below. The King with his field glass, and with the generals beside him one minute, messengers the next, surveyed the soldiers and commented on their performance to the Maintenon over his shoulder. But she, sitting in the carriage, was cold and had closed the window so that only a small crack remained, through which she carried on a conversation with the Duchess de Bourgogne who was sitting swinging her legs on the poles of the carriage which were tipped onto the ground, the horses having been unharnessed and led away. The King, who never felt the cold, would walk backwards and forwards to the carriage window to make observations and chat with his mistress until it was time for the horses to be put to again. As for myself, I delighted in every minute when I could watch the manoeuvres and the men forming up with such precision and splendour. No one would expect such a man as me to love the valour of war;

it is a contradiction between my body and my mind, and also between my dislike of violence and love of chivalry. In this, at least, I think I am typical enough. As far as John Law was concerned, being both taller than most other men and very strong, the contradiction was quite the other way around.

When I arrived in Paris from Versailles on the following morning, I went first to the Vendôme where the financial market and bank had been transferred. Several members of the parlement were there. I recognized them. If they thought they would be identified, perhaps they would eventually have been frightened into staying at home by the experience of the Mareschal de Villars who was stopped in his coach by a man in the crowd shouting out, "What about your advice?" And the whole mass of those around him took up the cry. I needed to ask someone what they were referring to, and apparently before the Battle of Oudenarde, de Villars had loudly advised the King to make promises to the common soldiers, but then to let them take the heat of the battle. Apparently, it is not safe to assume that the rude masses are ignorant, or that they have short memories.

The surrounding gardens were full of stock jobbers. Those who wished to consult with Monsieur Law or to request some preferment from the Regent went first to the Palais-Royal and returned to the Place Vendôme armed with pieces of paper which they would exchange with great urgency in the marketplace. Everyone wanted to deal in some way or other in order to secure paper which would hold its value, and in a collective fever of extraordinary magnitude the crowds dealt in millions, the jobbers buying and selling as fast as they possibly could. Many who successfully sold shares and were paid for them and actually had the patience to keep the paper banknotes they received for many months, left the market with millions with which to buy houses and live extravagantly for the rest of their lives. I actually watched a man, whose dress declared him to be a wig maker, exchange 6 rolls of folded share papers which he took in bundles out from inner pockets in his rusty coat, and sell them to a jobber who scarcely had time to turn around on his feet before selling them on again to three fine-looking noblemen lined up behind him. Then the wig maker, as he made slow progress through the crowd and, aiming at the gate, was constantly battered by importunate jobbers who saw he had paper money from the bank, and longed to take it off him again.

To see such commerce carried on with such disregard for social differences was in itself quite fascinating. Then, all at once, I saw Francis in the crowd. I told Gaudet to stand on the step of my carriage in order to attract his attention. At first, Francis did not see him. Instead, he was as intent as anyone else in exchanging certain papers, which very much puzzled, and then alarmed me. But then Gaudet caught his eye, and he came across to me. In the time that it took him to make his way through the press of people, he busily hid away the papers he still had, because in this crowd thieves were willing to risk being caught themselves if they saw a chance to snatch some booty. Some thieves had children working with them. Anything they got, they passed to those who were small enough to slip past the legs and under the arms of the crowd. But Francis got to me without mishap, and got into my carriage.

He was in a fine humour. "What a beautiful blue sky you have here," he said as he climbed up. "Thank God for the good people of France. I thought I would have to forget the loss when Climene said that her aunt had five hundred livres worth of shares in the Mississippi Company locked in a drawer, but I just sold them; every one."

I hoped his paper money would be worth what was printed on it when the time came. Perhaps it might take some time; a year or two. They say time is a great healer, and perhaps a sickness endured by a Bank is just as worthy of repair as a man with smallpox, or a broken heart.

I said I was on my way to the Palais-Royal, and Francis was pleased to accompany me because once there he might be able to have some conversation with Law.

"How was he looking after the riot?" Francis asked me, with a glint in his eye. And even before I could say anything he laughed. There was no malice in it. It just appealed to his sense of humour that such a huge strong man as Law should have once been frightened, and showed it.

Francis shared his sense of humour with the Regent. His Highness seemed to derive a great deal of enjoyment from laughing at Law on that account. Madame had complained to me bitterly. "They promise to kill my son," she informed me, "and they mean it. If they could get their hands on him, generous, hard-working and talented as he is, they would not hesitate, but he not only laughs at the fright Law got in when he was physically threatened, but he also laughs at all attempts on his own life."

Some days later, the bank was moved again to the Hotel Soissons where there was much more space, and such crowding as killed nine people after the recent edict could not happen again. And yet the crowds still attempted to trade, desperately trying to exchange what had lost value today for something else which would be useless tomorrow. Such trade continued with almost the same feverish activity for two more days. On the 17th of July – the year was 1720 – on my way to the Palais-Royal, I diverted to the Hotel Soisson where all the booths and tents were now re-erected in the garden and there was an atmosphere almost rivalling that of the *jours d'appartement* in the days of Louis XIV. Many tables were spread out under the trees and beside the pathways, lavishly decorated, with booths for traders to drink or even eat at. There was one man there, very old now, but I recognised him as the individual who made the famous fish soup of the Pont Neuf, which used to sell for one golden louis a bowl. I believe it must now have been his son, ladling out of a great cauldron. At the *jours d'appartements* in the days of the old King, all at Court were the guests of the monarch. We all wore our finest clothes and our most rich apparel and went from room to room for dancing, gambling or eating at the tables laden with food and wine. I think one day in each week was designated in this way, but suddenly I distrust my memory.

However, to find a similar scene in and around the Hotel de Soissons, when I knew how desperately deep was the chasm lying in wait to swallow up the celebrants in this frantic game of chance, depressed me. I admit that some made their fortunes there and then. They sold their Mississippi shares in exchange for banknotes, and eventually those banknotes were exchanged once more for coin, even if it took almost a generation to do it. And some paid on the spot for estates in the country without leaving the gardens, exchanging paper for stone walls and gardens which they need never lose. But others were still buying shares in the Mississippi Company, in the belief that they were still as valuable as they had been yesterday, and those who knew better were seeking those individuals out like wasps after jam.

Paper money positively bulged out of the pockets of some men. I watched one, in a fine blue coat, hand over five thousand livres in exchange for Mississippi shares. I knew how much he paid, because he handed it out with such care, naming each bundle as he did so. The share certificates that he got in exchange he held up to show his lady, before packing them away with a beaming face. The mayor of Paris – the Duke de Tremes – had arrived at the Hotel Soissons before me, and in a few moments afterwards, Law himself made an appearance on the balcony of the house.

Many were in tears in the street, one trying to find his wife, another trying to find her husband. Nobody wanted to have the paper money because it was discredited, nor silver because it was reduced in value every day. There never was seen such misery, simply because the shower of edicts were so badly administered that one intention clashed with another. A talented manager was needed to synchronise the minutiae of the administration, such as the problem faced by artisans needing to procure materials to further their work, but for which the suppliers could not take paper. Accepting banknotes involved the workers using unpaid time to get to the bank to exchange them for such small amounts of cash as needed, and that was just one example of the frustration suffered by the common people. A family was found dead in the village of Saint Eustache because the father had committed suicide after killing them because he could not buy food to feed them, although it was later found that he had 200,000 livres in banknotes but no cash.

The Duke de Tremes wasn't able to say anything to the people but, "Messieurs, what is happening?" He said this over and over again.

When Law eventually left, he somehow escaped in his carriage and went through the little market of Quinze-Vingts. One woman threw herself at the door of his carriage and hung there. She cried out, begging Law for her husband who, she said, was going to be killed. Law offered her some money, but she said, "I don't want money. I want my husband." Law's coachman at that whipped the horses as hard as he could. Many people were not aware that it was M. Law inside, but as he reached the entrance of the Palais-Royal the word circulated like a sudden violent draught, and the crowd realized that the very man who they considered at that moment to be the cause of all their misery was almost in their grasp.

They surrounded the coach and I myself saw John Law leap down and confront the crowd, calling them "scum" in such a strong commanding fearless tone that they fell back and allowed him to escape. No one could laugh at him for being fearful after that. The armed guards slammed the gates. The crowd vented their rage on the empty carriage when Law's coachman tried to drive it away. They threw stones at it, smashed the windows, and tore the leather at the back even though Law was no longer inside.

From that place, the whole crowd, carrying the corpses of those who had been stifled in the mob, went to Law's own house. The Swiss guard, who had been there for some time, defended it. They set guards around with loaded pistols in their hands. Such violence had never been seen before. Law's coachman had been seriously wounded. His servants fled.

The remaining servants and clerks stood at the windows of the Bank looking out, but the crowd started to throw stones at the windows, smashing them, and (in spite of the guards) especially those windows giving onto the street. The guards began to listen to the mob and to say that they too would gladly kill Law, but he wasn't there.

Meanwhile, Leblanc, Secretary of State for War, had the corpses carried inside the Palais-Royal, and threw some money at the crowd to appease them. By the time I arrived, Law's carriage was still stranded in the court of the Palais, where it had been dragged back, because the mob threatened to burn it. One woman in the crowd even said that they would attack the carriage of the King himself if they saw it.

CHAPTER TWENTY-FOUR

I SPENT the rest of that day with Monsieur Marais, at his place of work in the parlement building. He had a letter from the Abbé Terrasson, which turned out to be a learned essay attempting to prove that Homer was a bad poet, whereas he had promised to send notes on "A New System of Finances". Clearly, since the Abbé was an old man past his prime, he had confused the two manuscripts and sent the financial discourse to some unfortunate academic of the classics. Mathieu Marais always gave as much time to these gossipy matters as to the contemporary drama which so deeply interested me, and my friend Law. However, in vindication of Marais' character as a serious man, I must not forget to mention that during the same session he showed me a letter from the Abbé Tencin that went so far as to describe the bank as powerless, and to mention the King himself (for whom one should substitute the Regent) as one who planned the "total ruin of the State, and had even the intention of ruining the people." I am virtually quoting Marais when I say that the main fault was lack of administrative capability for the detail, for which Law himself simply had not time. M Marais then attended with equal relish to the previous day's doctrinal wrangles between the Abbé Dubois, the Regent and Parliament, which were extremely detailed and arduous, but my reward for following all this, when my copy paper was all but exhausted, was an account of the Regent's experience recently when taking the ferry boat to visit his mistress, Madame de Parabere. I suppose he must have been in high spirits because he was apparently amusing himself by violently rocking the boat. The ferryman had not recognized him, had no idea who he was, and remarked loudly, "This passenger will have us all in the river if he doesn't stop treating the boat just like the Regent treats the business of running the country."

Myself, I did wonder if the ferryman was disingenuous in pretending not to recognize the Regent, but with no other man in such a position of power as the Regent would a common man be safe with such remarks. I can see, in my mind's eye, the Regent himself laughing. What energy he must have, and pleasantness, to pursue the entertainment of his lust with such gaiety when so beset with treachery and many hours of contentious drudgery with his opponents.

I am not sure of where Marais gathered his stories, but I thank God for them, because I should have not been able to bear my task of spending several hours a day with him otherwise. I have no doubt that he included these tidbits in his journal, along with his assiduous record of all the conflicts and changes of direction which we underwent in those years.

Just as the legal profession seems to regard time and even money as being without the elasticity capable of responding to human urgency, so Mathieu Marais seemed a limited man; and yet he was not, as his journal so clearly will show. I liked and still do like the man. The Regent's extreme flexibility was a different matter. There were moments when I almost thought he perceived the occasional crack between fact and fiction, but simply denied himself permission to notice it. He believed emotionally in a version of reality which was different from that which he saw.

John Law, when later on I caught up with him, had spent the rest of the day with the Regent, devising several new schemes for altering the value of the banknotes, or the interest to be paid, or the rules by which the natural curiosity of the populace for seeing how much money they might be able to extract from the country's exchequer was to be constrained; and also, no doubt, whether the bank should be closed, or remain open for this fantasy of trading.

Each device they invented was tried one day and abandoned the next, but the Regent and Law were immersed in it. It was rather as if some flickering phenomenon had caught their eye, which had the power to ensnare their entire attention, and from which they could not escape. I asked myself what I expected them to do other than continue to pursue this wild fixation. I asked Fanette, but I could tell, from her joyful countenance, that all she thought of was Armand's return.

The next day I made my way unhindered up the now familiar secret staircase leading to the Regent's cabinet. There I found the Regent and Law together, working with mounds of paper beside them and as if there was no disturbance they needed to attend to. I, myself, was not needed at all. It was as if they were two gamblers, convinced that if they continued with unabated concentration on their game, they could still win; there was even a shred of that enjoyment between them, with which they had set out in the first place to conjure the economy. I swear I heard an echo of Law's voice as if running in my own blood, and repeating his remarkable comment of many months before, that he knew how to turn paper into gold. I excused myself and bowed, but I don't think they heard me. I waited in the ante-room until distant noises from the street dropped several tones, like a dog barking, which sounds so sharp until the moment when it begins to recede.

I could not go home to Fanette, where my state of mind would clash so unpleasantly with her preparations for the return of Armand. I went instead to the parliament building, and sought the familiar corner where Matthieu Marais was to be found. He showed some surprise at the sight of me. But his reaction was momentary, and he soon began to discuss the negotiations which had been entrusted to him, of the recent marriage of de Noce, the Regent's favourite. I have never been particularly interested in de Noce. For all his elegance and fashion I had never heard him say anything of interest, and I was not, now, very attentive, to the arrangement for the legal formalities of his marriage. Marais had the capacity to absorb boredom as paper will soak up water, and the man was actually interested in the legal terms attending the banal event between two individuals whom he did not know.

But I am very glad that I was there, because after about three-quarters of an hour I overheard a brief, but vital, exchange between two other advocates. I have the curious furniture of the desks and benches in the building to thank for this opportunity. Had they known that I was there, the men in question would certainly not have spoken of the treacherous measure which they were planning.

I cut my attendance on M. Marais short and escaped without too much delay. His Royal Highness the Regent had told me to come to him at once at any time of the day or night if I discovered a matter needing his immediate attention. I walked to the Palais-Royal and entered by the side door, unencumbered by the guard. I presumed that I would find the Regent and Law still at their work. In the ante-room was a footman wearing the livery of Madame de Parabere, and just as I entered one of the Regent's servants came from the inner room and handed him a note which he took and left.

The Regent's absolute inability to concentrate on matters of state to the exclusion of his mistresses was so like that quality in his uncle, Louis XIV, that my mind stumbled on it, as one's foot can so easily be tripped by a familiar stone.

Despite being to all intents and purposes fully occupied with my own mission, a remembered sighting of this beautiful mistress of the Regent somehow intruded on my inner eye so that for an instant I forgot why I had come.

His Highness looked toward me. I bowed to him, while Law continued to write. "Monseigneur," I said. I have just come from parlement where I overheard a matter being secretly discussed of which you would surely want to be informed. There is a conspiracy to pay an army of workmen to riot against the measures of the Bank des Indes being granted a commercial monopoly on all trade in France. There are certain men among the labourers organizing their numbers. The plan is already far advanced for two days from now."

To my relief – because I had considered the possibility of the Regent being so distracted by recent events that he might brush the danger to himself aside – he showed a rare response of passion, although immediately suppressed. He rested his cheek on his clenched fist in silence for fully two minutes before speaking again, and neither did I nor John Law speak. Finally, he said, "When was the Parliament previously sent to Pontoise?"

John Law looked hopefully at me, clearly seeing no connection with this question and the news I brought, nor having the faintest idea about Pontoise. But I had seen a document among the many hundreds forced on my attention recently, and was able to say "that was in 1652 Monseigneur."

"There must be accommodation for them there, in that case. And what better time for them to occupy it, than when members of parlement need to be separated from the loyal working men among the King's subjects in Paris? The entire Parliament will be sent to Pontoise. We will quote the previous occasion as a precedent. In Pontoise they will be separated not only from his Majesty but also from the common labourers of the city. They cannot execute their plan if they are forbidden to be in Paris." His Highness glared at me with approval. His right eye had been giving him trouble recently and he would put a patch over it when in public, but it was discarded just then, and I could see how the inside of the lid was red and raw looking. He shouted, "Leon!" and one of his clerks came running from several rooms beyond the cabinet. John Law was already gathering up the papers on which he and the Regent had scribbled their calculations. Leon was sent to fetch the lists of members of Parliament and where to find each one of them at home with his family. The Regent wrote another order to be carried to the commander of the Household Cavalry and another to the Commander of the Musketeers. At which point the Regent gathered up his wig, his cloak and the shoes he had kicked off from his stockinged feet, said good night to us, and left.

During that night the musketeers were busy delivering individual notices to every single member of Parliament, informing them that they were to remove to Pontoise within the following day and to remain there on pain of death, by order of the King, until recalled. Any failure to follow this order to the letter would be drastically punished. None dared disobey, and within the required time there was not one single member of Parliament left in Paris. The shock of the decision, the suddenness of finding that the Parliament was to be removed from all contact with the common people of Paris was great, and its thorough implementation more so. But they had absolutely no choice. Within a hair's breadth of them succeeding in getting rid of the Regency by having the King declared to be of age, and getting rid of Law and his financial system, the conspirators had their prize snatched away.

They must have already negotiated several preliminary legal difficulties without a word being disclosed.

The speed with which the Regent acted, and the extraordinary resolution shown by such a naturally indolent man, took me by surprise. And in this case, his action was entirely effective, both for the factual and the emotional result. By Monday morning the members of Parliament and their wives and children were seen to begin this grand exit. They suffered from inconvenient accommodation, uncomfortable beds and bad food all of which they complained about, and some absconded, despite the risk, to Hotels not actually in Pontoise. Two weeks later only just over half the Parliamentarians were still in the lodgings allotted to them, but none were in Paris and no riot took place at that time. However, like milk being scalded in a pan the temper of the people was continually seething, and threatened to spill over.

It was in the brief calm, two days after this crisis that the Regent invited Law to make use of his box at the opera.

At dinner that evening, I suggested to Law that he should not take advantage of the offer, but he was loath to risk offending the Regent, or to be accused of cowardice, and said that he would go. In spite of the fact that the traitors in parlement were no longer on hand to organise them, did neither the Regent nor Law himself realise that the common people had minds of their own, and should – like dried wood – be kept well away from any flame? I could not convince him of the wisdom of my advice. I was annoyed by it. It had not occurred to me to suspect Law of vanity; but at that moment I thought I saw the role that it had played, when he turned a slightly mocking smile on me and invited me to join Lady Caroline and himself the following evening. Of course I agreed. John Law did not have a monopoly of the vice I suddenly saw in him. But I said that I would not be accompanied by Fanette.

They were playing that opera by Luly the name of which, for the moment, I forget. I loved the music of Luly.

He was very popular at court during the reign of Louis XIV. I can recall some of the melodies now. In this silence, scratched though it is by my scribbling, I could hear them again if I were brave enough to listen. But I have to confess I cannot bear it. I can summon up a glimpse of Law's ankles as he mounted the stairs of the theatre, and Lady Caroline's silk skirt as she sat down and it settled around her so like the silks and ribbons of Climene in happier days when we shared a coach together. But I forbid my mind to hear again the music. It would be too sad, on this lonely vigil. So why does the restless shift of the bones of these trees, their skinny little branches and the sly breeze, set up such a simulacrum of the way in which the crammed audience that night began to signal their awareness of the presence of Law and his wife in the Regent's box? Someone must have looked to see the Regent, and spotted Law instead, and the whisper went around the whole house as this bitter wind does now, alerting every dead leaf to snap against the ground, and twigs to scrape so like the common people who got to their feet, despite the music, and turned towards us and shouted their abuse. It was no longer possible to hear a note of the music. After waiting a short while, Lady Caroline stood up. She was, I remember, as pale as this moon now. Reluctantly, John Law rose as well. Even he could not imagine that he could persuade so many to relinquish their position. We three left. The coach was still outside, but it would not have still been there if we had delayed. As I myself got into it, the news had already spread to the streets, and Law's coachman, who was a strong man and loved his master, used his whip and not on the horses. Law, who held the hand of his wife in both of his, laughed. "Berthon," he said, "you win."

The next day was like any other at that time. John Law worked in the Regent's cabinet with His Highness, and I clung to my position in the background quite unable to deflect my attention from the hypnotic scramble of devices with which they both thought to reanimate the currency. I think John Law imagined Parliament as his main enemy, without the interference of which his system would succeed; but in truth, it was the Regent himself he needed to be rid of. He must have known it. Even when the celebrated banker, Samuel Bernard, sent a message to say that he was never in favour of the system. But now that it was in place, if it were followed through without any hindrance, with no one touching the notes, or changing the figures, it could succeed. The Regent failed to realise that this proscription was aimed at himself. Bernard also offered money to supplement the butchers, the bakers and woodsmen, and the Regent read his letter with all attention, but almost as soon as he had finished it, he asked Law if the promised recovery would enable him to use the bank's money to pay the arrears of the Household Cavalry (Maison du Roi). I heard him myself. With all his intelligence, he simply could not understand the vital importance of the separation of the monarchy from the finances. He was so convinced that all belonged to the King. Others could see that this fatal delusion, which had been overcome in England while still extant in France, would forever foul the rigging of the French ship of state.

I must say, I had hoped from the first that the Duke of Orléans was intelligent and talented to the extent of being able to see this. But I was mistaken. John Law saw it, but he deluded himself, as did I.

Two days later, as if to illustrate the unregenerate failure of the Regent to either understand the finances or to refrain from interfering, His Highness insisted on enlarging the value of money. The louis, which was at 45, and which needed to be reduced to 35 by the first of August, was put up to 75. This immediately put up the price of food, and the market completely collapsed. A return to lower prices was promised for September but in such a wildly volatile market no sane policy could be implemented, or believed in. And yet Law's vigorous refusal to accept defeat was extraordinarily painful to witness. Torn between admiration for his spirit and despair, I refused to allow myself to recommend his surrender. With each new package of ideas by which he sought to rearrange the currency values, or the restrictions placed on the people or the markets, I was the witness of his valiant efforts to escape from the complex trap that he was in. Regardless of the fact that the Regent had largely manoeuvred these changes himself, the demands of the populace for Law's blood became voracious. The working sessions in the cabinet abated. The Regent still did not deny entry to John Law, but the bewildering game of mutual fascination with illusory solutions ceased.

I hardly knew how they spent the time. Or myself either. Armand returned. I found that I was now the father-in-law of a beautiful American Indian called Ashatea. I can hardly impress my account of how wounded my entire wellbeing was at that time than to say that his return mattered to me far less than the squandered opportunity that France had had, to be saved by the strong and devoted intelligence of a man like Law. The remaining question was whether or not Law would be murdered. My waking hours were tense with dread of all news; my sleep haunted. Had the Regent thrown him to the crowds I could not have borne it. But it was not in the nature of the Duke of Orléans to consider such a cowardly solution.

He continued to treat Law with respect and kindness, although he no longer made any pretence of working with him, until of his own accord Law decided to leave the Palais-Royal and return to his own house in the country not far from Paris.

This was actually the moment of undeniable defeat.

I wonder how generals on the field of battle conduct themselves in such circumstances. Do they also feel as if an evil dream has engulfed them? I was present when the Regent's footmen opened the doors for Law to leave the Palais-Royal, and the air of the outside world entered with a gust of flat and cloying emptiness, into which he strode with such courage. His intention was to go to his estate in Guermande, and he reached it safely the next day. The Duke de la Force visited him there. I did not.

EPILOGUE

AS I looked up from my book, to search in the darkness around me for shadows of memory from that tragic loss both to France and Law, I noticed instead a movement on the bridge below. Had I realized that in writing this I would be baring my heart to the cruel awareness of yet more pain, I should have desisted. But as I watched the gathering of flares in the hands of the servants following Madame's coffin and sensed the darker mass of her body moving soundlessly in the midst of them, from one side of the bridge to the other, I felt a strange relief. I felt that she knew that I was there. Like flotsam on the brink of the water as the tide turned, a detail of generous kindness brushed against me from somewhere. I felt wetness on my face. I was sure of the safe haven she was going to. This was her gift to me, this sensation of something accomplished, and not snatched away by an adverse fate.

BIBLIOGRAPHY

James Buchan, *Frozen Desire: The Meaning of Money*

Edward Chancellor, *Devil Take the Hindmost: A History of Financial Speculation*

Elizabeth Charlotte, Princess Palatine and Duchess of Orléans, *Collected Letters*, translated and edited by Maria Kroll

Elizabeth Charlotte, Princess Palatine and Duchess of Orléans, *More Letters of Madame*, translated and edited by Gertrude Scott Stevenson

Edward Faure, *La Banqueroute de Law* (not translated)

H. Montgomery Hyde, *John Law: The History of an Honest Adventurer*

Mathieu Marais, *Journal et Memoires de Mathieu Marais, Advocat au Parlement de Paris sur la Regence*. Manuscrit de la Bibliothèque impériale (not translated)

Duc de Saint-Simon, *Historical Memoirs*